Merchants and Warriors

Also By Camilla Tracy

Of Threads and Oceans

Of Flowers and Cyclones

Of Blood and Tides

Soxkendi: A Family of Dragons

Of Spools and Billows

Of Gates and Typhoons

Armoire of Adventures

Merchants and Warriors

Join my animal loving community and learn about my newest book releases by clicking below or scanning the QR code:

https://geni.us/CamillaTracynewsletter

CAMILLA TRACY

MERCHANTS AND WARRIORS

Camilla Tracy

Published by Pudel Threads Publishing

First Printing 2025

Tracy, Camilla, author

Merchants and Warriors

ISBN (paperback) 978-1-998506-03-3

eISBN 978-1-998506-04-0

B&N ISNBN 978-1-998506-05-7

Under a Federal Liberal government, Library and Archives Canada no longer provides Cataloguing in Publication (CIP) data for independently published books.

Technical Credits:

Cover Image: MiblArt

Editor: Bobbi Beatty of Silver Scroll Services, Calgary, Alberta

Proofreader: Lorna Stuber - Editor, Proofreader, Writer, Okotoks, Alberta

Created with Atticus

for Paul

CHAPTER ONE
Jinhua

"**I**S THAT A LETTER from His Royal Highness?" Fangyee dropped a piece of folded parchment onto Jinhua's lap.

Jinhua snatched it up and looked at the seal, surely Fangyee had already opened it. But no, the seal was intact. Jinhua broke it and scanned to the bottom of the letter. "No, it's from Qiao."

"Oh." Fangyee looked disappointed, but she sat on her bed opposite Jinhua, clearly waiting to hear the news from their sister.

"Qiao said the accommodations are as expected, and she is enjoying the challenge of re-establishing her rank amongst the other guards. They train at least twice a day, but most of their time is spent patrolling the halls of the female royals and learning new fighting formations for every possible occasion," Jinhua said. She had never been very close to her oldest sister, perhaps because of the age difference. But she'd been happy for Qiao—and secretly herself. If she moved to the palace, at least Jinhua would have family nearby.

"Does Qiao mention Prince Feng?" Fangyee asked.

"No," Jinhua replied as she scanned the letter again, "The Prince has not sent a single letter to me."

"Maybe Prince Feng is not the writing type," Fangyee said, patting Jinhua's knee.

Jinhua nodded. She didn't want to argue with her sister, so she didn't mention that this marriage wasn't her choice or what she really wanted-ed. A royal adviser had simply come to town one day and deemed her pretty enough to be considered a match for the royal prince. The adviser had commissioned a portrait, which he'd brought back to the palace, and the palace had sent a contract to Jinhua's family for her hand in marriage. It was a great honor for her family, but she didn't even know what the prince looked like. He hadn't sent her so much as a letter or a message. The palace had sent a sizable financial gift, but it was more to ensure she was appropriately adorned as a future princess than it was a gift.

"Do my hair for dinner," Fangyee said as she tapped Jinhua with her folded fan.

While Jinhua had been lost in thought, her sister had changed into her evening outfit for dinner, though they weren't technically required to change. Her brothers didn't even bother bathing after training. But Jinhua was expected to behave as a princess, so Fangyee took it upon herself to dress for dinner too.

Fangyee sat on her sister's bed again and handed her a brush. Jinhua smiled and brushed her sister's hair, then twisted strands together and pinned them in place. She took Fangyee's cherished jewels she had worked so hard for and placed them in her sister's hair with pins as well.

"Go get dressed, and then I'll do your hair," Fangyee said.

Jinhua nodded and put on her yellow silk dress. She had five dresses now and rotated through them consistently, not really caring which she wore when. She'd dine in her training clothes if she could. Jinhua shrugged, then stood in front of the mirror and let her sister do whatever she wanted with her hair.

"Jin, can I borrow this for tomorrow's dinner?" Fangyee asked as she tapped the comb she was securing into Jin's hair.

"Yes," Jin said. She knew Fangyee would take it as her own if it wasn't part of her royal trousseau Jinhua was supposed to bring with her when she moved to the palace.

"Are you excited to go to the palace? It will be so lovely to live with the other princesses and to have the prince dote on you all. Maybe you'll even see Qiao as she patrols the halls."

Jinhua nodded. It was her duty to do her family proud and move to the palace in a few weeks. If she was honest with herself, she was indifferent. She would miss teaching training classes here, and she would miss her students—mostly her brother Renshu—but her family was happy to send her away for the better life that palace life promised and the honor it would be to boast that they had a direct connection to the royal family.

"Come, come, our family will be seated by now. We can make our entrance," Fangyee said as she ushered Jinhua out their bedroom door.

Jinhua followed, letting Fangyee loop an arm around hers as they strode down the hallway to the dining room.

Dinner was as it always was. Silent. Once they were all seated, their cooks brought out the dishes for the evening and then it was Jinhua's duty to eat silently with her family. She slid a glance up to Renshu once, who grinned and winked at her before he looked down. Knowing he would look up again, she waited only a minute before peering up again and crossing her eyes at him. It was their custom to see how many looks they could get in before Amah noticed.

"One more look and I'll smack you both on the head," Amah said as they attempted another glance.

"I'm sorry, Amah," Renshu said. He sat on Amah's left as the favorite child.

She patted his arm and then added more meat to his bowl of rice. "It's all right, Renshu. Youth runs out eventually, so I'm glad to see you enjoying it."

Jinhua bit her tongue. Renshu got away with everything as the favorite.

"I'm sorry, Amah," Jinhua said quietly.

"It's not proper for a princess to disobey the rules. I will not have you shaming our family by being an outcast in the royal palace. Since you have so much youthful energy, you have patrol duty tonight," Amah said.

Jinhua nodded and swallowed whatever retort she might have uttered. She wouldn't get any sleep tonight while on patrol. And then she'd probably get blamed for the circles under her eyes tomorrow morning too.

CHAPTER TWO
Ranulf

R ANULF'S SHIP PULLED INTO the dock beside the largest merchant ship he'd seen to date. He stood on his own ship, awed, watching the bustling to and fro of the people at work on the enormous vessel. Over a dozen crew members were moving large crates back and forth on pulleys, carrying goods on and off the gangplank. His heart strings tugged, and he closed his eyes. "One day ..." he promised himself. He tore his gaze away from the ship and turned instead to the town before him. They'd barely made it across the vast, unforgiving ocean to Cerisa on their tiny vessel, and Crab was, for the third time, checking the knots he was securing their ship to the dock with.

Many curious eyes on the dock turned to him—until they shifted to the even larger man now appearing at his side. Ranulf's auburn hair, barely-there beard, and thick stature were a novelty in this part of the world. Crab's brown hair and dark eyes stood out a little less, but his sheer size attracted attention no matter where they went.

"We just going to stand' ere?" Crab asked.

"Just taking it all in, Crab. Can you believe we made it?" Ranulf asked. The excitement of a new place bubbled inside him.

"We should get goin'," Crab said, narrowing his eyes and looking around them as if expecting a monster to jump out.

"Let's go meet people!" Ranulf said, clapping his friend on the shoulder and stepping onto the gangplank.

If only his family could see him now. As one of their youngest children, his parents hadn't cared about his career choice as long as he wasn't dependent on them. They'd laughed when he'd told them he would become one of the greatest merchants in the world.

As Ranulf and Crab left the dock, they found themselves in a dusty village with high stone walls. The buildings behind the walls were tall and topped with angled roofs that sloped to barbed edges. The village hummed with motion. Whatever merchant ship had just arrived had awoken the villagers, who were pouring out in droves.

Crab and Ranulf continued down the main road, leaping aside when a cart came flying by. Suddenly, they heard shouts down a street to their right, and Ranulf ran to see what was going on. Crab followed closely behind.

They stopped at a large property with unusually low stone walls, low enough for them to see over. A group of at least fifty people stood in a cobblestone square, all in the same awkward position, in neat rows, and still as statues. Four figures stood on raised platforms on each side of the square. Suddenly, they cried out, and the mass of people moved in synchronicity into another position.

"It's a school for the fightin' arts," Crab said, the awe in his voice obvious.

"A school?" Ranulf said.

They continued watching from the edge of the stone wall. A figure on the closest platform glanced over at them, and Ranulf realized it was a woman. Apparently, men and women wore similar clothing here, and as Ranulf took in the others on the platforms, he realized that there were two men and two women teaching the crowd. Another man he hadn't seen until now walked along the rows, correcting postures, stances, and grips.

"It's amazin'," Crab said, "I'd heard of such a place, but I never thought I'd see it. There's so many people."

The woman who had first glanced at them now stared at them. Ranulf thought she looked beautiful as the light glinted off something metallic around her neck. He could watch her all day as she moved gracefully from one position to another, delicate and strong at the same time.

"We should get goin'," Crab said, taking Ranulf's shoulder and turning him away. They hurried back down the path to the main road.

"I wonder how many there are—fightin' schools, that is," Crab said. "Do you think they would take me?"

"She could take me," Ranulf said.

"What did ya say?" Crab asked as he turned to Ranulf.

"Nothing," Ranulf said. He shook his head to clear it, "Let's go find the market." He clapped Crab on the back.

They ended up following their noses to the market. This was supposed to be one of the biggest markets near this coast, and Ranulf was excited to research what was being sold, what was valuable, and what the market culture was like.

Ranulf was gathering information about what was valuable in this region. They'd come a long way for this, and he planned on being here for a few weeks to determine what he could buy at a low price to bring back to the Kingdom of Adanek and sell at a higher one.

So Crab and Ranulf observed. They walked up and down aisles, drawing gazes as they went, and watched deals being made. Ranulf noticed the haggling was fiercer here than it was back home, and there was more showmanship too. He also noticed he and Crab were at least a head taller than most of the people here. Plus, his hair and beard made him a bit of a spectacle.

They would return tomorrow in the early morning with fish to trade for local coin. Then he could start testing the waters. He liked the look of some of their fabrics. They were much more colorful than those that were made back home. He wondered how much they could bring back with them.

At that thought, he wondered how much time it might take for the villagers to manufacture more. He might as well bring back as much as he could afford or as much as his ship could carry.

Ranulf was so lost in thought as he absentmindedly wandered the aisles that he didn't notice the group lurking, slowly tightening the circle around him. When he finally did notice, he looked around for Crab and realized the true warrior of the two was off somewhere else.

"Look, I don't want any trouble. I don't have anything on me." Ranulf had long learned never to carry any valuables with him in the first few days in a new place. He was always tested. But as a fighter, he was the weaker one. Crab was the better warrior. Ranulf made a show of emptying his pockets as this group surrounded him and shouted something he didn't understand. They started to close in, and Ranulf wondered whether it would be better to run or to try and grab at one of their sticks. No one had brought out a knife yet, so at least there was that.

Ranulf made a mental note to come better armed next time and to really focus a little more when Crab was trying to teach him about fighting.

The circle tightened, and Ranulf knew he was in trouble. Then a blur of light-purple fabric caught his eye from the roof above; it leaped and landed next to him. He was so surprised that he just turned and stared at the woman from earlier that afternoon.

She said something menacingly. Then a blade shot out from each of her sleeves. This woman was magical. Ranulf stood off to the side as the group changed their focus to the woman in purple. She wore something like an embroidered tunic with large sleeves over long skirts. Before he even realized what was happening, she twirled and flew around the circle. The ruffians' sticks flew away. Ranulf had never seen such an extraordinary person in his whole life.

The men fled down the alley, and the woman brushed herself off. She carefully inspected her knives before tucking them back in her sleeves.

"Are you all right?" she asked slowly and carefully, as if testing the words.

Ranulf stood, still stunned and frozen. "You're incredible," he said, not fully realizing that the woman had just spoken to him in his own language. He moved slowly to not startle her into stabbing him, gently took her hand, and brought it to his lips. "Thank you."

His eyes traveled up her sleeve to her face, and her dark-brown eyes sparkled. Ranulf felt something inside him snap into place as his heart started to race. He bowed low and said, "My name is Ranulf. I'm eternally grateful for your appearance."

"The pleasure is mine," she said, dipping her head.

Ranulf still had her hand in his, and she didn't pull away, so he held it, gently tracing the delicate fingers with his own. "Your name?" he whispered.

"My name is Xu Jinhua," she said, smiling.

"There ya are." Crab appeared at the aisles' intersection. Jinhua and Ranulf jumped apart. "I just saw a bunch of guys runnin' the other way, so I knew ya must have been in trouble." Then he finally saw Ranulf wasn't alone. "Oh. Wait, aren't ya the woman from the fightin' school?"

Jinhua nodded to Ranulf. "Good evening," she said before hurrying away. After turning a couple of corners, she disappeared into the night.

"You all right?" Crab came and put his hands on Ranulf's shoulders as he looked him over for injury. "Ya look pale."

Ranulf finally blinked. "I just met my wife," he said dreamily. His hand still tingled where it had held hers.

"Ranulf." Crab shook his friend as he shook his own head. He steered him back toward the docks. They would sleep on the ship for a few days until they could better establish themselves in the village.

"Ranulf, I know you're noble in all official capacities, but ya said that was Xu Jinhua? Do ya even know who she is? Her family is legendary in the fightin' arts," Crab said. He sat in his hammock, hands moving quickly as he crocheted something. They were back on their ship settling in for the night.

"I don't care," Ranulf said. All he could think of was her, the way she moved, the way she smelled, the way the corners of her eyes wrinkled when she smiled.

"Ya don't understand, Ranulf. The Xu family has three sons and three daughters. I can't remember which one, but I'm pretty sure one daughter is engaged to the crown prince of Cerisa," Crab said.

"When did you become so knowledgeable?" Ranulf suddenly turned his attention to his friend and business partner.

"When ya were off gallivantin', I met someone originally from Adanek. We went fer a drink, and he filled me in on all the gossip. He's gonna meet us tomorrow," Crab continued.

Crab was quiet as he carefully examined his stitches, mouthing numbers to himself. Ranulf found himself drifting back to images of flying purple fabric and dark-brown eyes. He leaned back in the hammock he had hung in the corner. Even though he was technically captain, he'd worked on so many ships, he'd found it tough to sleep on a thin mattress instead of the hammock he was used to.

"I'm on first watch, so ya better get some actual sleep," Crab said. He jumped out of his hammock and pushed through the door.

Ranulf could tell Crab was annoyed, but he didn't care.

Chapter Three
Jinhua

"How was patrol last night?" Fangyee helped pull the pins out of Jinhua's hair as Jinhua sat on a wooden stool in front of the mirror.

"Huh?" Jinhua said.

"How was patrol last night?" her sister asked again. She shook her head. "You better hope the prince marries you before he notices how often your head is in the clouds."

"Maybe he'd love me more for it." Jinhua stuck her chin out.

"The only thing he'll love is the many children you produce for him," Fangyee said.

Jinhua stuck her tongue out at her sister as Fangyee slowly let Jinhua's hair fall and then started to brush it. Fangyee's lips moved as she counted out a hundred brush strokes, but Jinhua let her mind wander to the strange traveler she'd met and heard nothing of her sister's counting.

He'd been so kind and sweet. She hated ruffians who tried to take what wasn't theirs, so she'd gladly jumped into the fight. Yet she'd never met anyone so incapable of fighting. He intrigued her. Every time she closed her eyes, she saw the tall, wide man's gray eyes. His odd, dark, reddish-brown hair also intrigued her; she'd never seen hair like that before. And she would have thought gray eyes would look stormy and cold, but his were only soft and warm. She had felt that same warmth bloom from their connected hands. She knew it wasn't proper for a man to hold her hand, especially since she was betrothed to another man, but she hadn't wanted to let go.

"Little sister." Fangyee smacked Jinhua on the head with the back of the wooden brush.

Jinhua blinked. "Ow. What'd you do that for?"

"In the clouds again, are we? I'm done. Now do mine." Fangyee smacked Jinhua's shoulder, then butt, with the same brush to get her off the stool. Usually, they had help dressing and undressing, but Fangyee's temper made them lose maids more regularly than their monthly cycles arrived.

Jinhua stood up and shifted her voluminous sleeves as Fangyee sat down.

"Did you see how Renshu looked at Peng-li today?" Fangyee liked gossiping.

"No, I didn't. Was it lascivious?" Jinhua asked, playing along with her sister and using the new word she'd learned from their tutor the other day. She shoved the gray eyes from her mind for now, focusing on her sister's hair. Jinhua removed the pins one by one, careful not to wiggle them so they didn't poke Fangyee in the head, before loosening the twisted strands. Then she gently brushed Fangyee's hair as her sister continued to prattle on about how this person looked at that person.

"Did you see the travelers today? The smaller one is pretty handsome by foreigner standards. They stared at us like idiots." Fangyee laughed. "It's like they'd never seen a fighting school before."

A thought occurred to Jinhua and she spoke it before she could stop herself. "Maybe they hadn't."

"Now you're being an idiot. Fighting schools are everywhere, even in the rural areas," Fangyee replied as she shook her finger at her sister.

Jinhua focused on brushing her sister's hair. She'd lost track of her strokes a long time ago, but she knew she could just continue brushing for twenty minutes and she'd be done. It wasn't like Fangyee was counting given how much she was talking.

"They have such peculiar hair and eyes," Fangyee said. "I even overheard Peng-li say how handsome the red-haired one is."

Jinhua felt a wave of jealousy course through her and struggled to keep it hidden. She barely knew Ranulf, yet she promised herself she'd hit Peng-li really, really hard the next time they practiced together. "Oh? I saw them standing there, but I didn't notice anything extraordinary about them," Jinhua said, trying to keep her voice indifferent and even.

"I wonder if they'll stay long enough to cause a scandal," Fangyee said, practically salivating at the possibility.

"Just because they're foreigners doesn't mean they'll cause a scandal."

"They're foreigners. They *always* cause a scandal. They don't know anything about our ways," Fangyee said.

Jinhua had a few more minutes before she finished what must be over a hundred strokes; she couldn't finish fast enough. "Maybe someone should teach them."

"Why?" Fangyee snorted.

"So there's no scandal. Don't we aim for peace?" Jinhua asked.

"If you're so keen, maybe you should go and teach them." Fangyee laughed.

"Maybe I will," Jinhua said, hoping the heat in her cheeks was masked by the room's dimness.

Jinhua put the brush down and both sisters climbed into bed.

"You'll have the best access to the gossip at the palace. You'll have to tell me everything," Fangyee said.

"Of course," Jinhua said, noticing Fangyee hadn't offered to help tutor the foreigners. She wondered if Amah would even allow it. That prompted her to ponder the best way to present the idea to Amah. Maybe she should write to the prince.

She still couldn't believe she'd never met His Royal Highness. Though this was how it was done in her kingdom, and it was a great honor to marry the prince, she couldn't get the image of Ranulf softly kissing her hand out of her head. As she lay in the darkened room, her fingertips gently brushed the top of her other hand as if she could still feel the kiss lingering on her skin.

CHAPTER FOUR
Jinhua

THE NEXT MORNING, JINHUA was down in the training ring before Fangyee. She and Renshu always trained first. Sleeping little and rising before the sun was habit for them. She breathed in the fresh morning air, free of sweat that early. She went around to light her side of the lamps as Rennie did the same on his side. Walls of woven mats framed by dark-red wood enclosed this training space; it was a family training area. There was no way Amah would have allowed the intricately carved wood and woven mats in a training space for students. New punctures and tears would mar it every day.

"You have to keep a cap on your glances at Peng-li," Jinhua said as her morning greeting. She slid out of her shoes and sighed as her feet met the cool floor as she grounded herself.

"Fanny say something?" Renshu asked.

Jinhua nodded.

He handed her a staff as tall as she was, and they started their forms together, going through the movements like they had every morning since they were children. "I heard there was a disturbance in the alley last night. A foreigner was almost attacked, but a highly-skilled warrior came to his rescue." Renshu, a whole head and shoulders taller than her, raised his eyebrows.

"That group of boys is a nuisance," Jinhua said, careful not to admit or deny anything. "How did you know anyway?"

"I was around the corner when the boys ran by. I tripped one for you," he said.

They were silent as they leaped and jumped in the sequence they always followed.

"What are the foreigners like?" Renshu asked.

"They seemed ..." Jinhua thought about what she wanted to reveal. Of all her siblings, he was the one she was closest to; still, they all had their agendas.

Renshu stopped and waited for her to finish her sentence.

"They seemed nice enough," she said.

"Nice enough to kiss your hand?" Renshu asked, finishing the form with his staff.

Jinhua felt her cheeks warm and stabbed her staff at Renshu.

"It was nothing," Jinhua said. She faced her brother, ready to start sparring.

Renshu smiled. "If you say so." His eyebrows rose as he grinned, but he was kind enough not to push the issue.

Jinhua thought about her plan to teach the two foreigners. If Renshu helped her, it might be feasible. "What do you think of teaching the foreigners?"

He pursed his lips, thinking on it a moment. "What do you want to teach them?"

"Our culture, our language," she said, hoping her voice sounded as even as she wanted it to.

"Why?"

"So they don't cause a scandal. We strive for peace, no?"

"You'd cause a scandal if you did it on your own," Renshu remarked.

"Maybe," Jinhua said, not ready to ask him to help.

A gong sounded, and Jinhua and Renshu quickly put their staffs away before heading for breakfast. Amah would skin them alive if they were late.

They ate silently, quietly bringing their spoons of congee to their mouths. There was pork in this morning's breakfast, and she hoped that meant they'd get fish tomorrow. Fish was Jinhua's favorite.

"I'd like to start a new project, Amah," Renshu said after everyone had finished their breakfast. This was the only time the family could speak with each other before supper. Even then, they were usually joined by students, so breakfast was the only sacred time for family.

"Rennie, of course. What has piqued your interest this time?" Amah asked.

"Every time foreigners come here, they make mistakes, disturb the peace," Renshu said, sounding bored.

Their mother nodded at this, and Jinhua's brothers looked questioningly at Renshu.

"It's not their fault they don't know better. It's like the monkeys who wander in and take things. I would like to teach them, so they know better," Renshu said.

"My brave boy!" Amah said. "So kind and community driven. Why can't the rest of you useless children be more like Rennie?"

The other siblings nodded and bowed their heads. Jinhua knew they would be extra hard on him today for that.

"Amah, it is a big project. May I have help?" Renshu asked.

"Yes, of course. Foreigners are stupid. You will need much patience," Amah said.

"I think Jinhua should practice her patience. She will have to deal with many stupid people when she is princess," Renshu said.

"Such a smart boy. Yes, Jinhua should help you. She will indeed need to learn more patience to deal with all the stupid city people when she is at the palace. A princess should have infinite patience, with her husband *and* her subjects," Amah replied.

Jinhua bit down on her tongue, schooling her face into a neutral expression. "Yes, Amah." She bowed her head as her brother started talking about his expectations for the family at the upcoming sword competition.

Jinhua didn't hear much of the rest of the conversation. Her heart was fluttering at the thought of seeing Ranulf again.

After breakfast, they taught their morning lessons and then Renshu and Jinhua headed into town to find the foreigners. It didn't take long to learn they had returned to their docked ship for the night, so the siblings made their way to the dock. Even though Renshu and Jinhua had already been awake for hours, the sun was just rising above the horizon as they walked along the dock to the smaller foreign ship.

"Whaddaya want?" a skinny foreign man asked.

Renshu's eyebrow rose questioningly. It was a rather rude way to greet someone. "You owe me big time for this," he muttered to Jinhua before plastering a smile on his face. "We'd like to speak to the two men who came into town yesterday."

"Whaddya want wiv 'em?" the man demanded.

Jinhua saw Renshu's smile tighten, but before she could say anything, Ranulf came on deck and spotted them.

"That's no way to greet guests, Mouse." He turned to his visitors. "My apologies. Many of my men are nervous in these lands because it's our first time here." Ranulf stepped up to the rail and smiled widely, opening his arms wide, allowing Jinhua to see he was unarmed.

Jinhua's heart was doing somersaults.

Ranulf hesitated briefly as he looked at Jinhua standing next to Renshu. His gaze returned to Renshu a little more intensely than before, and he asked, "Would you like to board, or would you be more comfortable if I came to you?"

"I've never seen the inner workings of a foreign ship before," Renshu said.

So Mouse hurried over to help Ranulf lower the gangplank, and Renshu took Jinhua's arm in his before ascending to the deck. Once aboard, Ranulf moved some crates around to create some seating.

Jinhua saw now that there were actually more men on deck than she'd seen before, most on their hands and knees rubbing linseed oil into the wood.

"Never know when a storm might arrive. We waterproof when we can." Ranulf watched her gaze move around the ship.

Jinhua watched as Ranulf asked his guests to sit first before he did. The other large man arrived and joined them, preferring to straddle a chair he'd brought with him.

"I'm Ranulf, and this is my partner, Crab." Ranulf motioned to the man who straddled the chair.

Crab was a strange name, and Jinhua realized it was also the name of a sea creature she very much enjoyed eating.

"I am Renshu. And this is my sister, Jinhua," Renshu said.

Jinhua noticed Ranulf's tension ease when Rennie said the word "sister."

"You must allow me to compliment your mastery of our language," Ranulf said.

"Our grandmother believes in learning many languages, so communication is never a barrier," Renshu explained.

Jinhua kept her gaze down as was appropriate, but she snuck peeks at Crab and Ranulf through her lowered lashes.

"She sounds like a wise person," Ranulf said, his brow creased as if he was trying to put pieces together.

Mouse, the man who had greeted them so rudely before, brought out a few tankards of ale and placed them as delicately as he could on the crate between them. "My apologies fer my behavior before, m'lady," he said, dipping his head and bowing to Jinhua.

Renshu took the drink. As a lady, Jinhua couldn't. To her, it stunk like the back end of an animal anyway.

"In the past, when foreigners came, they've always caused problems. They disrespected our precious things or insulted our people because of their ignorance of our traditions. My family is a leader in this community, and we've decided to teach you some of our language and customs in hopes of preventing problems—if you are amenable," Renshu stated, never breaking eye contact with Ranulf.

"Oh?" Ranulf was busy looking from Renshu to Jinhua and back.

"Yes," Renshu said.

"We would be honored to learn anything you have to teach us," Ranulf said.

Jinhua glanced up to see Ranulf staring at her.

"Good. Then first things first. You will move to the inn in town. Being part of the community is a good first step. We have already arranged for two rooms for you and Crab. Um, I must ask though, isn't 'crab' an ocean creature?" Renshu asked.

"Yeah. It's a nickname," Crab explained.

"What is this word, 'nickname'?" Renshu asked.

"It's a ... name given to a friend that reminds both people of somethin' funny that happened in the past," Crab said.

Jinhua wanted to ask what had happened for a person to be named after such a lowly creature, but it would be rude, so she restrained herself. Her cheeks felt hot as Ranulf stared openly at her. So she decided to end the conversation. "We will train mid-morning every day. See you tomorrow morning." She nodded.

Renshu took her cue as she rose and held out an arm for her as they descended the gangplank and returned home to teach the afternoon lessons.

CHAPTER FIVE
Ranulf

RANULF LEANED OVER THE bow of his ship as he watched the beautiful Lady Jinhua walk away. She had acted so differently than the night before. Last night, she'd been bold and fearless. Today, she was shy and spoke barely a word. He wondered if it was a cultural difference or if he'd done something to offend her. He was glad she had come to see him today though. And he was excited at the prospect of seeing her every day. He could do without the brother, but he would gladly sit next to lions to spend another moment with her.

"Ya have to keep yer wits," Crab said.

Ranulf turned to see Crab staring at him, eyebrows raised.

Crab shook his head. "That was a warnin' as much as an offer. Why would one of the most powerful families in the area offer to teach little ol' us?"

"Maybe they like us?" Ranulf suggested hopefully. A small part of him hoped it was because Jinhua had wanted to see him again. That made the butterflies in his stomach take flight.

They were finishing maintenance on the ship later that afternoon when Crab declared, "If we wanna get to that inn before nightfall, we better get a move on." He looked around at the ship's crew and gave them all orders, and Ranulf went below to pack what he would need in town.

Ranulf hoped they would be able to sell some goods in the next two weeks because he only had enough coin to stay at the inn for that long. Though he had already secured supplies for their return journey, he had really hoped to gather as much product as they could before departing. He'd hate to dip into his personal budget for product or have to leave the inn and reboard his ship. The last thing he wanted was to offend the locals.

He shook his head and straightened before heading above deck to meet Crab. Together, they strode through town to the inn. After the owner had shown them to the rooms Renshu had reserved for them, Ranulf looked around. It was bare; nothing more than a hard bed, a small dresser and table, a desk, and a stool filled the space, but at least it was bigger than his room on his ship.

A small window sat higher up than windows at home, but he peeked out and saw a few people milling about in the streets.

Crab knocked and opened the door that connected the two rooms. He had taken the servant's room saying he didn't need much space, but Ranulf knew he was honoring Ranulf's role as captain.

They went downstairs and ate their supper as they pretended to ignore the hooded stares of the locals. But soon enough, rice wine replaced tea, and the room got louder as the patrons enjoyed themselves.

"Taverns are the same around the world. Isn't it amazing?" Ranulf asked Crab. He marveled at how similar things could be in such different parts of the world.

"Uh huh," Crab said, scanning the room.

At Crab's non-answer, Ranulf shooed them upstairs, knowing Crab wouldn't relax until they were behind a closed door. He always worried trouble was brewing.

CHAPTER SIX
Jinhua

J INHUA TRIED TO RESIST patting down her clothes for the hundredth time. She had been wide awake by the time the sun had greeted the sky and gone quietly to do her exercises before even Renshu was up. She'd left her staff out to let Renshu know she'd already been there and then returned to her rooms to get ready. First, Jinhua used the bathing chambers, borrowing some of her sister's jasmine-scented oils. Afterward, she dressed, having chosen her outfit the night before. She'd tried three outfits before coming back to this one. She huffed and went to breakfast.

So impatient to get through breakfast was she that she couldn't help but bounce her knee under the table, trying to keep her expression neutral. Fangyee shot her a stern look when Jinhua's elbow bumped her, making her drop her egg into her rice, where the yolk promptly broke. After that, Jinhua wriggled her toes back and forth. Renshu ignored her, probably on purpose to not give her away.

Unfortunately, she caught her mother's attention in the end. "Jinhua, you can barely sit still. Calm yourself," Amah chastised.

Jinhua bowed her head, trying to make her body stay still.

"Oh, she's just nervous about how stupid the foreigners will be. Don't be afraid to show them our strict ways, sister," Fangyee said, tapping two fingertips on the table next to her teacup as their youngest brother refilled it. Jinhua followed suit.

Jinhua paid attention to her breathing to calm her racing heart as she counted the seconds until breakfast was finished. She didn't focus on the conversation at all; she couldn't wait to get some of her energy out teaching the morning's first class.

In the training yard, she nodded to the students who had come early, and Renshu silently handed her her staff before joining his group. The students went through their forms, and Jinhua circled around to correct postures and stances, grips and foot angles. She enjoyed the work, and it absorbed her.

Suddenly, she felt a flutter in her stomach and an impulse to look behind her. When she did, she saw Ranulf standing with Crab at the gate of their training yard, watching intently. Renshu had seen them too and invited them to come and watch from inside the yard. They sat on an out-of-the-way bench, the same bench potential students sat on to watch the class.

When Jinhua glanced over, Ranulf waved enthusiastically. But Jinhua knew all her students were watching, and to show an enthusiastic reception of a foreigner would be a poor decision. She turned on her heel and continued instructing her students, refusing to look at him even though the butterflies were now jumping and leaping and swooping in her stomach like they were trying to wave back.

"Sister, we didn't get the opportunity to practice this morning. Would you like to help me demonstrate?" Renshu asked as she returned to supervising.

"What are you up to, Renshu?" she murmured as she bowed to accept his offer. The students all stopped practicing and turned to face them, eager to watch.

"Showing you off," Renshu said. He held his own staff loosely in his hands and tapped it twice on the ground.

"You mean *scaring* them off," Jinhua replied. She narrowed her eyes, but suddenly she couldn't continue talking as she defended against her brother's offensive strikes.

He came at her harder than usual, and she let her training kick in. She was angry at her brother for putting her on the spot as he had. So she focused that anger into every hit, not letting it get in the way of reading his body as he moved.

Her Amah had described it as that rare moment when all was in balance, as though time moved slowly and you moved faster than you ought to, thought faster than you ought to. It was a moment when everything was easy for a warrior. All the training, all the bruises, scars, and difficulties came together in this moment when you were in a zone of complete ease. While her brothers and sisters had awed about it and decided to work harder for the next several days after Amah's explanation, Jinhua had recognized that feeling given how often she slipped into it. She excelled at the martial arts and often beat her brothers. After two of her brothers had ganged up on her, though, she had realized she had to let them win or be constantly exhausted. Only Renshu accepted her superior skills and ability.

Only when she finally had the staff pushing firmly on Renshu's throat as he lay sprawled on the ground did she blink herself out of that mental state. Panting, she took Renshu's hand and helped him up.

The students all cheered and clapped, and Jinhua didn't dare turn to Ranulf and Crab to see their expressions. The students bowed as she walked by them, leaving Renshu to deal with the end of class.

She was now smelly and sweaty and decided she could afford to bathe again. Though she was angry that Renshu had made her work so hard, it felt good. It also felt good knowing Renshu had given her the chance to really fight to her level. She and Renshu were the best warriors in their family after all, aside from maybe their father.

Half an hour later, Jinhua sat in the tub, letting her tears fall as she thought of the horrible things Ranulf must think of her now. She didn't know much about Adanekian culture, but she knew most foreigners were disgusted with a woman who could fight as well as she could, as well or better than a man. She'd never be able to face him again. Once again, she'd lost her temper and beat her brother, a man, in combat. It was the farthest thing from ladylike she could imagine. Any man would ask that she temper her warrior ways before they marry—and the prince had already done so.

Oh my. The prince. How could she be thinking of another man and what he thought of her when she was betrothed to another man? She wanted so badly to serve her country, and the only way for her to do that was to marry the prince as promised. She had to be as honorable as her sisters. Fangyee had been to many fighting competitions and had a few warrior suitors from other warrior families courting her, and her oldest sister, Qiao, had joined the royal guard only last year. It was the greatest honor next to Jinhua's contract with the prince.

A soft knock interrupted her spiraling thoughts. "Jin-jin?" Renshu cracked the door open.

"Get out of here, Renshu. I'm naked," she said. Her voice cracked, giving her away.

"Jin-jin. I'm sorry. I wanted to show off how beautiful a warrior you are, that you don't need a man to protect you. In fact, you could protect him." Renshu laughed.

"It's not ladylike," was all Jinhua managed to say as she tried to hold herself together.

"How do you know what he appreciates?" Renshu asked. "You left before you saw his face. That foreigner would jump to his death for you. He's in love with you. I've seen it since that night I spied you in the alley with those thugs."

"Really?" Jinhua asked, her tears drying.

"Yes, really," Renshu said. "Now hurry up. You'll be all wrinkly. Men like wrinkles even less than warriors."

Jinhua threw a bar of soap at the door.

When he had gone, she pulled herself out of the cooled water. She dressed again in her special outfit, met Renshu in the hall, then walked to town with him, holding her brother's arm so they could speak privately in low whispers.

"What about the prince?" Jinhua asked.

"What about him? He hasn't so much as come to meet you since you signed the contract. And last I heard, he drinks too much and has too many nightly visits," Renshu said. His jaw was tight, and Jinhua wondered how he knew these things.

"But the family," Jinhua said.

"Our family will still produce warriors. People will still pay to train with us. That won't change. We just won't be sending people to their deaths in the army as required just because you married the prince."

"Amah won't like it," Jinhua said.

"Amah is an old lady and too stuck in the old ways, no matter what that means for her children. She might not like it, but I don't care. You're my favorite sister, and I want to assure your happiness, not hers. She's already lived a life. You have to live yours."

Jinhua paused to look up at her brother. "And you think I could be happy with a foreigner?"

"We'll find out, won't we? All I know is that foreigner looks at you like a worshipper does at a god that's descended to our mortal realm," Renshu said. "That indicates a better chance at happiness than being one of the many wives of a drunken prince."

Jinhua laughed; Renshu could always entertain her with his fanciful ideas. They arrived at the inn then, and Jinhua covered her mouth with her hand to hide her smile as Renshu nodded to the keeper who pointed to a side room.

Renshu opened the door for her while she put her basket down, and as she stepped into the room, Ranulf and Crab stood up. This room was often used for meetings of about a dozen people, so they had ample space with various tables and even a board on which to write.

"Good morning, Lady Jinhua." Ranulf bowed and Crab smiled as he followed his friend's lead.

"And Master Renshu." Ranulf nodded to Renshu and bowed carefully as if worried about offending him.

"It's good to see you again," Renshu said, and he offered his hand as he'd seen the foreigners do.

Surprise crossed Crab's face as he took his hand and shook it, then let Ranulf do the same. Jinhua thought she ought to be equal to them, so she offered her hand in the same way Renshu had. Ranulf took her hand and bowed his head over it, his lips brushing the top of her hand. Though she wished he'd held her hand longer than the brief moment he had, Jinhua froze.

"Lassie, he don' mean no harm. In Adanek, it's customary for men to greet each other with handshakes. But when men greet women, they bow an' kiss their hands as Ranulf does." Crab explained, eyeing Renshu as if expecting him to leap at Ranulf.

"I see. And why is this?" Jinhua asked.

"We are taught to treat women with precious gentleness," Ranulf said. Jinhua made the mistake of looking into Ranulf's eyes at that moment There she saw the soft warmth that always pulled her in.

Renshu coughed. "Here in Cerisa, you'll bow at the waist. We do not make physical contact with women unless assisting them. The deeper the bow, the more respect shown."

Ranulf and Crab nodded.

"We'll get started now if you like?" Renshu sat down and Crab did the same.

Jinhua tore herself away from Ranulf and went back to retrieve her basket. She sat in the chair Renshu purposely pulled out across from

Crab so she'd be further away from Ranulf and held the basket in her lap.

"First, do you have any questions from your first days here?" Renshu asked.

"Yes. If ya don' mind our bein' rude?" Crab asked.

"We will not consider any questions rude. We cannot learn about each other if we're too worried to speak our minds. In this room, we will speak freely and without judgment, yes?" Renshu asked.

Everyone nodded their agreement.

"We've noticed ya treat yer noble ladies as gently as we do ours, yet they spar an' teach in the fightin' schools. Lady Jinhua, for example, appears to have the same status and respect as the male instructors. Are we correct?" Crab asked.

"Yes, that is true. In the fighting arts, we are rated by rank and skill. As you saw this morning, our family runs a school of fighting arts, and Jinhua, me, and my two other brothers and sister have the same rank as the other teachers. But within our family, we are ranked by age. When it comes to skill, however, Jinhua is the most skilled warrior in our family. Don't tell my brothers though. They are incredibly arrogant," Renshu explained.

Jinhua felt her cheeks warm.

"Are all women trained to fight?" Crab asked.

"No. It is popular, or fashionable, for nobility to send their children to our school for private lessons. Though most nobles will never use the fighting arts, they enjoy learning for exercise and entertainment. On the other hand, some women seek accomplishment in different ways, like poetry and painting," Renshu replied.

"Do you enjoy it?" Ranulf suddenly asked, looking only at Jinhua.

Jinhua looked at her brother, who only raised his eyebrows as he awaited her answer. "I enjoy the physical exertion. And the movements. It is like dancing," she said.

"Ya seem very talented," Crab said.

"That is kind of you. I am only as good as my best teacher," Jinhua said, deflecting the compliment and bowing her head.

"Is humility an admired trait in yer culture?" Crab asked Renshu.

Renshu nodded. "You are correct. Arrogance is a great sin. Direct eye contact is considered aggressive when you pass someone in the street or meet someone briefly."

"What is the polite way to greet people then?" Ranulf finally turned his attention to Renshu.

"It depends on how well you know them. If you do not know them, you do not acknowledge them unless you've bumped into them. And even then, only acknowledge them if they belong to one of the great houses," Renshu said. "But if you meet someone you are acquainted with, say if you were to run into us in the street now, we might stop, nod to each other, say hello, and ask how you are. Now, if you were in the street and encountered someone you'd only met once or twice, the owner of this inn, for example, you would nod your head like so"—he tilted his head and nodded—"as you passed each other."

They continued to discuss customs and greetings and cultural differences for the next few hours until Renshu and Jinhua left with promises to return the next day.

"Why didn't you say anything?" Renshu asked Jinhua as they walked home.

"What do you mean?" Jinhua asked. She thought she had joined the conversation sufficiently.

"You were like the serene maiden of the matchmaker in there," Renshu said, his expression puzzled.

"I …" Jinhua paused as she thought back. "… I was being polite."

"Polite? They wouldn't have understood that as being polite. From where I sat, it seemed like you didn't want to have anything to do with that entire conversation."

"Are you just angry because you had to do all the work?" Jinhua raised a skeptical eyebrow. Renshu had never had a problem doing all the talking before.

"I know I usually do the talking, but I could have seriously used some help back there. I can only teach from a male point of view. And for that matter, be yourself! Those two aren't hampered by our cultural need for ladies to appear demure." Renshu's voice gentled.

Jinhua studied her brother's face, "You like them."

"I do. They're refreshing, earnest. Exciting even. They're respectful, not bawdy and loud, and they don't drink too much," Renshu said.

"Tomorrow. I promise I will be more helpful tomorrow then," Jinhua said.

"Good." Renshu looped his arm in hers, and they turned the corner onto their street and changed topics. They would have to help with afternoon classes and then train with their siblings as they always did.

Jinhua's heart felt lighter. Though she knew all her siblings would be harsher on her today for having missed her mid-morning duties, excitement bubbled within her for the rest of the day. She was excited to get to tomorrow and see the handsome man with the kind, sparkling gray eyes.

CHAPTER SEVEN
Ranulf

RANULF SWALLOWED HARD SO he wouldn't swoon after Jinhua and Renshu had said their farewells. Then he and Crab made their way to the docks to see to their ship and check in with Mouse.

"Well, that was unexpected," Crab said. He rubbed the back of his neck and looked around at the crew as they suddenly sped up, rubbing linseed oil into the deck boards. He knew they were all listening to the conversation. The crew was excited for any and all news.

Ranulf nodded and closed his eyes. If he closed his eyes, he could almost pretend she was still here. He breathed in slowly, trying to remember the delicate smell of jasmine and lemongrass. He took two more slow breaths before opening his eyes to see his best friend staring at him with wide eyes, waiting. "What?" Ranulf asked.

"Ya can't seriously tell me ya didn't notice how cold she was," Crab said.

"She came to us, didn't she? Maybe that's just cultural. Maybe she was just being polite," Ranulf suggested.

"Maybe. Or maybe that was her version of goodbye," Crab said.

"She'll be back. She has to come back," Ranulf said. He grinned like a fool and leaped up from the crates suddenly. He put his hands on his hips and looked around at his little ship, watching his crew waterproofing the deck.

"We still goin' to market today?" Crab finally piped up after Ranulf had stared at the same poor new crew member for a solid three minutes.

"Yes. Let me gather more of my things," Ranulf said.

"Why?" Crab asked.

"We should probably stay at the inn for the duration as they suggested, and I only brought enough for one night. I wasn't sure how this would work out."

"Ya really wanna do that?"

"Yes, I do now. Though perhaps tomorrow we can ask more about why."

"So, yer just gonna to jump when Renshu says 'jump' and duck when he says 'duck'?" Crab asked.

"Yes, if it means I get to see her again."

Ranulf nodded enthusiastically, then headed below deck as he heard Crab mutter, "Goddesses help us."

"Do you have everything you'll need, Crab?" Ranulf shouted from below.

Crab looked up and made eye contact with Mouse. With one nod, command seamlessly passed from Crab to Mouse as the small ship's crew continued their afternoon work.

Moments later, Ranulf came back on deck and spoke to each of the six crew members individually, reminding them of his expectations. Then he came to Mouse. "You're in charge while we're at the inn. We'll be sure to check in at least once a day," Ranulf said. "Do you remember the tasks that need completing while we're away?"

Mouse nodded. "Yes, Captain. Continue to oil everythin': the deck today, the mast, every wood surface. Then the sides above the water."

Ranulf nodded, waiting for him to continue.

"Then the ropes, inspected an' cleaned an' dried. New ones made. Polish all metal parts until we can count our teeth in 'em," Mouse said.

Ranulf nodded again. "Good. If you need us, you know where we'll be. I hope to return to all of you with many wares and lighter pockets," Ranulf said.

"May you be successful," the crew replied in unison. It was a little saying they'd created for whenever Ranulf went off to the markets and had now become a tradition, even a superstition, given he'd always been successful thus far.

"Ready, Crab?" Ranulf asked as he swung his pack over his shoulder and Crab also exchanged quiet words with Mouse.

Crab nodded and they strode off their small ship and onto the dock, heading into town and turning toward the inn. They walked through the open doors to their rooms to the left of the tavern.

Ranulf looked at the keys. There were no numbers on them, only symbols. Maybe it was just how they wrote numbers here. Either way, he and Crab strode down the hallway, past the meeting room they'd met Jinhua and Renshu in earlier, slowing at each door and looking at each door's symbol and checking it against their own keys. Though they'd found their way to their rooms the night before, Ranulf still thought it was a curious labeling system.

"Let's ask them about numbers and symbols tomorrow," Ranulf said.

Crab only grunted as he held his key up to the symbol on his door and raised an eyebrow.

They pushed their doors open at the same time, and Ranulf went and put his additional belongings in the drawers. No sooner had he finished when he heard a knock on the wall by his bed, so Ranulf left his room and popped into Crab's. When he walked in, a small part of him deflated despite himself. Crab's room was much bigger and had many more luxuries, such as a lamp and softer bed coverings. That was odd, given these were supposedly the servant's quarters. Perhaps the owner had explained it wrong, or perhaps something had been lost in translation.

"I'll switch if ya like," Crab said.

"No, that's fine. We're partners in this. Besides I have the big room on our ship."

Crab looked as if he might say something, but then he nodded. "The market then?"

Ranulf nodded and they left, passing the silent barkeeper on the way out with only a quick dip of the head. They passed a few old men engrossed in what looked like a card game but with blocks. Ranulf would have been content to sit and watch, but Crab pulled him along.

They entered the market from the side entrance today. As soon as they stepped among the tables, Ranulf's heart leaped. This was what he lived for. Ever since he had been a small boy at the market with his mother, he'd loved it. The swirl of different smells hitting him from all sides as they walked down rows of vendors, the colorful wares, the people of all walks gathered to purchase, trade, and barter all combined to create a heady feeling. He could never decide what his favorite part was, the textiles or the food. Or perhaps it was the hustle and bustle of people ready to find that little something that would make their lives better or the many sellers standing behind their tables trying to catch people's attention by yelling, being flashy, or demonstrating the wonders of their wares.

This time, Ranulf and Crab took a closer look at the stalls and tables and how many there were in each category. The two noted the numbers and then went back and walked the aisles again. They inspected the variety of goods. That told them much: which vendors were middlemen, which vendors made their wares themselves, and where the deals lay. Those vendors who created their own wares usually had less variety but were more willing and able to make deals because they took all the profit. Middlemen needed to make an additional profit to pay their supplier, so there were fewer deals to be had but more to choose from.

Finally, Crab and Ranulf watched the vendors themselves on the third time around, observing how they behaved, especially when customers weren't looking.

Ranulf had it in his mind to make long-term friends. He dreamed of establishing a merchanting empire, and he and Crab had spent many hours talking it over, what they wanted to trade in and how valuable having friends all over the world would be. *Perhaps,* Ranulf thought, *having so many connections will result in an invite from the King of Adanek to bring my newly acquired jewels and other riches to him for purchase. Maybe the king will even commission me to bring back rare, exotic products from faraway places.*

Ranulf's gaze had landed on fancy jewels as he thought of them, and the next thing he knew, a young man stood beside him. The man was about the same age as Ranulf, maybe a little older. He was thin and tall with tan skin and dark hair and had a beard that could rival Ranulf's father's own in length.

"Hello. I couldn't help but notice you also aren't from around here." He bowed to them, and Ranulf noticed that even though the man tried to dress plainly, all his clothes were still beautifully and finely made.

"Hello," Ranulf said. He bowed back, thinking of his lessons, and offered the man a wide smile. "I'm Ranulf. This is my partner, Crab. We are merchants from Adanek."

The man bowed his head. "It is nice to meet you both. My name is Mupto, and I am from a small island to the southeast of Adanek."

"What brings you here?" Ranulf asked. He looked around. Everyone in this kingdom was at least a few inches shorter than him, so it was nice to have to look up at Mupto.

"I am here on behalf of my kingdom, training in the fighting arts," Mupto said.

Crab nodded. "We're staying at the inn in town. Would ya like to join us fer supper there?"

"That would be lovely, thank you. I will leave you to your business this afternoon and call upon you then." Mupto bowed his head and turned to go.

"That was strange," Ranulf said after Mupto had left the market.

"I think he's homesick. It must be difficult to be thrown into a new culture and language. Besides, ya have yer beards in common." Crab grinned.

Ranulf knew Crab never cared to grow such a long beard, but he was such a large man that it didn't matter much. No one would mistake him for a youth.

Only when the market vendors started to pack up their goods did Ranulf and Crab make the trek back to the inn. They washed up, then went to the common area, hoping that the inns in this country were like the inns they'd been to before and served dinner.

Crab and Ranulf took seats opposite each other in the large room that at least looked much like other taverns around the world with its simple furniture and hard-working folks.

"Do you think our friend from earlier will come?" Ranulf asked, feeling a little nervous.

"Yes," Crab said.

"Should we wait for him before we order?"

"Probably best," Crab said.

At that moment, the doors opened again. Though the room was starting to fill, Mupto was unmistakable when he walked in with his height and large, full black beard that seemed almost too full for someone so young.

"Good to see you again, friends," Mupto said with a smile when he reached their table.

"You as well," Ranulf said as the two friends stood and shook hands with their new acquaintance.

As they took their seats, the barkeeper came out of nowhere, putting three large dishes down, not in front of them but in the middle of the table. Then he placed small bowls in front of each man and left as suddenly as he'd appeared.

CHAPTER EIGHT
Ranulf

"WHAT DO WE EAT wif?" Crab said. He looked around, as did Ranulf. All the other patrons were enjoying their meals using nothing more than a couple of sticks.

Mupto leaned over and took a cup full of sticks from the edge of the table. He plunked it down between Ranulf and Crab before asking, "Have you not eaten with these before?"

"What are they?" Crab asked as Ranulf, his eyebrows knit together, observed the other diners.

"I don't understand how they're holding them," Ranulf said. But he took two sticks and tried to imitate the other patrons.

"Here. Like this," Mupto said matter-of-factly. "You have to hold this one here—brace it with the bottom of your thumb—and put this finger there." He put one of his sticks between the second joint of his thumb and over the first joint of his bent ring finger. "Don't move this stick." Then he took a second stick and held it with his thumb, index finger, and middle finger. Moving it up and down with his fingers, he said, "This is the one you move. You move it up and down to grasp things."

Ranulf focused, tongue sticking out, as he practiced holding one stick and moving the other.

Mupto nodded. "It'll take practice."

Crab maneuvered his sticks, then went to grab a dumpling. As he lifted the dumpling from the dish, it came crashing down and skidded along the table, landing next to his bowl. He snapped at it again with the sticks as he picked the dumpling up again. Ranulf could see Crab's knuckles turning white from gripping the sticks so hard. He got the dumpling in his mouth, though, and grinned widely.

Ranulf practiced moving his sticks once more before he went to grab a dumpling. He saw the rice dish next to it but didn't even want to attempt that. He opened his sticks and closed them around a dumpling. Then he lifted it a couple of inches above the dish so that if it fell, it'd land back in the bowl without the dramatics of Crab's attempt. But it stayed where it was, held firmly between his sticks. Holding his breath, his hand slowly made the arduous trek from dish to bowl. His hand was already starting to cramp. The dumpling started to slip, and he rushed the last few inches to his bowl, but the dumpling fell and hit the side of his bowl before landing on the table.

"It'll take time. I had to tighten all my pants when I first arrived," Mupto said. He took a dumpling and popped it into his mouth without any effort.

"I'm going to starve," Ranulf said, finally fishing the dumpling from the table and onto the bowl and then to his mouth with his fingers. His shoulders slumped as he stared at the pile of dumplings and the rice dish.

"Here, soup is much easier," Mupto said. He gathered their bowls and put them beside the large bowl in the middle of the table. Using a brown bowl similar in size to their personal bowls, he scooped up a clear broth, gently pouring it into each of the ceramic bowls and placing them in front of Crab and Ranulf.

"It's acceptable to drink it like this." He grasped the edges of the bowl, bringing it to his lips and drinking straight from the edge.

Ranulf brightened, his whole being excited as he grasped the edges of his own bowl and drank the soup directly. Crab had already emptied his when Ranulf emerged from his now-empty bowl of soup. Finally, he had something in his belly.

Mupto had helped himself to the rice, and now he grasped the chopsticks in his hand, using them more like a shovel to get the rice into his mouth.

"That I can do," Crab said as he followed Mupto's example, bringing the bowl to his mouth and shoveling the rice into it with both sticks. Ranulf took another look around, wondering if Mupto was being kind to put them at ease. But no, most of the patrons were eating their rice the same way. This, at least, would allow him to eat.

After he'd shoveled down a whole bowl of rice, Ranulf was better able to concentrate on things other than his growling stomach. "How long have you been here?" he asked.

"I've been here for a few months," Mupto said.

Ranulf was impressed that Mupto had managed to keep his beard free of rice grains, even soup. He thought of his own beard and self-consciously patted it, looking for rice or other bits.

"And I remember ya mentioned yer a warrior. Why exactly did ya come here to learn?" Crab said.

"I am a soldier in my country. It's a small island called Bulstan. I was tasked with coming here to learn the fighting style of the area and bringing it back to my home country."

"And you found a school willin' to take ya?"

"Our king can be very ... persuasive," Mupto said, smiling.

Crab's shoulders sank in disappointment. "So what 'ave ya learned so far?"

"Much. The style here is very fluid. While we practice a lot of sparring at home, they learn routines first here, and there are many routines. It's a brilliant way to teach the body movements. Then it's up to the fighter to apply the routines to a situation."

"Interestin'," Crab said. He opened his mouth to ask another question but didn't get the chance.

"I've never heard of Bulstan," Ranulf said.

"I'm not surprised. It is a very small island. The only reason we're known at all is because of the trade we do with the world," Mupto said. He seemed more excited to talk about fighting than his own kingdom.

"What is it that you trade in?" Ranulf asked.

"Gems," Mupto said.

Ranulf and Crab's eyes went wide. A whole kingdom that traded mostly in jewels.

"You are merchants, yes?" Mupto asked.

"Yes. Though not at the level of trading jewels. We'll be dealing in common goods for a while," Ranulf said.

"Ah," Mupto said, "You'll have to forgive my ignorance, but what do you mean by 'common goods'?"

"Well," Ranulf said, puffing out his chest, "Instead of bringing back lots of high-priced items, we want to find something that this country makes well and is cheap and unavailable in our country. Then when we bring it home, we can sell it as a higher quality item. It might be something different, something that works better, or something that looks better. But in that way, we can sell it for a higher price than the same item made at home. Or perhaps we can purchase and sell something that serves a purpose, something that make people's lives easier and isn't available at home."

"That is a very good line of thought," Mupto said.

"We've been thinkin' 'bout it a long time," Crab said.

It was a strategy he and Crab had been planning for the last five years.

Normally, Ranulf would worry that they were spilling their plans to a stranger, but the truth was that this was completely unexplored territory. Most other Adanekians didn't explore this far away from home. To his way of thinking, if he had made it this far, taking another chance couldn't be a bad thing.

"To all our adventures!" Mupto raised his teacup, and Crab and Ranulf mimicked him as they had watched the other patrons do.

The barkeeper came hurrying over, shaking his head and taking their teacups away. He replaced them with equally tiny cups and put a jug of a clear liquid on the table. He poured them each a half a cup and then urged them with his hands to do their toast again.

Mupto had a grin on his face as he repeated, "To our adventures!"

When all three raised their cups, the barkeeper pushed their hands together to clink the cups. Then they drank what they thought was water.

Ranulf almost spit it out and Crab's eyes went wide. It was definitely not water.

"Alcohol is much stronger here. And it is clear," Mupto said. His eyes sparkled as he grinned.

The other patrons roared with laughter. They had all turned to watch the foreigners drink their first cup of alcohol.

The barkeeper smiled as he filled their tiny cups again. "On the house tonight."

Crab looked at him, surprise on his face. Ranulf hadn't realized the barkeeper could speak their language. He shrugged as Crab lifted his cup to the barkeeper. "Thank you, good sir."

They lifted their cups to the whole room, and they all took a sip of the drink this time instead of throwing it all back.

The room erupted in raucous laughter before the patrons turned away and ignored their little table, continuing instead with their own festivities.

"What's the drink like in Bulstan?" Crab asked Mupto.

"We have wine, much like other kingdoms. We also have stronger drinks like this. They take a long time to make, but we use them for special occasions. Most times, we drink a mint tea. And in Adanek?"

"We 'ave much weaker drinks than this," Crab said, already looking a little bleary-eyed.

"We have wine, and we have a honey-based drink, sweeter than this, and ale," Ranulf replied for him. He'd stopped taking anything more than tiny little sips because he knew Crab was probably forgetting to pace himself.

"And is it normal for men to go and drink at establishments?" Mupto asked.

"Yes." Crab nodded. "Yes, yes. Just men."

Mupto grinned, looking over at Ranulf. "He will be difficult to get to bed."

"That he will," Ranulf said. While he was a large man, Crab was even larger.

"In Bulstan, it is common to have a drink after dinner, part of the socializing. But men and women eat and drink together. It is often a family event."

"Even the children?" Ranulf asked.

Mupto nodded. "We only drink a small amount after dinner. It is shameful to drink too much."

"It is ... well, mostly shameful to drink too much, but it's always the men in the tavern. I can't say I've ever seen children at a tavern."

"Oh, we drink mostly at home, at parties or dinner parties. We eat, drink, and catch up on comings and goings and other events."

"That sounds wonderful," Ranulf said. He thought back to his own childhood, the madness of having so many siblings running around. He'd found his own little quiet area in the woods out back and played there alone or with his sister and brother. But mostly he'd read about faraway places in the library. The adults almost lived a separate life from the children. He usually saw his parents only once a day, either when presented to them or at the required weapons practice with his family's small army.

He blinked then, coming back to the conversation. Mupto was looking at him with open curiosity. "My apologies," Ranulf said, "I was just thinking of my family and how nice it would have been to converse with each other growing up. We only saw my parents rarely, maybe once a day."

"Why? Who raised you?" Mupto asked.

"My siblings. I have many brothers and sisters. And we had tutors and lessons."

"Oh? I have two siblings myself."

They heard a grunt then, as if Crab was trying to reply. But when they turned to look at him, their eyes went wide. Crab had joined another table of patrons—the loudest—who had started singing.

"Should I ..." Ranulf asked.

"No. I think it might be to your benefit. Bonding with locals and all," Mupto said.

They silently watched the spectacle and Ranulf wondered how Crab knew the words. But then he realized Crab was half a second late with each word; he was repeating what he heard. No one seemed to care though. And the barkeeper didn't seem to mind his patrons getting a little wild. Ranulf even saw him grin at the men, who had swung their arms around each other's shoulders, some standing on benches to reach around Crab's shoulders as they swayed back and forth and sang.

Ranulf turned to Mupto. "Do you ever miss home? Your family?"

"My siblings, yes. But I joined the army to provide for them. My father had an accident at work in the mines, and my mother passed from illness."

"I'm sorry. That must have been difficult."

"I enjoy the brotherhood of the army. Most young people join the army anyway, unless you like to work in the mines. The army, I think, is easier."

"Oh?"

"I know I'd much rather be outside, sparring and exercising and riding around, than in the caves, where it's dark and dirty and your eyes hurt from looking at all the shiny jewels."

"Are there really that many?"

"There were when I left. We also have crops, though, and can feed ourselves."

"It's sounds like you have a big army. Why so large?" Ranulf asked.

"Many countries have tried to steal the jewels we produce. So our island is more like a fortress. We actually have a channel with three gates we control to allow ships in or out."

"I'd love to see that one day," Ranulf said as he tried to imagine what that might look like.

Mupto grinned and leaned closer. "Our warriors are some of the best in the world," he whispered quietly.

Ranulf grinned when he realized Mupto had said that quietly not to insult any listening ears and perhaps start something too big to control.

Chapter Nine
Jinhua

J INHUA HAD LET RENSHU land two hits on her this morning at their practice and had to stick her hands in her pockets to stop her fidgeting as she taught her morning classes. They would meet Ranulf and Crab this afternoon, and she had to focus extra hard on keeping her movements calm so none of her siblings picked on her.

"Jin, would you help me demonstrate this move? These ones say they can't tell the difference between what I'm doing and what they're doing," Fangyee said, pouting, as she turned with her young students. She held her staff out in front of her at an angle. The kids, too, held their staffs in front of them, some straight, some angled.

"You've all got the first part right," Jinhua said. These were young kids after all. "Now, can you make your staff stand straight like a tall tree?" she asked.

All the students squinted at their staffs as if trying to imagine them as trees. A few more straightened, but a few still leaned over.

"Let's do a little test to see if they're straight, shall we?" Jinhua said. These kids were so little that Jinhua wondered if they really understood what a straight staff really meant.

"Let's put our staffs on the floor like this." Jinhua put the flat base on the ground and then let go. The staff remained upright. "If it stays standing, that means it's straight up and down like a tree. Perhaps it will even grow roots?" Jinhua grinned at the kids, and they all smiled. They were a strict school, so it wasn't unusual for a child to cry at some point in the day because one of her siblings said something mean. But Jinhua always tried to be gentler to the little ones.

They all started to put their stick on the ground and let go for a moment, but they tried to do it so quickly that their staff would start to lean and fall.

"That's it, keep trying," Jinhua said. This would probably occupy them for the next twenty minutes.

"Amah wanted the little ones to be able to do a simple strike and block by the end of the week," Fangyee said quietly.

Jinhua narrowed her eyes. That would be difficult. They could barely hold their staffs properly.

"If you trade me groups this week, I'll brush your hair first for the rest of the week," Fangyee murmured under her breath.

Jinhua didn't really care about her hair, but she didn't want to see one of these kids cry. She nodded and Fangyee disappeared.

"Well, you're stuck with me for the rest of the week now," Jin said, and the children only looked at her with wide eyes. Some had forgotten about their staffs, and one fell and bonked a boy on the forehead. He blinked and then started to bawl.

"So much for not crying ..." Jin said as she went over to him to get him reorganized.

By the time the gong for the midday meal sounded, the kids could all balance their staffs on the floor for several seconds. They had also learned how to hold their staffs in the middle and at the third. Jinhua wondered whether Fangyee had spent all her time yelling at them or whether she'd actually taught them anything. But Jinhua felt accomplished because the kids all left smiling and showing each other what else they could balance their staffs on as they ran out for lunch. Her brothers would have them for the afternoon as they practiced balance and conditioning. With a jolt, Jin realized it was time for her to eat and then go meet Ranulf and Crab.

She hurried back to her rooms, changed her clothes, then joined her family in the main dining room. As they all sat at the low table, she was glad that at least she wasn't the last to show up.

"Thank you for taking the brats. I can barely stand them, and today, I just couldn't," Fangyee said. She rubbed her temples as if she had a headache. Jinhua hadn't seen Fangyee do much more than walk around and flirt with some of the oldest students, but it wasn't for her to judge. Jinhua herself had been thinking of another man that wasn't her betrothed. That made her wonder if Ranulf and Crab would visit her at the palace. Would she even be allowed male visitors?

"Jinhua," Amah said as Fangyee elbowed her in the hip at the same time.

"Yes, Amah," Jin said. She knew Amah must have had to repeat herself, which is not something she liked to do, so Jinhua hoped Amah was in a generous mood today.

"You did well with the young ones today, Jinhua. The prince shall be pleased you are so good with children," Amah said.

Jinhua bowed her head. "Thank you, Amah. I only hope to be half as good as you have been in raising us."

Amah's smile grew wider, and Jinhua was glad she'd said the right thing. If she didn't give Amah enough credit or bow in return, a compliment could result in extra chores or bleeding hands—or both.

The gong rang again as Jinhua scooped the last spoonful of rice into her mouth.

"Ah, Renshu, how are the foreigners? I have not yet heard scandal, so you must be teaching them well. Just as I expected."

"Thank you, Amah. They seem willing and excited to learn our culture," Renshu said. His face was solemn, just as Amah liked it.

"I'm sure they are very stupid, but even if they do cause a scandal now, it won't be as bad as it would be if you weren't helping them. Don't be afraid of ensuring they're kicked out of this kingdom if they step out of line, Renshu. You know that harbor master owes our family his life," Amah said.

Renshu nodded his head. "Though it is challenging, I will strive to do my best."

Jinhua bit her tongue to keep from laughing.

"Good, good. Jinhua, have you packed up your supplies? You will need chalk boards and a cloth for their many mistakes," Amah said.

"I will go do so now, Amah," Jinhua replied. She kept her head down as she rose from the table and brought her dishes, along with Renshu's, to the servants lining the wall.

She hurried quietly to her rooms to collect a basket and then to the classroom to collect two small chalkboards, chalk, and a few other things she thought they might need this afternoon.

Jinhua met her brother in the entryway of their family home. He offered her his arm, and she took it as they started into town together. She stayed quiet until they were far enough away. "How much do you think they will be able to learn?"

"What do you mean?" Renshu replied.

"I mean, we know younger students learn faster. That's why we don't usually take older students, why we turned that soldier from Bulstan away from our school."

"I think if they're motivated enough to learn even some, then it will be better than learning nothing at all," Renshu said. He grinned as he turned away.

"What?" Jinhua squeezed his forearm.

"Motivation is important, and Ranulf is very motivated." Renshu slid his gaze her way.

Jinhua couldn't help the heat that crawled up her neck. But she held her chin high. It wasn't something she was ready to talk about, and she wondered if Renshu could feel her heart hammering in her chest. "I don't know what you're talking about, Rennie," Jinhua said.

They passed someone they knew then, so Jinhua looked at the ground as Renshu greeted them and exchanged a couple of words. They continued to the inn in silence. It was too easy for someone to overhear them and send word back to their mother.

Chapter Ten
Ranulf

RANULF WOKE QUITE EARLY to the quiet of the morning. Fortuitously, Mupto had the room next to Crab's because it had taken them both to put Crab to bed. So, Ranulf made his way downstairs as softly as he could to write a letter to his sister back home. At the same time, he ate his breakfast of rice soup—more of a gruel, really—and tea. It had taken him half an hour to finish two sentences when Mupto came down and sat across from him. The barkeeper brought over hot water in a teapot and another bowl of rice soup.

Ranulf stared as Mupto poured brown grains into the teapot and wondered what he'd just mixed into the tea. Mupto didn't speak and looked much more ruffled than he had the previous night.

Ranulf scratched out another line of text, realizing it didn't make any sense whatsoever. He looked at his letter and thought about how terrible it looked with more than half of it scratched out. He would have to rewrite it to not feel ashamed of sending it to his very tidy sister.

After Ranulf had spent much time staring at the letters on the page that seemed to float and dance around, Mupto poured the contents of the teapot into two cups and pushed one toward Ranulf, who smelled it immediately. It smelled dark and burnt. "What is it?"

"It's called coffee. It comes from roasting the beans of a special fruit grown in hot places. These are from Bulstan. It helps to stimulate the body, wake it up," Mupto explained. He sipped his own cup as quickly as the heat allowed before pouring himself another cup.

Ranulf brought his cup to his lips and took a careful sip. He felt the hot liquid slide down his throat and the warmth radiate from his center. But he couldn't help but make a face as the bitterness of the drink made his tongue pull back.

"Here, try it like this." Mupto took a small bowl with some small rocks in it and plunked one in Ranulf's cup. He took a stick from the nearby cup and stirred the liquid around, then slid it back to Ranulf.

Ranulf tried another tentative sip, the sweetness balancing out the bitterness this time. He had to admit he enjoyed the feeling of it sliding down his throat and warming him up from the inside out. He drained the rest of the cup. Mupto filled Ranulf's cup with the dark liquid again, plunking another small, sweet rock in before sliding the cup back. Ranulf drank that cupful too, starting to feel the world coming back into full color instead of the sluggish swirl it had been. He reached for the pot to pour himself a third cup when Mupto's hand shot out and stopped him.

"You shouldn't have too much the first time," Mupto said.

As if on cue, Ranulf's stomach gurgled, and he knew he'd have to make a trip to the privy sooner rather than later.

"That's another effect of coffee," Mupto said as he drank a third cup himself.

Ranulf nodded as he rose and left for the privy, quickening his steps as he got further away from the table.

When he returned, Crab was at the table, head between his hands. Ranulf sat down and rewrote his letter to his sister, realizing how quickly his thoughts were now coming to him and running down his quill.

"That's... coffee, you said?" Ranulf threw Mupto a glance, who nodded. "It's very useful."

Mupto nodded; he poured Crab a cup before finishing off what was left in the pot. "It's often used when soldiers have to keep watch all night." He patted the tea pot. "I started drinking it when I was on night patrol, but I find now I cannot go without it. My day doesn't start until I've had my coffee."

"Can we use the grains a second time?" Ranulf asked, reaching for the pot.

"No, it's much more bitter the second time, and it doesn't seem to be as effective either," Mupto replied. He eyed the table, underneath which Ranulf's leg was bouncing up and down.

"What time is it?" Ranulf finally asked.

"Almost midday," Crab mumbled.

"We have to get going. Renshu and Lady Jinhua are coming in a few minutes," Ranulf said. He leapt up and tried to shake Crab awake. His friend only tucked his head further into his elbow.

Ranulf turned to Mupto. "I'm going to change. Can you see if you can wake him?"

"I will try," Mupto said. He glanced at Crab fearfully as he signaled the barkeeper.

Ranulf ran up the steps two at a time to his room and threw his clothes around as he tried to find something clean to wear for Lady Jinhua. Ten minutes later, he took a deep breath before exiting his room and going back down the stairs as calmly as his heart would allow. He saw that Crab was now awake and looking around. "Hi, Ranulf, you-look-good-do-we-need-anything?" he asked as rapid fire as an archer's arrows in battle.

Ranulf looked to Mupto, who shrugged. "How many cups did he have?" Ranulf asked.

"Four," Mupto said. "I figured he'd need more because of his size, so I made more."

"I need to use the privy right now," Crab said quickly as he dashed away.

"Oh my," Mupto said. "I don't think I've ever seen a man that large move that fast."

"Indeed," Ranulf said. His own heart was thumping in his chest.

"I'm off to train. I'll see you later this evening?" Mupto asked.

Ranulf smiled broadly and nodded. "We'd be honored."

Mupto bowed and left, hurrying out the door. Ranulf wondered if he wanted to avoid Crab.

Crab made it back to the table only a moment before Renshu and Jinhua walked through the doors. They approached, and the barkeeper nodded at them.

"Good morning, Master Ranulf and Master Crab," Jinhua said. She bowed her head.

Ranulf felt his heart leap and pound hard against his rib cage.

"Did you sleep well?" Renshu asked.

"Very!" Crab sang.

Renshu tilted his chin, looking like he was wondering whether he'd heard the response correctly. He looked cautiously at them, then said, "Come, we'll be in the back room today." He and Jinhua walked down the hall toward the back of the building.

Coffee made Crab a different person. Ranulf had never seen him so enthusiastic. As Ranulf guided him toward the back room, he thought he could feel a tremor in Crab's arm.

"The barkeeper has been kind enough to lend us another back room," Renshu said, and he held the door as Jinhua walked inside first. She snuck a glance at Ranulf, who caught her eye before she turned to sit at the table.

Renshu and Jinhua sat first, with their backs to the wall and facing the door, and Ranulf helped Crab into his seat so he didn't fall since he was starting to tremble more.

"How was your first evening in town?" Jinhua asked.

"It was ... interesting. We learned many things, including how to use sticks to eat and the dangers of clear liquids." Ranulf said, waiting to catch Jinhua's eye again. When he did, he held her gaze as she giggled, covering her mouth with her hand.

Renshu grinned. "We heard of no disturbances, so it must have been a minimally enthusiastic, successful evening."

"Crab here made friends," Ranulf said. He felt like a little boy reporting to his parents.

"Crab seems ... not himself, if I may be so bold to say," Renshu said.

They all turned to watching as Crab jiggled his leg under the table.

"We've also made a friend of another traveler, who gave us a beverage called 'coffee' to drink this morning," Ranulf explained.

"Ahh ... coffee," Renshu said. He nodded.

Jinhua sucked her lips in, looking as if she was trying hard to contain her laughter.

"Ya know it?" Crab said in one blurted breath.

Renshu smiled. "Yes. And it seems that you've had too much of it."

"I don' mean to be rude but if ya'll excuse me I 'ave to—" Crab said, rising suddenly from the table and nearly running out the door. A moment later, they saw him hurry past the window and break into a run.

"He'll be back shortly. I'm sure he's just trying to calm himself," Ranulf said. Smiling and hoping he was right, he found himself distracted by Jinhua's grin.

"Ranulf, do you have any questions about the customs you've seen?" Renshu asked.

"Yes, I have to ask if there's another way to eat," Ranulf said.

Renshu looked puzzled. Jinhua put a hand on her brother's arm. "I think he means without sticks."

"Ah, yes. What do you use in your kingdom?" Renshu asked. He looked a little perplexed.

"We use a few utensils. The fancier the meal, the more utensils are laid out, but basically, there are three. There is a spoon—for soups—and a fork, which looks like this." He took the small chalkboard from the basket Renshu had set on the table and drew four tines on a handle. "There's also a knife, like this." He drew a butter knife. "We hold a fork in one hand and the knife in the other and eat like this." Ranulf pretended to cut something on a plate, then stabbed the food and pretended to eat it with the fork.

"Oh." Jinhua looked genuinely surprised. Renshu leaned over and took two sticks from the cup and gave them to Ranulf. "Why don't you show us how you've been using these, and we'll give you suggestions on how to improve."

Ranulf nodded and tried to remember how Mupto had taught him the day before.

"Hm," Renshu muttered before reaching over and adjusting the chopsticks a little. Then he scrunched up a few small balls of paper for Ranulf to practice with.

Ranulf failed a few times before Jinhua got up and retrieved a second pair of sticks. She grasped them both correctly, then took one out of her hand to demonstrate. He imitated her grip. Then she did the same with the other stick.

"The key is to keep the bottom immobile and move only the top one," Jinhua said.

"Your hand will cramp at first, but it will recover quickly," Renshu said.

"How do you know that?" Ranulf asked.

"My brother grew angry with me one time and broke my right hand, so I had to do everything with my left for a few months, including eating. My hand was sore and cramped for about a week before it got used to the movement.

"Your brother broke your hand?" Ranulf said.

Renshu nodded. "This hand." He pointed to it. Then he added, "And this shin"—He pointed to his left leg—"and sliced this side of me." He swept his right hand along his left side from arm pit to the bottom of his ribs.

"Your brother?" Ranulf repeated, incredulous. He'd had a few broken bones from playing too roughly with his own siblings, but Renshu's injuries seemed deliberate.

Ranulf turned to look at Jinhua. He wondered if the same had happened to her and found himself quite angry that anyone would hurt her.

Jinhua slowly grinned, exchanging a look of pride with her brother, unaware of the concern in Ranulf's eyes. "I have a scar on my torso from when my sister was angry with me. And I have several broken toes, and I've broken this wrist and that thigh bone." She pointed to her left wrist and right leg.

"All from your brother?" Ranulf asked.

"No. We have three brothers and two sisters. Most of Jinhua's injuries are from our sister, Fangyee. She's always been jealous of Jinhua's natural talent and skill as a fighter."

"Then how did you get those injuries?" Ranulf asked. He had always thought the weaker warrior ended up injured.

"Well, I was only three, five, then six."

"But you were just a child."

Jinhua nodded. "We start training very young. I used a staff to help me take my first steps."

Renshu looked at her and they exchanged fond smiles while Ranulf's eyes went wide as he realized they were proud of the injuries they'd received as toddlers.

Chapter Eleven
Ranulf

MUPTO HAD SAID HE would meet them again for their evening meal, so Ranulf looked around the room, wondering if they'd missed him or if the Bulstani had been so beaten in training today he didn't have the energy to so much as raise a hand in greeting. Crab looked around too.

"Do you think he's just late getting back?" Ranulf said.

"Maybe. But it's already later," Crab said. His brows were knit together, and Ranulf knew Crab was as worried as he was.

"Do you think we should go search for him?" Ranulf suggested.

"All right. You go out front and look around, and I'll go out back."

Ranulf nodded. He saw Crab scan his belt and nod. In a town full of warriors, Ranulf was aware he must be armed at all times.

Crab left through the back door as Ranulf went through the front. The sun was setting, painting the sky with rays of purple and pink amidst the blue of night.

Ranulf looked to the left and the right of the inn, searching for any sign of dark hair and a dark beard. To the left, men were trudging home or to taverns, and to the right was the same. No women or children were out.

Suddenly, he heard many shuffling feet to his right, and without thinking, dashed off that way. Ranulf didn't know for sure, but something inside him said the sound was unusual. He ran past two buildings and then stopped, listening again for the shuffling. He took off between two buildings and came upon a familiar man with a large dark beard being closed in by three older teenagers.

"Hey, we were wondering what was taking you so long," Ranulf said as he strolled into the situation, pretending he didn't know what was happening.

"Ah! Yes, well I was just conversing with these lovely young gentlemen here," Mupto said. He was crouched, looking ready to leap into a fight even as the pleasant words left his mouth.

Ranulf took out a dagger ready to launch at the three teenagers as they also crouched in a fighting stance. He put himself between Mupto and the teenagers; if he hadn't spent his coin earlier for supplies for his ship, he would have tossed it at them and hoped they left.

"We have no money," Ranulf said as he made a show of emptying his pockets.

The teenagers watched, but they didn't move.

"I think these boys are just looking for a brawl," Mupto said.

"I guess that's what we'll have to give them," Ranulf said. He wished at this moment that his lessons with Renshu and Jinhua had included combat. Crab had ensured he knew enough to swipe at attackers and defend himself in dire situations, but fighting was definitely not Ranulf's strong suit. He never felt bothered enough to learn until he was in a bit of a jam.

Ranulf took a closer look at the three teenagers and realized they might be men. They looked young and were not bearded, but here, it wasn't common for men to have beards. As he looked at them, he felt the fear rising in his stomach. On closer inspection, these looked like trained young men. They didn't look like random hooligans trying to prove themselves.

"Do you know what they have against you?" Ranulf asked.

"No. I was just walking back like I do every day."

"Ah, the first rule of merchanting is to always take a different path home every day so you don't become predictable."

"Well, I'll remember that for next time."

"Think Crab will get here in time?" Mupto asked as the three men started to circle them again, fanning out and closing the circle around them. Mupto and Ranulf stood back-to-back now like prey.

"No, but he'll be sore for days about missing out. He likes fighting as much as I hate it," Ranulf said.

"Why did you leap in then?" Mupto asked.

"I wasn't about to let you face them alone," Ranulf said. "That's not what friends do."

Mupto nodded. "Thank you, friend." Mupto suddenly charged at two of the men then, swinging his dagger at one and sliding to knock the other off his feet.

The third man charged at Ranulf, who sliced down with his dagger, catching the man's arm. But the man swung with his other fist, and Ranulf barely managed to bring his other arm up in time to block it. The man shoved him against a wall and slammed his hand into it; the dagger clattered on the cobblestone. A quick punch to Ranulf's face, then another, made his nose start to bleed.

Ranulf swung his arms blindly while hot liquid gushed down his face, just trying to land something. Then he remembered he could use his knees and legs to kick the man wherever he could and managed once to land one between the legs. That gave him only a second's reprieve. Repeated punches to Ranulf's middle were ensuring he could barely catch his breath when a sharp voice to his left made it all stop. He folded to the ground, trying to catch his breath, the world spinning and stars exploding in his eyes as he stared at the stones.

"Good. You all belong to our school. You can go to the training yard now and start punching the stone dummies if you're so keen. If your knuckles aren't bloody by the time we get back, you'll regret the next tasks." Renshu's smooth voice floated over to him, and Ranulf breathed out a sigh as he stayed on the ground, glad that friends had found them.

The smell of jasmine reached his nostrils, and he tried to open his eyes to see if he was dreaming. They had already swollen shut, however, and he tried to say hello, but all that came out was a groan.

"Oh, Rennie, they really hurt him," Jinhua said.

Ranulf felt a soft hand touch his arm.

"I assumed he knew what he was doing," Mupto said. "He came and rescued me."

Strong arms—surely Crab's arms—helped Ranulf stand. Then two more strong arms slipped under his arms, one on each side, and half carried him, stumbling, as he tried to walk. Finally, Ranulf recognized the raucous laughter and shouting of the inn and knew from the dampened volume that they must have come in the back door. There, he was gently sat on a hard wooden bench.

"Can ya remain sittin'?" Crab asked.

Ranulf nodded. Both his eyes were swollen shut, and he could feel warm liquid oozing out of his nose.

"You. Run up to my house and hand this note to my sister, Fangyee. She will give you a few things, and you are to run right back here with them, understood?" Renshu instructed.

Ranulf couldn't see much, but he listened to the worried people around him until warm, delicate hands touched his own.

"I'm going to start cleaning you up," Jinhua said. He heard a cloth being dipped in water and wrung out, then felt the stinging sensation of a cloth on his face.

"He never trains when I ask 'im. Says he don't need to when he's got me," Crab said.

"Foolish of him to come to my rescue then," Mupto said from beside him. "Ouch!"

Ranulf realized Mupto must be hurt too. While he hoped Mupto wasn't badly hurt, Ranulf also hoped Renshu was tending to Mupto and he had Jinhua all to himself.

"What did they want?" Renshu asked.

"A fight," Mupto replied.

"They didn't take any coin?"

"I have no coin to give them."

Ranulf heard a more-forceful-than-necessary splash of the cloth in the water before it was wrung out again, and he braced himself for the sting of the cloth on his face. He inhaled the jasmine as Jinhua sat in front of him, gently wiping away all the blood. It was his favorite smell now. He tried to crack open an eye, and his heart raced when he saw her face only inches in front of him.

"You're all right. My sister makes the best salve. It'll have all this cleared up in no time," Jinhua murmured. It felt like a secret, one Ranulf would cherish forever. If her brother wasn't so near, he might have moved closer to her.

A knock on the door pulled everyone's attention in that direction when Renshu went to answer it. Ranulf only knew it was Renshu for the green cloak he wore and the way it shone in the light. Renshu had returned with a few jars.

Renshu opened the ceramic jars and Jinhua dug her fingers into them. "This will sting when I first put it on. But then the pain will go away. It will help your cuts heal."

Ranulf nodded, and Jinhua applied the sticky salve to his face, the stinging sensation making him realize he must have a cut on his face and a split lip to boot. Then she pressed a cup of warm liquid against his lips. "Drink this," Jinhua said. "It will help the pain—and don't you dare spit it out."

It was his only warning before the most bitter taste filled his mouth.

Only Jinhua's proximity kept him from spitting out the contents. It tasted like an old man's boiled shoe.

She pressed the cup against his lips again, and he drank only because she asked him to. But this time, he gulped it and then pressed his lips together so he didn't spit it back out. Next, she pressed a little rock of sugar to his lips, and he gladly let that roll around in his mouth.

"I'm impressed you kept that vile stuff down," Renshu said. "Most people can't help but spew it all over the place the first time."

Ranulf tried to smile in response but felt his lip crack and bleed.

"Oh, I'm going to murder those boys," Jinhua said softly with so much anger that it surprised Ranulf.

"I am curious to hear why they decided to pounce," Renshu said.

"Because we're foreigners and easy prey," Mupto said.

"Well, Ranulf is, but you, as a Bulstani soldier, aren't," Crab said.

"They didn't know that until now," Mupto replied, puffing his chest out proudly.

"I will flay them," Jinhua said under her breath.

Ranulf put a hand on hers resting on his knee as she painted more salve on his cheek. "Don't. They didn't mean anything by it. They were just a group of kids looking for something to do," he said.

Jinhua froze. Renshu, however, wasn't as forgiving as Ranulf. "They'll have something to do from now until the end of time, that's for sure."

Ranulf started to feel very sleepy. "I think I need to go to bed now," he said to no one in particular.

"I'll take 'im," Crab said. "Thank you fer all yer help."

Ranulf heard Crab step forward and Jinhua rise and back up. When he felt Crab beside him, Ranulf stood up and put an arm over his shoulders as Crab helped him to their rooms. Mupto, too, bid Renshu and Jinhua good night and hurried ahead of Crab, opening doors for him as they went.

CHAPTER TWELVE
Jinhua

J INHUA HAD SEEN HER fair share, maybe more even, of beatings. She herself had been beaten plenty of times when sparring with her siblings or when they had been angry with her for something or other. But when she'd seen Ranulf tonight, her heart had broken. He looked like a baby bear, bloodied and bruised. She was kicking herself for not having found him sooner. Had she been there, that fight never would have happened.

"You can't be everywhere at the same time, sister," Renshu said as they packed up the bandages and supplies the runner had brought from their home. "Mupto knows how to handle himself at least."

"Yes. I think he's been attending the Wong family school," Jinhua replied. She was seething inside but trying to keep the conversation light until she got home and could deal with those boys.

"It was foolish of Ranulf to step in. He doesn't know how to fight. I'm sorry to say it, sister, but it's badly affected my respect for him."

"You've lost respect for someone who hasn't spent his entire life training yet still bravely steps into a situation he knows he can't win just to help a friend?"

Renshu rubbed the back of his neck. "Well, when you put it that way ..."

"He's the bravest man I've ever met," Jinhua said. She took the basket of supplies and stood up, brushing herself off.

"I think we should include some combat lessons in our sessions then. Though those boys won't dare try anything else, the story will get out and he'll become a target," Renshu said.

"Not when they see what I'm going to do to those boys," Jinhua said.

"Oh? And what is that?" Renshu said.

"You'll see." Jinhua pressed her lips together, her anger simmering for a few moments before she could calm it enough to continue her conversation.

"Ready to go then?" Renshu asked. He had been staring at her, head tilted.

"Yes." Jinhua left and Renshu followed. They passed the barkeeper in the hallway on the way out the back door. "I'll see you tomorrow morning, Ling," Jinhua said. "If anything happens, send a messenger up, please."

Ling nodded. His eyes were wide and filled with sympathy.

Renshu was almost running to keep up with his sister as her tiny legs hurried through the streets to their home. When they neared the courtyard, they heard three people huffing and puffing as they punched stone dummies.

"Rennie, will you take these in for me?" Jinhua asked, shoving the basket at him.

"I will, but I'll be right back," Renshu said as they entered the training yard. "Don't kill them." He continued past the men and into the house.

Jinhua didn't reply. But she did turn to the three young men. "Stop," she commanded.

The three boys all stopped and looked at her. They looked determined. She smiled. "Let's see your hands."

They turned and showed Jinhua their wrapped hands, blood seeping through in a couple of places.

"Take off the wraps. You didn't have wraps on tonight when you decided it would be fun to beat up complete strangers." She smiled again. One man whimpered, but the other two clearly still didn't understand they were being punished.

"All right, continue with the stone. I will cause a distraction," Jinhua instructed as she started to pace beside the men. "And know that if you quit, if you stop, you will be kicked out of this school. Is that understood?"

"Yes, miss," they said in unison. It was an honor to be chosen to join Jinhua's family's school and a great shame to be kicked out before they completed their training. They would be completely written out of society, ineligible for apprenticeships or jobs and be forced to live hidden away forever.

The three boys glanced at each other and then started punching the dummies again. One gave only a lackluster effort.

Jinhua grabbed a staff from the wall nearest her. She struck it on the heel of the boy who punched with minimal effort and slid his foot out wider. They all maintained a wide stance already, but now she wanted a wider one. So she made each of them spread their legs wider and wider until they were practically doing the splits while punching the hard stone. Blood now marked the stone, which was not unusual.

Renshu returned with blocks. He placed them beside their feet. "Ankles on the blocks, boys. Do not move the blocks."

Now each man was almost doing the splits on only the sides of their feet as they continued to punch the bloody stone, opening more and more skin with each hit.

Jinhua was quiet as she watched them for the next several minutes. Then she asked, "Who can tell me why you decided to pick a fight with foreigners tonight?"

One boy let out another whimper, but the other two shot him a look.

"Very well. It's too easy, is it?" Jinhua asked rhetorically. She collected some smooth, round stones with flat bottoms. After placing the stones in front of wooden dummies with many protruding pegs, she instructed the men to each stand on a stone while they did the third form with the wooden dummies.

It appeared the boys thought that would be easier because they gladly left the stone dummies. When each stepped onto their smooth rock, though, they discovered it was slippery and keeping their balance would prove difficult.

"Every time your foot touches the ground, you will run ten laps." Jinhua smiled. She was enjoying this way more than she should. "I will keep count, but you know how much I hate numbers. So you will run until I tell you to return."

They all slipped on the rock then, and Renshu sent them running around the training ring. They ran twelve laps before coming back and stepping back on the stones, now impossibly slippery as Jinhua had added more polish to the stones while they ran. The men were becoming visibly exhausted. But Jinhua wasn't done teaching them a lesson. So when the first one slipped off again, falling to his knees, she had no sympathy when she and Renshu pointed to the training ring.

Renshu kept watch as the student ran; then another joined him. The third, the now-clear leader of the group, slipped but pretended he hadn't.

"Go run. I saw you slip," Jinhua commanded.

"No," he said.

"What did you just say?" Jinhua said, her voice sickeningly sweet.

"No. We did nothing wrong. They are foreigners. They do not deserve the same rights as we do."

"Go. Run," Jinhua said, gritting her teeth as she spoke.

"No. I will not," he said, and worse, he stepped off the stone, turned, and faced Jinhua, ready to fight.

Jinhua only smiled. "So you want to challenge me?"

"Yes. I'm stronger than you. I'm male. We're built stronger than women," he said.

Renshu whistled. "Make sure you don't kill him, Jin," he said.

The boy squared off with Jinhua, who still held a staff. She reached behind her and grabbed a second staff for him, just to make it less of a slaughter.

He came in with the stick and slammed it down hard. Jinhua redirected it and slammed the end of her staff into his stomach. Air whooshed out of his lungs, and he started to crumple. But instead of letting him catch his breath and try again, she went in for the kill. She thwacked him on one shoulder and the next, then smashed each side of his knees before shoving the butt of her staff against his ankles and hips. She was bruising joints and bones, if not breaking some. Jinhua wouldn't stop until he lay motionless on the ground. She didn't hit him in the face but hit every joint and then every squishy spot.

Renshu finally threw his arms around her. "Enough, little sister."

Jinhua stilled. Her anger was still seething, only some having abated as she had beaten this boy to a pulp.

"You two. Take him home and inform his family he is no longer welcome at our school. Should any of you ever attack foreigners again, we will do ten times worse to you than what you do to them. Is that understood?" Renshu demanded.

"Yes, Sifu," they answered. They picked up their friend, who only groaned, off the ground and left the training field, leaving Jinhua and Renshu alone.

"I didn't hit anything vital. He'll just have lots of injuries," Jinhua said.

"You did well controlling your temper," Renshu said, though he kept his arms wrapped around his sister. When she trembled, he guided her toward their family's private training area and said, "Shh. You're all right. Let's go have some tea, yes?"

Renshu poured them some tea and sat, removing the staff from her stiff hands. He threw a blanket over her so she'd stay warm as she worked through her emotions and let the adrenaline drain out of her.

Jinhua sat, focusing on drinking the tea. She didn't fully understand why she felt so angry. It seemed so disproportionately angry on behalf of some near strangers. It felt as though someone had hurt her family and needed to pay. The problem was she'd only really known Ranulf for a few days and Mupto hardly at all. "How can I feel so angry for someone I just met?" she finally asked.

Renshu rubbed her back, then refilled her teacup. "There are some people in this world we feel an immediate connection to the moment we meet."

Jinhua turned to face him. "Has this happened to you?"

"Yes, a few times, most importantly when you were born. I knew we'd be best friends, even more than any of my other siblings."

She reached out and he grasped her hand in his. "Amah has hidden you within these walls and this town. I knew that one day, you'd want more than that," he said.

Jinhua felt her temper easing. She was no longer angry, and she knew those young men would never pick on another foreigner again. "What do you mean?"

"I mean you are much too clever and skilled to remain here for the rest of your life like we will."

"Is that why you were so happy when you learned of my betrothal?"

"Yes, I was very happy to hear you would have the opportunity to live in the big city and be able to explore it from the safest seat: the royal family." He paused, putting his cup down and rubbing the back of his neck again. "But there are other ways to live, to see the world, ways in which you'd be able to use your fighting skills too. Sailing with a merchant, for example." He looked at her sneakily from the corner of his eye.

"What about the prince?" Jinhua asked.

"I hear he is not a respectable man. I know I've said this before, but he drinks too much, enjoys too many carnal pleasures. He hasn't come to visit you, to try to get to know you. He just sends you a gift once a month, and I bet someone else is doing it on his behalf."

"But—" Jinhua started.

"But nothing for now. Just consider it. We're still a long way from either path, and the light is starting to fill the sky. I need my beauty sleep, and you do too. We're going back to see Ranulf in only a few hours."

Jinhua was quiet for a few moments as they made their way into the house. But then she thought of something. "Mupto must really be a spectacular warrior. He barely had a scratch on him."

Renshu nodded. "It's too bad he didn't come here to study with us."

"He's too old. Amah rarely takes older students."

"I heard he brought an offering of a chest this big"—Renshu opened his arms wide and wiggled his eyebrows—"full of gems."

"Why don't we invite him to practice with us?" she asked.

"Because he's with the Wongs. We'd start a war if we did that," Renshu said. He kissed his sister on the cheek and left her at her door as he disappeared across the hall into his own bedroom.

Jinhua pushed her door open and found her sister already asleep, snoring like a bear. She changed into her sleeping clothes and fell asleep moments after her head hit the pillow.

Chapter Thirteen
Jinhua

Jinhua walked into her bedroom the next evening and dodged a flying hairbrush.

"How dare you throw it all away!" Her sister threw another brush across the room. Jinhua caught this one because their brushes were expensive.

"What are you talking about?" Jinhua asked. Her heart was pounding impossibly fast. There was no way her sister could know how she felt about Ranulf. She'd barely admitted it to herself. Renshu had guessed, but he'd never have said anything.

"I was in town earlier today, and I saw the way you looked at him. How dare you throw it all away?! What about the rest of us? What about your family?" Tears streaked her face, and she swiped her arm across the tabletop, scattering everything to the floor.

"I haven't done anything," Jinhua said.

"You will though, I know you will. You always do whatever you want. No one ever tells you no," Fangyee hissed at her.

"That's not true."

"It is. I was the one who wrote to the imperial matchmaker. But she came here and took one look at you and didn't even want to see me. You stole my prince. But I made peace with it. I figured with your connection to the prince, I could at least find a rich and decent husband. And you don't even want it. I've watched you squander all the power you could have wielded in town. You're betrothed to the prince of the empire and you don't even dress like it."

Jinhua was stunned. She hadn't known Fangyee had written to the matchmaker or what her sister's plan was.

Fangyee stared at her, seething with anger. Jinhua imagined steam coming out of the top of her head.

"I'm ... I'm sorry," Jinhua said.

"Promise me you won't choose him, won't run away with him. You'll wrap up these lessons or whatever Renshu has you doing and then you'll focus on the prince?" Fangyee begged.

A pang of fear struck Jinhua's heart. She had never thought about it, running away with Ranulf. But now that the question had been asked, she knew she would. To spend a single day with the kindness, the thoughtfulness, and the gentleness that was her Ranulf, would she give up a lifetime of luxury? The answer came easily.

There were no guarantees Ranulf would make it, that they would make it. But they would make a fearsome pair, and he could promise her a life of adventure and meeting new people, discovering new cultures.

Suddenly, an image flashed in her mind: a young boy, maybe twelve, hugging her waist and a young girl around eight pressing into Ranulf's side as they stood on the bow of a ship, sailing into the open ocean. She blinked. Now she was getting way too ahead of herself. "What do you want from me, Fangyee?" Jinhua asked quietly.

"I want you to marry the prince and find me a husband who can give me the life I deserve!" Fangyee yelled. In her defense, though, that was her normal volume.

"And what about my happiness?" Jinhua said.

"You *will* be happy with the prince. I wish you could see it. The dresses, the fashions, the gold, and so many ladies in waiting. You would have everything you ever wanted. How could you not be happy?"

"I cannot promise you anything, Fangyee. But I can tell you that's not where my happiness would come from, not from things. It would come from people, from family," Jinhua tried to explain.

"That's foolish. Have you seen the beggars on the street? They'd kill each other for a few coins. Tell them they wouldn't be happier in a palace." Fangyee only dismissed Jinhua's words. Somehow, Jinhua had calmed her fears enough that Fangyee had returned to her arrogant self.

Fangyee huffed, then changed into her night clothes and went to bed as if nothing had happened. Jinhua, on the other hand, couldn't sleep. She went to the training ring and dug the polish out from the back cupboards. She didn't feel steady enough to train, but there was always polishing to do.

"Can I join you?" Renshu sat down with a cloth of his own, pulling the next piece of armor over.

Jinhua shrugged, focusing only on the task at hand: polishing the shiny surface until she could see her reflection. "Did you hear everything?" she asked quietly.

"Only because I was in the hallway. The others are still out for the night."

"Did you know?" Jinhua asked.

"Know that you and Ranulf are in love with each other? Yes. Know that Fangyee wanted to marry into a life of luxury, no. Though I can't say it surprises me as much as it must have you."

"She ... she works as hard as we do. As all of us. How could she want to live a life of partying and gossiping?" Jinhua said quietly.

"She hordes the pretty things whenever she can. Just because she works as hard as we do doesn't necessarily mean that she wants to. I can see she'd prefer to be doing something else," Renshu said. He looked up and gazed at the middle of the training space as if he was remembering something. "One time, we were playing hide and seek, and I ran to find a hiding spot in the alcoves downstairs. Fangyee yelled at me and shoved me down a hallway. I went back later that night to see what she wanted to keep secret and saw that she collects things: pretty things, shiny things, anything with jewels in it or that looks like jewels. She even had a dress she must have painfully stitched together one patch at a time to make this incredible patchwork dress."

"Really?"

"Yes, but it's all gone now. I used to take a look every week or so just to see what she'd added or if she was finished with the dress. And a couple of years ago, it was all just gone. The dress, the bits, the shiny things. Come to think of it, that was when you became betrothed to the prince."

Jinhua's shoulders slumped. That made her feel terrible. She didn't know she'd crushed her sister's dreams when she had accepted the betrothal. "Wait, how do you know about—"

"I know you. I've seen the way you look at him. And the way he looks at you—there's no denying you two are in love with each other."

"Argh," Jinhua said. She picked up another piece of shiny metal, a cuff of some kind, and started rubbing the polish on it.

"He's not a terrible person to be in love with," Renshu said.

"Oh? Besides the facts he's a foreigner and I'm betrothed already?"

"I'm not saying it's ideal. But has the prince given you any reason to remain loyal? He doesn't visit, he doesn't write, and you won't even be his first, second, or third wife. You'll be his eighth wife. Something tells me he won't miss you."

Jinhua shook her head; the prince was as much a mystery to her now as he had been when she'd heard of the proposal.

"Fanny might be all right with living a secluded life in the palace. But you? You were born to adventure and deserve a partner to adventure with. You need the excitement. And you are definitely the jealous type. I'm not sure you'd survive the palace without being miserable."

"How do you know what palace life is like?"

"I know things."

Jinhua looked at her brother. It was on the tip of her tongue. She wanted so badly to ask it. But it wasn't her secret to tell. She did, however, wait to see if he would offer the information, offer the piece of himself she knew he kept tucked so far inside she wasn't completely sure it was actually real.

Renshu met her stare and held it for a minute before coughing and returning to polishing the cuff in his hands. "I'll love you no matter where you are," he said instead.

"If I choose him. And he hasn't even given me a choice. But if he did, what do you think would happen, here, with the family?" Jinhua asked quietly.

"You'd be disowned—don't worry, I'm not one for following rules, so you'll still have me—but you wouldn't be allowed to return home ever again."

"And the prince?"

"You might never be able to return to Cerisa. Though I imagine if he hasn't taken a huge interest in you yet, he probably won't care. Maybe he'll just keep marrying until he has a hundred wives."

"You really think he'd have that many?" Jinhua said.

"I wouldn't be surprised. How he'd even keep their names straight is beyond me."

"Maybe they'd wear numbers."

"Maybe he'd just rename them with numbers," Renshu added.

They were quiet for a while. The humor fell flat given the seriousness of the conversation.

"You'd have to be sure Ranulf could make you happy because you'd only have him. Your family, except for me, of course, will not exist to you. And if I get kicked out by association, by the way, I'm coming to live with you. So I hope Ranulf has some space."

Jinhua grinned. "I think we could find you a free hammock."

The horror that crossed Renshu's face was priceless. It gave Jinhua things to think about though. Would she be able to live without her family? Would she be able to count only on Ranulf? Was it fair to him to put all that pressure on him to be her only family? Ranulf and Crab were practically family to each other, but would Crab allow her in? Would she be the outsider forever?

Plus, Jinhua had heard rumors that it was bad luck to have women on board a ship. Would the crew even let her aboard? Would they accept her?

She did know one thing though. In the palace, as one of the prince's wives, there was no need for fighting or sparring or training. She would have to quit. But on the ocean, faced with thieves and pirates in foreign lands, she'd have a chance to do what she loved most. On top of that, she felt like a future on the open ocean was an opportunity just waiting for her to step up and take it.

"You're going to need to hand me more polish if you want me to help you finish that pile of cuffs." Renshu interrupted her thoughts.

Jinhua looked over and saw the pile she'd dragged out. It was too bad she had started the task because now they would have to finish, and it would be late into the night when they did. She leaned over and grabbed another cuff, handing it to him and sliding the polish between them.

"It's going to be a long night." Renshu smiled.

Jinhua grinned back at him.

Chapter Fourteen
Ranulf

"**I**'LL BE RETURNING HOME at the end of this week," Mupto said. They had finished their evening meal together and were about to start a wild night of tea and clear alcohol.

"Is that a good thing or bad? Is it because of the letter you received today?" Ranulf asked.

"It's a good one. The school I train at sends regular reports to my captain, and he has asked me to return to share my knowledge. He thinks I have learned what I need."

"Congratulations!" Ranulf and Crab chorused together so loudly and suddenly that the whole inn turned their attention to them. The group waved them off.

Mupto's cheeks—what you could see between his thick beard and hair—turned pink. "I will be sad to leave you, my friends."

"It was never going to be forever. We've already stayed much longer than we'd planned," Ranulf said, at the same time thinking that, logically, he should make his own plans to leave soon. Something pulled at his heart at the thought.

"Sometimes it takes longer than planned to woo a woman," Mupto said. He grinned at Ranulf. It was Ranulf's turn for heat to flood his cheeks.

"We're runnin' out of funds though," Crab said.

"Ah," Mupto replied before silence fell.

"You should come and visit me in Bulstan when you can. You will come and stay in my tiny home, meet my fellow soldiers," Mupto said. Then he smirked. "And I promise, we will even find something for you to trade."

At that, Ranulf and Crab laughed. "We would be honored to come and visit you in Bulstan."

"And should you ever run into any trouble, I would be honored to assist you," Mupto said.

"Thank you, but we're hoping not to run into trouble."

Crab nodded in agreement. They were quiet a moment longer, and Ranulf wondered about the tugging in his heart. The thought of having to leave Jinhua made him miserable. But they'd only just met, and he wasn't even sure she felt as he did.

Mupto narrowed his eyes. "Do you not realize the ramifications if a certain lady decides to leave with you?"

Ranulf narrowed his eyes. He wasn't embarrassed of his love, only a little surprised it was so obvious. Ranulf deeply loved Jinhua. He would always love Jinhua. But he also understood that she would probably be disowned by her family, which he knew could be very hard on someone. So he hadn't pressured her; hadn't asked her to leave with him yet. Ranulf wanted her to make the decision. He would love her until the end of time, he knew, but he was giving up nothing. She would be giving up everything.

"Do you mean her family?" Ranulf asked, leaning in. He wanted to know if Mupto knew more than he did about what she would have to give up.

"Yes, but she is also betrothed to the emperor's son, the heir of the empire," Mupto said.

"They haven't married yet. Jinhua told me they haven't even met," Ranulf said.

"Still, she is supposed to be his eighth wife. It's an honored position. I've heard rumors that she's supposed to leave for the palace at the end of this week."

"Wait, eighth wife?" Crab interjected.

"Yes. Here, royalty takes as many wives as they can fill the palace with as a way to show the people they care. They try to wed from as many regions as possible. It's a great honor to be the eighth in any set," Mupto explained.

"Whaddaya mean by 'set'?" Crab asked.

Mupto's eyes filled with sympathy. "I mean eighth, eighteenth, twenty-eighth, all of them honored positions."

"Wait, how many wives does the current emperor have?" Ranulf asked in a whisper. Strangely, he found they were all whispering as they leaned closer together in the middle of the table.

"Forty-three," Mupto replied.

Ranulf's and Crab's jaws dropped. That was a lot of wives. How could one person manage, never mind love or even have affection for them all? Ranulf's heart broke for Jinhua's future. He wanted to tell her right away how he felt and convince her to leave with him. He couldn't guarantee the luxury the emperor offered, but he knew he'd love and cherish her every moment of every day.

Seeming to read his face, Mupto spoke up. "It's not about love, Ranulf. It's about status, honor, and tradition." He paused. "If Jinhua leaves, you could have an army chasing you. The royal family is not forgiving in these circumstances. For her to run away with someone else could be considered treason."

Ranulf tried to steady his rapidly beating heart. He would face an army for her, but was it fair to ask her to face such adversity?

"If you ask her to come with you, you'll need to marry her first. But you will need to do so quietly and leave quickly. The only chance you might have is being gone before the news reaches the royal family. And you must hurry away from here. They have a very large army." Mupto hurriedly spat out his advice, even though it was whispered.

Ranulf's eyebrows knit together in thought as he tried to put all of this information together.

"I'm sorry to leave you with so much strife," Mupto said, "I personally hope to see you and Jinhua married and visiting me." He reached into a vest pocket before putting his fist on the table. His eyes slid around the room before he said, "And I want to gift you this, to help." He turned his hand over and opened it. Inside was a shiny diamond. It wasn't huge, but it wasn't tiny either.

"How, what ..." Crab began as he put his hand in front of Mupto's so no one spied the gem.

"Bulstan's main resource is gemstones. That's how I came here and paid for my spot in the school. But this I was holding back in case I needed it. I think you have greater need than I do," Mupto explained.

Crab looked between Mupto and Ranulf. Mupto pulled his hand away, leaving the diamond on the table behind Crab's hand. Crab turned to his partner. "Have ya even asked 'er?"

"No. I wanted to give her a chance to make her own choice before putting pressure on her," Ranulf said.

Crab pulled his hand back, the diamond inside, as he closed his fist.

"You need to ask her to marry you. That may be the only way she sees she has a choice," Mupto encouraged Ranulf.

Ranulf nodded. He would ask at the next opportunity. They had lessons with Renshu and Jinhua the next day. He'd never felt more sure about anything.

Before Renshu and Jinhua arrived, Mupto, Ranulf, and Crab were waiting in the room they always used for lessons.

"Gimme your hand," Crab said as he looked at Ranulf.

Ranulf opened his palm, confused. He trusted his partner though, so he waited. Crab plopped a tiny thing in his hand, and Ranulf blinked. In his palm was a small ring, the diamond Mupto had given them yesterday secured to it with some wire.

"It ain't fancy, but you should have a ring if you're going to propose," Crab said.

"You're pretty handy with a bit of wire," Mupto said as he peered over Ranulf's other side.

Crab nodded, and Ranulf stared at the ring. A beautiful little diamond wrapped in wire sitting in his hand made the future feel real. He felt so giddy about the possibilities, he couldn't help the grin that spread on his face. Jinhua could be his to cherish and love.

The door opened and Ranulf palmed the ring into his pocket. Jinhua and Renshu walked in, and Ranulf felt his heart soar. His smile was unstoppable as she walked into the room and smiled before averting her eyes and sitting across from him. Renshu started the lesson after he greeted them in their fashion.

Ranulf had a difficult time focusing, and the other two tried their best to cover for him during their lesson. As their lessons came to a close, Mupto, Crab, and Ranulf enacted their plan. Mupto and Crab tried to keep Renshu occupied on the other side of the room by asking him many questions. Ranulf and Jinhua remained on the other side of the room, alone.

"Good afternoon, Ranulf," Jinhua said, smiling.

"It's a beautiful afternoon," Ranulf said. "How are you? How were your classes this morning?"

"They were good. We had a few new students join the school this week, and they're always so cute when they're toddlers," Jinhua said.

"How many children would *you* want?" Ranulf blurted out, covering his mouth as he realized how personal that question might be.

"At least two," Jinhua said. She turned a bit pink in the cheeks as she started to pack up her basket.

"I—" Ranulf looked over and saw Crab and Mupto still busy talking with Renshu, so he took his chance. "Jinhua, I love you." He swept her hand up in his, rushing to continue in a low tone. "I've been waiting for you to make a choice because I didn't want to put pressure on you. I know you'd be turning your back on your family if you chose me, and now I realize you might be turning your back on your whole kingdom. But if you choose me—if you love me and want to choose me—it would be my honor to strive every day to make you as happy as you make me. Would you make me the happiest man in all of history and marry me?"

Ranulf turned his other palm over in her hand. The ring sparkled. Jinhua stared at the ring. It might not have been fancy, but she glowed anyway as she looked from it to him and back again.

"I would pick you, every time," she said so quietly Ranulf didn't know if he'd imagined it.

Ranulf's heart was pounding out of his chest. He took both her hands in his and grinned from ear to ear. "Mupto's leaving at the end of this week to return to Bulstan. Do you think you could leave by then?"

Jinhua nodded. "I'm supposed to leave for the royal palace at the end of the week. We would need to leave before then." She closed her fist around the ring and pulled her hands back, holding her fist to her chest.

CHAPTER FIFTEEN
Jinhua

JINHUA COULDN'T STOP THE whooshing in her ears. What just happened? She'd just accepted a proposal from a foreign man while still engaged to the prince. Yet she was happier than she had been in a long time. She'd been taught to mask her emotions from an early age, but now she had to press her lips together to keep from smiling.

To leave this kingdom and meet new people, to find actual opportunities to test her skills as a warrior, these were all things that excited her, not fancy clothes and jewels and luxuries.

She glanced over at Renshu; he stood a little straighter, so he'd obviously heard their conversation, but she couldn't see his face. Was he happy or offended? A heartbeat later, she answered her own question. Their previous conversation and the fact that he hadn't come over yet told her he must approve.

"I promise, I will get you a much better ring. This is not fit for your beautiful finger, but it represents my love for you," he said.

Jinhua laughed. "I don't care about the value of the ring."

Ranulf exhaled. "Thank goodness," he said. "Because while my family has a large piece of land in the Far Northeast, we won't get a share of it. When I ran off to be a merchant, they decided to split it amongst themselves since I wouldn't be there much of the time."

"I'm sorry," Jinhua said, putting a hand on his arm.

"I know it won't be easy. I also know I'm asking you to leave your family and possibly any chance of ever returning here. But I promise you with all my heart that I'll do anything I can to fix the situation. If you change your mind, I'll understand."

She put her hand back on his. "I love you," was all she said. It was terrifying, but it felt right. Still, part of her thought this was crazy. She'd only known him a few days, but it was like the world finally had clarity. A vision of their hands holding and the smell of a sea breeze flashed before her eyes until she blinked again and returned to the dusty old room.

Ranulf nodded. Renshu finally turned around, and they dropped their hands. He gave nothing away, but Jinhua knew he must know. Was that a glint of amusement in his eyes?

Either way, Jinhua finished packing up her basket of supplies, and they began to say goodbye. She almost leapt out of her skin, though, when Renshu said, "Before we leave, I feel we ought to teach you the customs of courting and marriage in our kingdom."

He glanced over at Ranulf, who turned a deep red. "It is not customary to court one another here, but it is to arrange a marriage between two people. Marriages are alliances between houses and families. Rarely, two people will fall in love upon meeting, but if their families do not approve, if the contract is not negotiated to both parties' standards, or if one or both have no family, then they become part of the poorest caste." Renshu looked directly at Jinhua, his eyes telling her she had to be completely sure of her decision and willing to accept the consequences. "But I am a little jealous because I hear in your kingdom, people usually marry for love," he finished.

"More often than 'ere perhaps, but we also have marriage contracts to join two families together. It usually happens in war or among noble families that want to join their estates," Crab said.

Mupto looked like he was trying hard not to laugh as he looked at Jinhua, then Ranulf, then Jinhua again. Ranulf's face flicked from white to red faster than Jinhua thought possible. He would give everything away if they were not careful.

Renshu

Renshu thoroughly enjoyed watching Ranulf and Jinhua squirm. Jinhua looked like she wanted to smack him. Trying hard not to chuckle, Renshu studied Ranulf's face again. He had planned to talk about marriage in hopes that it would show him what kind of man Ranulf was. Was he the kind to play around and break his sister's heart, or was he the kind to marry and worship Jinhua for the rest of his life? The answer was easy. Both his embarrassment and the way he looked at Jinhua shouted he was the latter.

Satisfied, Renshu asked, "Ranulf, do you have any brothers and sisters?"

"I do. I have six brothers and sisters," he said.

"Wow. It's rare to come across someone who has more than our five. What was it like growing up?"

"Well, I got to do a lot of whatever I wanted."

"And what did you choose to do?" Renshu asked.

"I read lots of books and climbed trees and hid in them," Ranulf said.

Renshu saw his sister soften with that comment. "Why's that?"

"I was small for a young lad, and my siblings often taunted me or tried to take my things. It was safest to hide."

"I see. Did you not learn any fighting arts?" Renshu asked.

"It's not as common at home as it is here, and we have no schools for it like you do here. But we do have to defend our lands every few years, so I learned some."

Renshu and Mupto stared at him. "Your family trained you in combat?" they asked at the same time.

"Just not his specialty," Crab said as he glanced between the two.

"I'm not very good at it." Ranulf said almost at the same time. He shrugged his shoulders. "Combat and fighting don't come easily to me."

Renshu was impressed that Ranulf was willing and open to saying so out loud. It was rare for a man, especially one as large as Ranulf, to admit his faults without so much as a blink.

"That is very bold of you to admit," Jinhua said. She looked at him doe-eyed.

"You all saw me get beat up. What's the point of denying it?" Ranulf said, shrugging his shoulders.

"You are a good man," Mupto said. He put his hand on Ranulf's shoulder.

Renshu thought Mupto had read his mind.

CHAPTER SIXTEEN
Jinhua

THEY STOOD, NOSES NEARLY touching, under the roof behind the inn, hidden from view. Jinhua was at the same time afraid to move and aching to close the gap.

"Jin, are you ready? Are you sure? I will love you always, but I do not wish to make you unhappy if you treasure your family and your home over me," Ranulf said.

Jin could feel the beating of her heart in her ears. Ranulf was silly and kind and made her happy just by existing. She smiled and nodded. She'd taken the ring from her pocket and placed it on her finger. He reached for her hands, and they intertwined their fingers. She could imagine standing beside him just like this on the bow of a ship, sailing to the next adventure.

A cough interrupted them. Renshu stood in the alley with a bag on his shoulder. "Hi, little sister," he said.

Fear speared Jinhua's heart. Then she realized Renshu was smiling the way he had as a kid when he had his visions.

"You knew?" Jinhua said.

He shrugged. "I saw it—you know me—but I'd already guessed. But you're going to have to hurry. I think Amah knows." Renshu held the bag out to her.

"You packed up my stuff?" Jin said. She had been ready to leave with nothing. She shared a room with Fangyee after all, who certainly would have stopped Jinhua.

Renshu nodded.

"What about Fangyee?" Jinhua asked.

"I suggested to Amah that Fangyee deserved an extra chore, then snuck into your room to pack a few things. Fangyee will be busy until dinner, but you'll be discovered for sure then," Renshu said.

Ranulf took the bag, strapping it across his chest. His hand lingered on the strap. "Are you sure about this, Jin? Once we board, I don't think we can turn back."

Jin saw Ranulf's selflessness in his eyes. He was only thinking of her happiness. But she'd thought about her family and their wishes for so long, she had forgotten what she wanted.

Renshu's face wrinkled earnestly. "He's right, Jin. I'm sure the family will disown and dishonor you if you leave. And I can't begin to think what Prince Feng will do."

Jinhua nodded. "I know. But I owe it to myself to be happy." She rolled her shoulders back.

"Then let's go," Renshu said.

"What do you mean?" Jin said.

"Peng can marry you. He used to be a priest. If you're serious, then let's do this quickly before you leave," Renshu said.

Jinhua's heart started to beat even faster. She turned to look at Ranulf's face.

"It would be my honor. I was serious when I said I wanted to marry you. I don't care when."

"But your family—"

"Doesn't care about me anyway," he said. "The only family that matters is you, and maybe Crab."

Jinhua nodded. Ranulf was so confident in his decisions, it perplexed her sometimes. She usually had to think at length before making decisions.

When they walked into Peng's courtyard, Crab was already there. "Was sent a note to meet ya here," he said.

"Thank you," Ranulf turned to Renshu.

Renshu nodded and they stood in a line as Peng approached.

Peng, a weapons maker now, ensured Ranulf and Jinhua were both marrying willingly, then dove into the simple ceremony. When the couple finished their vows, tears came to Jinhua's eyes as Peng pulled out two simple rings.

"Where ..." Ranulf began to ask.

"I forge weapons, but my father made me practice my craft on smaller items. This is my gift to the newlywed couple," Peng said as Jinhua and Ranulf placed the rings on each other.

And then in a blur, they were married and standing on the dock, hidden by Ranulf's ship as the sun began to disappear over the horizon.

Renshu smiled. He took two steps forward and wrapped Jinhua in a hug. "Be safe, sister. I'll always be here for you. Send a note to Peng whenever you're in town and I'll come find you."

Jinhua felt the tears gathering in her eyes and squeezed Renshu tighter before pushing away. "Be safe, Rennie," was all she could squeeze out.

Renshu shook Ranulf's hand, muttering a few words that made Ranulf pale before his expression hardened and he nodded.

Renshu looked one last time at Jinhua and smiled, nodded, then turned and walked away. He couldn't be seen with her, or he would be dis-owned too.

"Ready?" Ranulf asked, holding a hand out. They stood a moment as Jinhua turned to look at her home one last time. Ranulf waited until she was ready. Then she took a deep breath, turned away, and stepped toward the gangplank.

"Together, my darling wife?" Ranulf asked, raising his outstretched hand.

Jinhua smiled and put her calloused hand in his softer one and nodded. Together, they climbed the gangplank and pulled it up.

"Happy to have ya, Jin," Crab said, coming up from belowdecks. He'd hurried back after the ceremony to prepare the ship for a quick departure.

Jinhua nodded. She didn't trust her voice as, for the last time, she watched the village slowly start to quiet. Everything would be different from now on.

"Ready?" Ranulf asked. His small crew stood frozen, waiting for word from their captain.

Jinhua swallowed, then nodded. "I'm ready."

"Let's get going, boys," Ranulf said.

Crab went to the helm in Ranulf's stead, so Ranulf and Jinhua moved to the bow, watching the open ocean as they glided past all the other ships in the harbor before making their way to the opening.

"Is that opening getting smaller?" Ranulf asked.

Jinhua narrowed her eyes. "I think it is."

"Crab?" Ranulf said.

"I see it. They're closin' the gates, hopin' to cut us off," Crab said.

"Are we going to make it?" Ranulf asked.

"Maybe?" Crab said.

"Drop the sails," Ranulf said. He led Jinhua back to Crab.

"I know you're capable, but the ship is unsafe right now. You need to be careful. There are lots of swinging parts on a ship, and I know men who've died from being hit in the head by a swinging cross mast," Ranulf said.

Jinhua smiled and nodded, sitting down next to where Crab stood. "I'll watch this time, help next time," she said.

Ranulf nodded, then turned to his crew as they dropped the sails.

"Ya better take the helm, Ranulf," Crab said.

Ranulf grinned and took over as Crab leaped off to help with the ropes and sails. Jinhua smiled to see her new husband so happy. He was in his element. This is where he shone. He reached down and grabbed a long pole, then wove it through the wheel. "It's easier to handle than the wheel," Ranulf explained without looking back at her.

The sails all unfurled then, and Jinhua was thrown back as the wind filled them, billowing the fabric out and taking the ship along for the ride. Ranulf held the helm steady, aiming for the gap between the enormous walls that were slowly closing.

"We're not going to make it," Jinhua said. She felt the incredible disappointment and shame of almost having her adventure before having it snatched away. "Look, you can drop me off at the gate, and they'll probably let you through," she suggested.

"Do you want to go?" Ranulf asked, his face paling, his eyes widening.

"No. No, I love you. I have no regrets about marrying you, but the only person with the power to close that gate is the prince. He must have discovered our plans and ordered that I be recovered."

"Ye of little faith," was all Ranulf said as Crab pulled the rope of another sail, a small one at the bow.

Suddenly, the ship lurched forward, gaining yet more speed. As they pushed through the gates, the sides of the ship scraping against them, Jinhua watched the gates' masters yelling and beating the workers who were pushing the giant wheels that controlled the gates. In the moment they drew even with the gates, mere feet away, the eyes of the beaten men stayed with her. She was leaving a life of oppression behind.

And then they made it through. Jinhua had never been so happy and sad at the same time. She was free but she would likely never see her family again. She blinked the tears away as they sailed into the open water, away from everything she knew. "Where are we going?" Jinhua asked.

"To Adanek," Ranulf said.

"I thought you were from the Far Northeastern lands?"

"I am. My family has no need of me. But I do have a friend in Adanek. He has this beautiful property overlooking the seas. He will want first pick of what we bring back."

"Do you have enough stock?" Jinhua asked.

"We sure do. We moved the merchandise a week ago just in case we had to make a run for it." Ranulf winked at her.

"You are amazing."

"No, you are," Ranulf said.

Crab returned to the helm. "I hate to burst your beautiful romantic bubble, but we have a problem," he said.

"What is it?" Ranulf asked.

Crab pointed behind them. A dozen or so ships were following them.

"You don't think it's a sendoff, do you?" Ranulf asked.

"Definitely not," Crab replied as he turned to Jinhua. "Ya don't happen to know how fast their ships can go, do ya?"

"No, I'm sorry." Jinhua said.

Crab nodded and looked to Ranulf. "So whaddaya wanna do?"

"Let's outrun them. Once we get a day's travel between us and land, they'll have to turn back. They don't have nearly the supplies we do, not with that many people on board and no time to prepare."

Crab nodded and hopped back down to the main deck and issued instructions.

The winds picked up then, and their ship was the first to speed forward. "May the winds be with us," Ranulf muttered, tapping the helm three times. "For luck," he explained when he turned around.

And so the anxious waiting began. They continued to check behind them, watching the ships get smaller, then bigger, then smaller. Their ship, though laden with cargo to trade, was lighter than the other ships. They did not have cannons as the Imperial war ships did.

"Would you like to go and rest? I can get Mouse to show you to my quarters," Ranulf said.

"No. I'd like to stay with you," Jinhua said. She stood up and wrapped her hands around his waist, pressing herself to his back.

Ranulf took one of her hands from his waist and brought it to his lips, then pulled her around to stand in front of him. She stayed wrapped around him like a koala, and he kissed the top of her head. "I'm the luckiest man in this whole world."

Jinhua pressed her face into his shoulder and squeezed him. She kept her eyes closed, her face against his chest, as he maneuvered the ship in the wind, staying within it as tightly as he could to go as fast as they could. She enjoyed feeling his corded muscles twist and contract as he shifted one way and the other. She could stay here for all eternity.

However, she felt his nerves as he checked behind them every few minutes, felt the tension in his body as he looked down at the crew, the crew she hadn't even been introduced to yet, her future family. Somehow, though, she knew they would be all right, knew they would outrun these Imperial ships. Her hope was their captains were not particularly motivated to chase a ship across the ocean.

Eventually, with a tinge of regret, Jinhua turned around. She watched them slide across the ocean like a sharp knife. The crew all worked together to create as much speed as they could muster. Crab came back periodically to discuss the best direction to take, where the fastest wind could be found, where there might be dead zones. They never discussed what to do when they did hit a dead zone, though. Perhaps they hoped their momentum alone would be enough to propel them through.

It was a whole day and night later before they saw the ships getting smaller and smaller until they were tiny blips on the horizon.

"I think they finally stopped following," Ranulf said.

Crab made his way to the helm then. He held his breath, then said, "I think you're right." They all waited, not daring to stop, not daring to slow, until those ships disappeared over the horizon.

It wasn't until mid-morning the next day that a cheer and a whoop went through the crew. They'd been alone on the ocean long enough to declare themselves escaped and were on their way to friendlier territory.

"I'll gather the crew?" Crab said from below.

Ranulf nodded. Jinhua had stayed with him almost the entire time. She had, though, wiggled her bag off him and wandered the cabins until she found Ranulf's captain's quarters and tossed her bag in there. But aside from seeing to some needs like eating and finding the privy, she had been there next to him.

Crab came back and coughed. Jinhua spun around out of Ranulf's arms, surprised to see the entire crew standing before her. Crab took over for Ranulf at the helm, so she and Ranulf climbed down to the deck.

"I'd like you all to meet my wife, Jinhua," Ranulf told the crew. "Jinhua, I'd like you to meet some of the crew. This is Mouse, Dog, Shelley, Turt, Spinner, and Carthy. Carthy feeds us, so she's generally in the galley. There's a couple more up in the ropes, but you'll meet them later."

Jinhua bowed as Ranulf had to her many times. "It's an honor to join your family."

Mouse came up to them and bowed, presenting her with a silver-and-gold coin. "It was forged by mistake many years ago. I used it for luck, but it's the prettiest thing I 'ave to offer ya."

Dog stepped up then. He was a bit of a burlier man, but he bowed low and presented Jinhua with a bracelet of leather. Jinhua bowed in acceptance. Shelley approached, bowed, and gave her a necklace made from shells. When it was Turt's turn, he bowed and gave her a silver chain bracelet.

Carthy, at the end of the line, bowed and gave Jinhua a gold ring with a tiny ruby in it. "We 'eard it's Cerisan custom to 'ave a tea ceremony where the family gives the bride jewelry or somefin of value for 'er to take into 'er marriage. We don't 'ave tea, but we wanted ya to feel welcome," Carthy said.

A tear rolled down Jinhua's cheek. She was surprised at the crew's acceptance and overwhelmed with their generosity. "Thank you, all of you. I'm so flattered." Jinhua put on every single piece of jewelry she'd been gifted. She would never take them off.

Ranulf coughed, his own emotion evident. "Are we ready to eat?" he asked Carthy.

She nodded. Half the crew stayed on deck, including Crab. The rest followed Carthy into the galley's tight quarters, where slices of meat, vegetables, and fruit were laid out. As they all sorted and divvied up utensils, Jinhua had her first idea. Why not teach everyone to use sticks? They were much easier to clean and store. She would tell Ranulf her idea later.

When they had all settled, Jinhua asked, "When do you train? For fighting?"

"Sorry?" Turt asked.

"When do you practice your fighting arts?" Jinhua asked again.

"I practice when I'm off shift, sometimes wiv Crab if he ain't working," Mouse said.

"Well, then, we'll practice every morning," Jinhua said.

The others looked a little skeptical, but Ranulf backed her up. "It will be mandatory. If I learned anything in Jinhua's kingdom, it's that it's necessary to know how to defend yourself." He grinned, and though it made her heart skip a few beats with fear, she was proud of Ranulf for admitting his faults.

CHAPTER SEVENTEEN
Crab

THEY HAD BEEN ON the open ocean for two weeks. Jinhua's new routine was to wake up early in the morning and train—usually with Crab, their best fighter—and then together they would train the rest of the crew.

"He's never tried so hard for me," Crab said.

Ranulf had just finished sparring with Jin, even though he'd taken the helm overnight and was soaked with sweat.

"Ya don' look like *that*," Shelley said.

Crab cuffed him on the back of his head. "You watch your mouth. You're lucky she didn't hear you."

"She's pretty is all I'm sayin'!" Shelley took a step back, his palms up. "I don' mind havin' another woman on board. She smells nice, she's nice, and—"

"Shelley, start your laps. You're training with me today," Jin said.

"And she heard you," Crab said, raising his eyebrows and waving his fingers at Shelley, who went to run around the ship a dozen times.

Crab was astounded at Jin's ability. She moved quickly and fluidly. It was a pleasure to watch her practice and an honor to train with her. She beat him every time but was never smug about it and always willing to teach him where he'd gone wrong. She'd even asked him to teach her to use a longsword. It had caught him off-guard because it wasn't a weapon she was accustomed to, and it was heavy. He was the only one who even carried one. Ranulf used a cutlass and Jinhua often borrowed it to practice with too. Though she could probably take down ten men on her own, she was already learning how to adapt her moves with different weapons, always learning.

Crab wiped his brow and then dove into the fray; the whole crew was learning the same form. Truly, Jin ran her own mini school. He admired the way she taught a crowd because anyone could join. Whether it was your first class or hundredth, there were variations: harder moves, different stances, and focuses such as power, angles, and distances. Jinhua would start the form and when she turned around, Crab would take over so she could fix a stance or challenge someone with a more difficult version.

He noticed that even Mouse and Dog, who hadn't been pleased to have another woman on board, were going through the form. Crab kept an eye on them. He knew that despite their outward demeanor, they were days away from expressing themselves to him, Ranulf, or Jin herself. Crab wanted to avoid the latter. He imagined it was difficult enough to leave your family and everything you knew behind you, never mind be a woman on a crew of mostly men. He'd heard Dog gripe about how unlucky it was to have yet another woman on board. Crab had silenced him by putting him to work with Carthy peeling onions. A few hours of crying would teach him.

"Good, Mouse, but you should stand a little wider. We call it 'horse stance.' It's nearly impossible to knock over a horse given how wide they stand. If your opponent can't knock you over, then you're on your way to winning the fight," Jinhua said.

"But aren't ya also makin' yourself a bigger target?" Mouse asked, lifting a brow.

Crab wondered if this was it.

"Not in close combat. As such, if you were being shot at with arrows, then I'd suggest running away. In one-to-one combat, your enemy is right in front of you. You don't need to try to make yourself smaller," Jin replied calmly.

"Who put you in charge of trainin' anyway? Crab's a better teacher," Mouse muttered.

"Ah. I suppose we did just install me here as teacher without explanation. Crab, please, correct me if I'm wrong." She looked over at Crab.

He nodded, recognizing the look in her eyes. It was one of confidence and readiness. She had clearly been hoping he would challenge her.

"You didn't ask me to teach you. I know some of you have seen Crab and I practice, but I suppose I've never given any of you the opportunity to learn why I might be a good teacher." She picked up her staff and looked at the crew. "Why don't we clear the ring?" Turning back to Mouse she said, "Mouse, if you beat me, then you can teach. How about that?"

Mouse grabbed a staff off the ground. "My pleasure." He grinned and Crab wanted quite badly to smack him into the next ocean.

Ranulf came over to stand with Crab. "I wondered when this would happen."

"So she knew," Crab remarked.

"Yes. She's been trying to incite them. She thinks it will release some pressure."

"I think so too," Crab said.

"Are you going to, I don't know, stand by in case she needs help?" Ranulf asked.

Crab lifted his eyebrows. "Apparently, it's been a while since ya saw her fight too. She could take 'em all down without breaking a sweat."

Jin held her staff next to her. "Whenever you're ready, Mouse."

Mouse took his staff with both hands and held it horizontally. He charged in, coming from above and aiming to hit Jin's head. She brushed it away with her staff but did not jump into the offensive. Mouse pivoted around to hit her other side. She held her ground and let his staff bounce off, moving away from the blow. He rotated and swung, trying to sweep her feet, but Jin only moved to the other side. Mouse was getting angrier, so he slid his staff up Jin's to hit her hands, but she only let go, knocking it aside with her feet as she pushed Mouse's staff. He still gripped the end, and she looked surprised to see his skill as he arced it over her and swung to hit her square on the shoulder. With a foot still under the wooden staff, she kicked it up to her hands, blocking Mouse's attack with ease.

"I ain't used to a staff. Course ya'd be better," Mouse grumbled.

"Please, choose whatever weapon you prefer. I don't mind," Jin said. She picked up her staff and waited.

Mouse let his staff clatter to the ground, and Jin kicked it aside. Mouse went to a box of weapons and picked out a longsword and a dagger.

Ranulf swallowed.

Crab said, "Trust me. She'll be fine. I'm more worried 'bout Mouse. But it looks like Jin hasn't lost her temper yet."

"She's making Mouse angry enough."

"She's letting him air his grievances," Crab said. "Smart woman."

Ranulf beamed as Mouse approached Jin with his double-edged weapons. Jin held her staff in both hands but had donned leather gloves that covered her palms and wrists but left her fingers free.

Crab leaned over to Ranulf, unable to contain himself. "I'll bet ya night watch that she'll end this with Mouse in four moves."

Ranulf kept his gaze on Jinhua. "I have faith in my wife. I think she'll do it in three."

"Yer on," Crab nodded.

They turned their attention back to Jin and Mouse. The entire crew was watching now. Jin and Mouse circled each other. Jin held her staff calmly, not crossing her feet as she moved but shuffling sideways.

Mouse lunged with his left hand first. Jin neatly lunged and hit the crossguard of the longsword, making him drop it. When he stabbed the dagger from her right, she flicked her staff and sent the dagger flying too. Mouse's temper flared and he rushed Jin, grabbing her staff. Jin gave it to him and let him throw it aside. Then he stood facing her again, both with no weapons at all.

"We don't need fancy weapons to settle this," he jeered.

"Man to man?" Jin asked, grinning.

Mouse fumed and he rushed at her, aiming to tackle her, but Jin simply stepped aside. Mouse couldn't stop his momentum, so he rushed right past her before slowing and turning around. He looked as angry as a wet hen. He ran at her again, and this time, Crab realized she was going to intercept him. Mouse had enough sense not to tackle her this time; instead, he threw a punch with his whole arm. Jin caught his fist with her open hand, rolled her shoulder, and used his own momentum to flip him onto his back.

Mouse lay unmoving, looking stunned. Then he flipped over and rose onto all fours, a hand pressing his stomach. Another moment later, he gasped for breath.

"Have you had enough? I don't want to have to waste our limited supply of bandages on you," Jin said.

Crab grinned; she was starting to lose her patience.

"Yeah. I admit it, you're a better fighter," Mouse said, still wheezing.

"Anyone else?" Jin asked.

"I think I could do better," Dog said. He had a big mouth and a bigger stature. He was a brute of a man, as large as Ranulf, with wide shoulders and a face that showed he'd been in many a brawl. Dog was short for Bulldog. "Yer just a wee thing."

Jin bowed her head. "Then please, pick a weapon."

Dog went over to the weapons in the box and picked a practice cutlass. Jin chose a pair of short swords about the same length.

"I'll bet ya night watch she don't slice him," Crab said.

"You're already on night watch. I won the last bet," Ranulf said.

Crab conceded.

"Do you think we're going to need to hire new crew when we get to our next destination?" Ranulf asked.

"No. I think this'll settle it. Though I ain't convinced Dog is the sort to behave honorably," Crab said.

Ranulf nodded.

Dog didn't waste his energy circling Jinhua like Mouse had. Jinhua conserved hers too. This was her fourth match this morning. Crab saw sweat beginning to drip down her back but after fighting her so often knew she relished the buzzing in her muscles.

Jin waited patiently for Dog to initiate. He finally gave in and slashed the cutlass at her. It was a half effort, and he didn't even bother putting his body into it. She stepped back, giving the cutlass the clearance it needed plus a few inches. He swung again, this time lunging. Jin knocked it aside with a short sword and flipped the other short sword over in her hand as she spun, knocking Dog in the temple with the pommel as he leaned into his swing. He landed face first on the deck. She was impossibly fast.

"Well, at least his face might look better now," Turt said.

Jin grinned. She looked around at the other crew members now surrounding them. They started clapping.

"I'm glad you're on our side," Shelley said.

"So you're telling me that if I do the routines, I can move like you?" Turt asked. He was the youngest member of the crew at fourteen.

"The forms are to train your muscles, your body. In an actual fight, it's about knowing when to use what," Jin explained.

Even though so much had happened, Crab could already feel the tension that had been building over the last two weeks ease significantly.

"I guess I better get back to my routine then," Turt said.

Jin smiled, but Crab saw she was a little disappointed that there wasn't another opponent. "I'll have a go," he said.

Everyone turned in surprise. They looked first at Crab, then at Ranulf.

"I'm not thinkin' I can best her, boys. I just wanna give her a better lamb to beat on," Crab said.

"You're a pretty big lamb," Ranulf said out of the side of his mouth.

Crab knew he was nervous, but even he wanted to show Ranulf what his wife was capable of. "You looked ready to pounce," Crab said.

Jin shook her hands as if shaking water off them. She nodded.

So he took a staff and handed hers to her. "Take it easy on me. I'm not used to going more than once."

Jin grinned, but this time, pleasure gleamed in her eyes.

She moved like a flag in the wind. And Crab moved like a lion. But together, they danced across the ship, staffs *clack-clack-clacking* a rhythm. She would spin to stab at his toe and then Crab would leap, barely moving out of the way in time before she rained down a blow from above. After a full eight minutes, Crab tossed his staff and threw up his hands, sweat drenching his previously dry shirt, his chest heaving.

Jin wiped her brow, though she wasn't huffing and puffing like he was.

"Wow," Turt said. He picked up his staff, took his spot, and dove into the routines Jin had been teaching them, as did half the crew. The other half stood there, blinking.

"You're looking much better, Crab," Ranulf said, approaching them.

Crab still hadn't caught his breath, so he just bowed his head and waved at Jin.

"And you looked like a flower spinning and floating in the wind," Ranulf said. He wrapped an arm around her, and even though she was sweaty, kissed the top of her head.

"Thank you, husband." She grinned up at him.

Crab knew without a doubt these two were madly in love and was so glad for his friend.

"But," Jin continued, "I won't let you get away with skipping your own practice, so hop to it." She slapped his behind playfully, and he jumped away, giving her sad puppy-dog eyes as he slinked away to his own spot and started copying Turt's moves.

"His form is getting better," Crab said, after a few moments of watching Ranulf.

"I can't believe he's survived this long with such little combat ability," Jin replied.

Crab laughed. "Well, wait till you see 'im dealin' wiv the nobles. He charms 'em right outta their gold."

"I look forward to it," Jin said as they parted ways to make the rounds, fixing postures, angles, and movements. It was a full hour later before they called a halt to it, bringing up buckets of water from the ocean to rinse clothes and body parts.

"I'm going to wash in our rooms," Jin said.

Ranulf nodded. "Can I come and help?"

Crab coughed. "You gotta take the helm."

Ranulf looked at Crab, pleading in his eyes. Crab just rolled his eyes.

"I need to bathe. I said I would help Turt with some arithmetic before he rests ahead of his nightshift," Jin said.

Ranulf nodded sadly, moping as he climbed up to the helm, and Crab looked around at the crew. They had only dunked their hands and arms, waiting until Jin left to undress. Crab smiled. They would have a new normal in no time.

CHAPTER EIGHTEEN
Jinhua

THREE WEEKS AFTER LEAVING her home, Jinhua was trying as best she could to put on a brave face. The crew, most of them anyway, had been kind and thoughtful. They'd not rejected her, but she didn't quite fit in either. She missed her family terribly, and high-quality training too. Even Crab was just barely advanced enough for her. And Ranulf was busy getting them safely to their next location, so she was often alone.

She stared up at the ceiling, feeling like she could be doing so much more. Though she was excited to see Adanek and wondered what it would be like, how different it would be from Cerisa, she was lonely and unfulfilled. "Ranny?" She smiled as she looked at the large burly man curled around her, asleep.

"Mmmhmm," was a sleepy Ranulf's reply. He nuzzled into her chest.

"Ranny, I think I need a job. Give me something to do," she said. At least she knew he enjoyed being married. She'd heard that some husbands acted differently once they married; they turned violent, unresponsive, or even insulting. But Ranny was even sweeter, even kinder, and she was impressed with how he handled his crew and ship.

"You have a job," Ranny said. "You train us all."

"I want to do more," Jinhua said.

"Like what?"

"Could I learn how to steer the ship?"

A deep rumbling laugh reverberated in his chest.

"What, am I overreaching?"

"You can do anything. But you should know that the crew would take issue with you taking the helm. It's an earned position that requires being the first mate or more sailing knowledge at least."

"And what do you have to do to earn it?"

"You start from the bottom and work your way up," Ranny said. "You earn everyone's respect. Then they nominate you."

"Why didn't you say so?" she asked, leaping out of their bed.

"Where are you going? I was hoping we'd repeat last night..." Ranulf wiggled his eyebrows. He reached out like a bear grabbing at fish, trying to pull her back to bed, but Jin danced just out of reach.

"I'm going to work my way up," Jinhua said. She got dressed and paused before exiting their quarters. "Outside this door, I will be just another minion to you." She grinned then leaped out and sprinted down the hall to find Crab.

He was at the helm, so she climbed up and stood beside him, waiting for his attention.

"Yer quite early to kick my butt around the deck," Crab said. He raised an eyebrow, obviously smelling something brewing.

"I was actually hoping you could kick my butt around the deck." Crab narrowed his eyes, so she continued. "Ranny just said that everyone works their way up on a ship. I don't want to be the exception. I want to work my way up too." She flicked her eyes toward the other crew members.

"Are ya sure?" Crab asked.

Jinhua nodded.

"Then first things first. Go polish anythin' that shines. And yer not to be on this level unless given explicit permission, understand, Swab?" Crab said.

Jin nodded excitedly. She leaped down the stairs, ran straight to the weapons, and gathered what she needed, darting out of everyone's way to find her own little spot at the bow to polish weapons. This was something she was used to, and if she was being honest, she missed it dearly. Eventually, she lost herself in the rhythm of polishing and sharpening blades, moving quickly and swiftly though the men snuck their own weapons into her pile; their dozen or so weapons were nothing compared to her family's stock, and she had cleaned and polished all those many times.

When she finally finished, she looked a little suspiciously at the pile of finished weapons. Many had disappeared as the crew had recollected theirs.

Crab stood in front of her, his shadow now blocking her light. "I'm impressed ya did it all in such a short time, but let's train now."

Jin put her polishing gear away, then grabbed her staff before meeting Crab in their usual practice spot.

"Ya should wear these, slow ya down." He handed her a couple of sandbags, half filled.

"Any place in particular you want me to put them?" Jin asked, not at all bothered.

"Wherever ya like," Crab replied.

Jin didn't tell him that she'd been training with various weights and objects since she was five, all attached to her in different ways. She flattened the sandbags as much as she could and used the rope, securing their tops to wrap them around each leg. The lower the weight, the more tired her legs would get, but the positioning would allow her to swing them to her advantage too.

"Ready?" Crab asked.

Jin nodded and they began. She tested the way the weight changed her movement and readjusted.

"I thought those would slow ya down a little more," Crab said. "Maybe I should have borrowed a couple of bags of potatoes from Carthy too."

They danced around each other as they always did before Crab moved in. Soon the *clack, clack, clack* of their staffs drowned out everything else. Jin could really feel the weights slowing her down, and she made a mental note to start wearing weights once a week. Crab was showing signs of tiring, and Jin knew she'd also have to finish soon or she'd be completely out of energy. She moved quicker, but Crab must have picked up on the change because he grinned. Instead, she slowed her movements, hoping to pull him into her trap. When he finally did fall for it, he slowed his own movement, and she swiped her staff downward onto his side.

"And I thought that'd tire ya," Crab said.

"It did," Jin said. She felt herself breathing harder.

Jin had been working nonstop. And if she was honest with herself, she loved it, loved the physical labor of scrubbing the deck and focusing on a singular task, loved everyone ignoring her as she put her elbow grease into the work.

And Crab had given her lots of work. She had been scrubbing all the small spaces the men couldn't get into, then polishing and waterproofing them by rubbing linseed oil into the wood. She'd polished every metal surface on the ship and done so with all the gusto she'd learned to bring to the task for the many years her siblings had made her do their work.

"Are you sure you don't want me to take you off that task?" Ranny had asked when Crab had told her to clean out all the privy buckets.

"No," Jin had said.

"You're sleeping with the captain. Surely that gives you some kind of immunity from privy buckets." Ranny had made a face.

"I'm enjoying the work, Ranny. It's all part of learning how this ship runs. Besides, I'm sure you have a better appreciation of the person emptying the privy buckets after you've done so yourself," Jin had said, smiling.

Ranny had grinned at her. "Just wait till after."

He'd been right. Emptying the privy buckets was something she definitely didn't want to do again—ever. It was probably the most singularly disgusting thing she had ever experienced. Men were gross. She felt so disgusting afterward, she brought up a dozen buckets from the ocean to scrub and wash, and she still couldn't get the smell out of her nostrils.

"Hi," Ranulf said, making her jump as she continued to scrub.

"Hi. You should stay there. I smell," Jin said.

"You're still beautiful," he said. Then he smiled. "Dog doesn't have a sense of smell. Did you know that?"

"That explains why he can still find joy every day despite emptying those things," Jin said. She scrubbed harder.

Ranulf took two steps and took her hands. "You're going to scrub your skin off."

"Will it help with the smell?"

"It's time you learn the ways of being at sea," Ranulf said.

Jin raised an eyebrow, wondering what Ranulf had up his sleeve—literally—as he slid something down his sleeve. It was a small tin of salve.

"We cover the smell," Ranulf said.

Jin took the tin, opening it cautiously. She looked inside and the smell hit her before she even moved it. "It smells like... you," Jin said.

Ranulf smiled. "It's my secret."

"What is it?"

"It's a salve, made of mint and lavender and vanilla."

"Where did you get it?"

"From an apothecary," Ranulf said. "Though Crab gave me my first tin."

He gently took some salve and rubbed it into her arms. She melted at his touch as she let Ranulf rub the salve into her arms and her shoulders. Then he produced another tin from his pocket and rubbed it into her hair. She sat on a crate and Ranulf combed his hands through her strands, separating it as he worked the salve into it.

When he started pulling at sections of hair, she closed her eyes. "I didn't know you knew how to braid."

"Best one in my family. My sisters all demanded I do theirs."

"Hmm. Do you miss them?"

"I do. But they weren't always kind to me, so in some ways, I don't."

"Do you think you'll ever go back?"

"Maybe when I make something of myself," Ranulf said. His hands were incredibly gentle for such a large man.

Jin's thoughts turned to his new family—their new family. "How did you meet them all? Your crew?"

"Crab and I have been friends since we were wee lads. He's a couple of years older than me, but we're from the same place. His father was a sailor, so we spent a lot of time playing on a ship. My family, having so many kids, they never really cared to keep track of us much."

"I'm sorry," Jin said.

"No, don't be sorry. When we have kids..." Ranulf turned pink.

Jin smiled and took his hand. "I want kids too. Fewer than my family had though."

"Me too. Two?" Ranulf asked.

Jin nodded.

"Well, when we have kids, I want to bring them along. I want to be a real family and keep them with us," Ranulf said.

"It would be more difficult."

"I know. But I would help. And honestly, I think Crab would practically become a nursemaid. You should see him around babies," Ranulf said.

Jin grinned. "Want to start now?" she asked. She fluttered her eyelashes at him, and he jumped up.

He scooped her up in his arms and barrelled down the stairs and the hallway to their quarters, slamming the door closed with his foot. She was already kissing his neck and nibbling on his earlobe as she'd discovered he liked the other night.

CHAPTER NINETEEN
Jinhua

"**I** DON'T THINK I want you on privy duty ever again," Ranulf said.

"But—" Jinhua started.

"Nope. This is purely selfish. I don't ever want another whiff of the privy when we're in bed together again," he said as they snuggled in bed, her head on his chest.

"Aye aye, Captain," Jin said. She giggled into his chest and ran her hands along his chest hair.

Ranulf smiled, as did Jin. She couldn't be happier, and for the first time in a long time, despite the challenges, despite missing her family, she was excited for her new life and what tomorrow might bring. Jin put her hands on his chest and pushed herself up.

"I don't think I'm quite ready for a second sailing," he said.

She rolled her eyes at him. "I have to go finish cleaning the mess I left on deck."

"Ohhh, but I really want you to stay here."

"And who will clean up the mess I left?"

"Crab."

"And that won't help my case with the rest of the crew."

"But you're not the rest of the crew. You're my wife."

"But you're all a family, and I want to be part of that family," Jin said. She stood up, stark naked. But she liked the way Ranulf's eyes roamed over her body. She slowly pulled on a new shirt and pants.

"If you were really crew, you'd be sleeping in the bunks with them. But you're not because you're my wife. You get to sleep right here." He pointed to the empty space next to him.

Jin shook her head, pulling her hair back and tying it with a piece of leather.

"What if I said it was an order?" Ranulf asked as Jin reached the door.

"I have to give you a chance to miss me," Jin said, winking and disappearing out the door. She couldn't bare to look Crab in the eye as she slinked to her spot and cleaned up the buckets of water she'd hauled up. She returned everything to its place and then mopped up the mess she'd made before finally going to face him.

She climbed the stairs and waited on the top step. Crab was looking out at the ocean. In the distance were great rock formations jutting out into the ocean. Mist settled among them, giving an eery air to it all.

"Come an' join me," Crab said. "You know what those are?"

"The Misty Mountains. It's said that this place touches the spirit world, and on misty nights, you can walk among the spirits. Many make the journey to seek answers." She walked toward him, but he told her to stop when she was three feet away.

"Ya stink, lassie," Crab said.

"How are you, Crab?" Jin asked, hoping he hadn't noticed when Ranulf had scooped her up and they'd disappeared for half an hour.

"I'm good. I enjoy peaceful nights like these," Crab said.

It *was* quiet. Only a couple of crew members moved about on deck.

"I understand …" Crab paused and frowned. "Jin, yer in a strange spot. But I think yer doin' a good job. I hear less grumbling and more laughter when your name is mentioned lately."

Jin nodded, feeling her cheeks warm at the compliment. "Do you think I should join the crew and sleep in the bunks?"

Crab took a deep breath in and then out. "I think it would create a great bond with the crew if ya hack it down there. But I also think you and Ranulf need some time together—with as many doors as possible between ya and the rest of the crew." He slid his gaze to her, and Jin felt like her cheeks were on fire.

Crab grinned, turning back to the dark open ocean. "Have ya ever known anyone to go to the Misty Mountains?" he asked.

"A man from our village did. He had finished training at our school and was planning to join the army but decided to go to the mountains first."

"What happened to 'im?"

"He came back a different person. He was brash and impulsive before. But when he returned, he was peaceful. Some didn't recognize him, and some say he was taken over by another spirit."

"Did he join the army?"

"No, he actually joined the monks for five years and has since opened a temple in the hills beyond our kingdom for traveling monks."

"That musta been an incredible journey."

"Sometimes, I wish I was a man. Then I could have gone to ask him or gone on my own mountain journey."

"I can't pretend to understand what it's like to be a woman, but I do understand not being able to do what ya want because of things out of yer control."

"I'm sorry you've had to feel that way," Jin said. A thought occurred to her. "Crab, how do you and Ranulf know each other?"

Crab grinned. "I'm two years older than 'im. When I was six an' he was four, he got lost in the forest. Everyone searched far and wide for 'im. But he was nowhere to be found. Next mornin', he appeared on my doorstep. He was dirty an' his hair was matted with leaves, but he had berries in his pockets. He'd come to sell them."

Jin smiled to think of four-year-old Ranulf already trying to trade.

"He was shiverin' mighty fierce but tryin' hard not to show it. His lips were blue, so my father invited 'im in to show off his wares. Then my father told me to choose somefin while he went out to find somefin to trade. In truth, he went to let the big house know we'd found their son, or rather, he'd found us."

"And you've been best friends since?"

"That afternoon, I showed 'im how to tie knots. I didn't know what to do wiv 'im. But he was so unlike the rest of the family, not at all above us, just filled with curiosity."

Jin smiled.

"He ended up comin' back a week later to ask about a knot I'd taught 'im. Then he came every other day, and then every day. And then his family started sendin' us word us if they needed 'im. My father took 'im in like a second son. I was excited to have a friend to play with, so we grew up more like brothers than friends."

"It shows, your brotherhood."

"Thank ya," Crab said. "I fill his head with knowledge, and he fills me life with adventure. Did ya know he got this ship by making a bunch of deals that began with only a seashell he found on the beach?"

"No way."

"Yep. He traded a seashell to a lady who collected 'em for a pair o' socks. Then it was socks fer a cup, a cup fer a bowl, a bowl fer a broom, a broom fer a chair, a chair fer a table, a table fer a cart, a cart fer a horse, and a horse fer a field. He kept half the field and traded the rest fer a ship."

"That's incredible," she said.

Crab nodded. "There's nothin' more to do tonight if ya wanna get some rest."

"Thank you, Crab, for sharing that story," she said before heading back down the stairs and belowdecks to her room. She wasn't surprised to see Ranulf already snoring, his barrel chest heaving up and down with each breath. She stripped and snuck into bed in the space still waiting for her. The moment she did, his arms and legs wrapped around her, pulling her against him. She settled into her husband and the man she loved, happy and content.

Chapter Twenty
Mouse

MOUSE GLANCED UP AT Ranulf, their captain, manning the helm but watching Jin as she coiled rope. It was as big as she was, but she hid her struggling. Never mind that it usually took two to coil that particular rope.

"Whaddaya think?" Shelley asked without looking at him. They were close enough for conversation as they worked, so conversation was had.

"I think she's 'ere to stay, and I think she could beat us all to fish chum if she wanted," Mouse replied.

"I appreciate the work she's puttin' in, but ya really think she'll stick?"

"I do. I look at my wife the same way they look at each other," Mouse said.

He'd recognized it at Ranulf and Jinhua's first lesson. Mouse had met his own wife when they were kids. But even then he knew they would be each other's. This was the same.

"Ya don't think it's bad luck? Another woman on the ship?" Shelley said.

Dog sidled up to them, snorting. "You say that near Carthy, you'll be eatin' rotten fruit for the next two weeks."

"They're permanent. So we better get on 'er good side or it'll hurt," Mouse said.

"She really is that good." Dog sighed as if he was admiring a new dagger.

Shelley whistled softly. "She took Crab down without breakin' a sweat. I don't even think she breathed any harder."

"She moved so fast tying up the ropes the other day, I thought for sure she was part bird," Mouse said, keeping busy so it didn't look like they were gossiping.

Another newer crew member, Spinner, came within earshot. "Think he'll share?"

Mouse turned and smacked him upside the head. "Say that louder. I dare ya. She'll gut ya before ya finish the sentence, and you'll be fish food before yer last breath." Shelley and Dog glared at the new sailor.

Ranulf and Crab didn't tolerate lewdness. Mouse knew Ranulf would challenge any man who was vulgar and now knew his wife would inflict even more damage.

"I'm scared of 'er," Turt said.

"Good," Dog retorted.

Turt, as their youngest sailor, was still learning the ropes, and they were raising him as much as teaching him. Mouse was glad to see he was being smart.

"Heard back in Cerisa that she was engaged to the prince. Think he'll come after us again?" Shelley asked.

Mouse shrugged. "Didn't you sign up for adventure when you joined up?"

"We can't defend ourselves against a navy. We're not a warship," Shelley said.

"Why worry 'bout what might happen?" Mouse said, "If it happens, it happens. Yer not goin' to accomplish anythin' by worryin' bout it now."

"We're not terribly far from Adanek now. You think if they're comin' after us, they'd have caught up by now," Turt said.

Shelley nodded and so did Dog. Mouse knew they didn't want to say it aloud because the superstition said that would make it true.

"Time to polish." Crab came over, tossing cloths and polish jars, and they parted.

CHAPTER TWENTY-ONE
Crab

"WE'RE ALMOST THERE. ANOTHER day or two and we'll see land," Crab said.

"Good. I think the crew has cabin fever," Ranulf said. He looked down and watched the crew laughing and trying to toss a bucket of water from one person to the other. Water sloshed all over them, and Ranulf laughed as they tried again.

"All right, missy, you show us. How do ya toss a bucket o' water without sloshin' it?" Dog asked.

"Like this." Jin took the bucket, poured half the water out, then swung it around in a circle. She tossed it to an open barrel, and it landed, right side up, water sloshing, but not a single drop went over the edge.

"She's a smart lass *and* she can kick all our butts," Dog said. "Ya sure ya won't marry me instead of Cap?" He smiled his most charming smile, but he was missing many teeth, so it looked more like a bulldog growl.

Ranulf leaned forward, waiting to hear Jin's answer.

She grinned and walked right up to Dog. She leaned toward him and kissed him on the cheek. "I'm already married, but I'll get back to you if it doesn't work out," Jin said. She winked at him.

"Oy." Ranulf ran down the steps. "She's my wife, boys, and ... and you'll have to fight her and win before I step out of the picture." Ranulf grinned and they all laughed. He scooped Jin up and carried her up the stairs to the helm. "Mine, you hear me, you scallywags? All mine." He placed her on the ground and wrapped his arms around her, kissing her head, then her neck and shoulder before working his way back up. Jin couldn't stop giggling, and the crew below laughed before turning away red-faced and going back to their tasks.

"I think you've won 'em over," Crab muttered under his breath.

Jin was trying to catch her breath as Ranulf continued to hold her—without the incessant kissing—so all she could do was grin at Crab and mouth, "Thank you."

When Ranulf picked her up to return to their quarters, Crab only rolled his eyes and shouted orders to keep the crew busy so no one giggled and listened at their door.

When he spotted Jin back on deck, rubbing more oil into the wood surfaces, he watched as some of the crew teased her, only enough to make her turn pink, though, not to the point of crudeness. And he knew this crew knew how to do crude.

CHAPTER TWENTY-TWO
Jinhua

THE NEXT DAY, JINHUA woke in the arms of her dearest husband. She smiled. It was her birthday, though she was sure Ranulf didn't know that. But she was all right with that. She had him and her new family. Besides, if he knew, he would try to do something wild like throwing a party, and she didn't want to take attention away from the crew's excitement to get home tomorrow. As much as she enjoyed being a new wife to a man as wonderful as Ranulf, she knew their trysts had a certain ... effect on the crew; they would be in search of companionship as soon as the ship docked.

"What are you thinking about?" Ranulf asked.

"I'm just thinking how incredible it is that I've come so far in such a short time. I lived my whole life in that town, eighty percent of that within those walls. Now I'm across the world."

"Mmm ..." Ranulf pulled her closer and pressed his lips on top of her head. "Oh, Crab mentioned last night you were to be on crow's nest duty for the first two hours this morning."

"Crab should suck an octopus." She flung Ranulf's arm aside and leaped out of bed and into her clothes and ran out, racing up the ropes to the crow's nest. She was almost late for her shift.

"Mornin', Jin," Turt said.

"Morning," she said cheerily.

"I'll head down unless ya need anyfin?"

"Nope. Have a good sleep, Turt."

He nodded and shimmied down the ropes, clearly exhausted after his overnight shift. Jin stood and looked around, tying herself to the crow's nest as safety dictated. It was so peaceful up here, ocean around her, sea and salt and wind in her hair. She undid the leather tie and let her hair whip around in all directions. She breathed deeply, then looked around and breathed deeply again. Then she felt a tickle in her lower regions.

Oh no, she thought, *I forgot to use the privy before I came up.*

Jin looked around for the bucket. It was strange, to pull her pants down and pee in a bucket so openly on a ship full of men. She was protected by the crow's nest walls, but it still felt odd. Looking around after yanking her pants down, she squatted over the bucket. Then she pulled her pants back up as she glanced around anxiously. That had felt strangely exhilarating. Smiling, she squinted at the horizon.

Wait—was she seeing things or was that land ahead? It would still take them a day to get there, but she could make out mounds and shapes that could be buildings.

"Land!" Jin shouted as she pointed.

Crab and the crew all turned the way she was pointing. A cheer went up.

"A day ahead!" Crab said, his voice booming across the ship.

Jin kept her gaze ahead, leaning over the nest as far as she dared and squinting at the formation. Though she couldn't see details, it was breathtaking just to see the silhouette. It was beautiful. And it might be her new home.

Chapter Twenty-Three
Ranulf

J IN, LIKE THE REST of the crew, was busy running around the ship and trying hard not to stop and stare at the land ahead.

Instead, she worked hard to focus on the tasks at hand. She completed them quickly and flawlessly as she did her best not to let her gaze stray and linger on the approaching shore. As they neared, though, Jin's jaw dropped. What looked to her like a rocky cliff topped with a beautiful castle came into view. However, they were aiming for the harbor just south of it. A new place was so close. Last night, she could hardly sleep, not that Ranulf minded filling the time.

"So, we're going to see a friend?" Jin asked Ranulf once her tasks were done.

"We're going to visit the lord of Densria. He's a good friend. He owns all this land, and he was the one I bought my ship from."

"Wait, I thought Crab said you traded for your ship," Jin said.

"I did. I'm trading with Lord Densria."

"What are you trading?"

"Something entertaining."

"And that is ...?" Jin asked, pushing herself up to stare at him.

"Lord Densria is the kind of lord with much wealth who needs entertainment. He's lived an amazing life and no longer enjoys travelling. So when I told him I wanted to travel to faraway places, he said he would trade me a ship for some entertainment and exotic goods he'd never seen before."

"Am I what you're trading?" Jin asked suddenly, her face draining of color.

Ranulf's eyes went large. "No. No, no, no, not at all. Not in a million years!"

"Then what did you bring to entertain him?" Jin said.

"Stories. And a few things Crab and I traded for."

"And I suppose me, in a way."

"Yes, you'll love him, and he's going to love you."

"So how did you become friends with the lord of Densria?"

"I,... uh, met him when Crab and I drooled at the beauty of this little city after we'd been drinking. I might have tried to trade him for the city and his lordship."

Jin's eyes goggled. "He could have had you killed!"

"Yes, he could have," Ranulf said looking somber.

"What happened?"

"He was entertained. He decided to invite me to dinner instead."

"You're one lucky man."

"I know. So please, be excited! He's going to love you."

"All right. How should I dress?" Jin asked.

Ranulf looked at her blankly.

"Should I dress in my finest? Or for my position on the ship? Or as your wife? Or what?" Jin asked.

"Umm... I suppose as my wife? What does that even look like?"
Ranulf asked.

"You'll see," Jin said.

The next morning, Jin worked hard on the ship, but Crab finally
sent her off, saying he had no more for her to do so she better go
get ready for their arrival. Jin let herself stare off the ship for a few
more minutes before doing just that. There was space here for so
many docks, but only two were built in a cove where a low rock
wall had been built to protect the ships tied to the docks. It was
beautiful. For a merchant, it was perfect. She could almost imagine
all the docks they could build there, a storage building on one side
for goods and barracks on the other.

A gondola system moved goods up to the city, and a staircase built
into the rock to the left zigzagged this way and that. It wasn't the
safest route but was surely the fastest to get to the big castle at
the top. The edges of the city sat nestled in the "V" amid the cliffs,
with the castle on one side and the sheer cliff on the other. Lantern
light was already starting to glow as the sun started to set.

Crab coughed and Jin jumped. She looked back and ran down the
steps to her quarters. She pinned her hair up, then changed into
the one outfit she'd been sad to see packed. It was her best dress. It
was the dress she was supposed to have worn on her journey to the
prince of the Cerisan empire. Her parents had paid a fortune for
it to be made, and she was half hoping to sell it instead of wearing
it. But if she wore it just for today, she could still take it apart and
sell the textiles. The gold thread alone was worth more than the
rest of her wardrobe combined.

She went light on the makeup. If there was one thing she knew, it was
that this country's women didn't wear nearly as much makeup as they
did back home. So today, she used none of the white paste to coat her

skin, but she did pinch her cheeks a little and dab some berry stain on her lips.

When she was finally dressed, she felt the crew slowly pull the ship closer to the dock and knew Ranulf would come for her soon. As predicted, there came a knock on the door just as she put one last coat of berry stain on her lips. "Come in," Jin said.

Ranulf opened the door, and his face froze. "You look beautiful, Jin. Like a bride."

Jin smiled. "See? You do get it."

He looked puzzled but offered her his arm, and they made their way through the cramped hallway to the deck. He went up first, blocking her, but when he stepped aside and she took the last step to the deck, she heard a collective gasp.

"M'lady," Shelley said. He knelt on one knee and bowed low.

One by one, the crew followed suit, bending a knee and bowing as they ushered her forward.

Ranulf glanced at her; he looked anxious. But his face relaxed into a smile when she smiled at him.

Crab coughed, so Jinhua headed his way. His eyes looked shiny as he looked at the little pin she'd attached to a fold of her skirts. She'd taken all the gifts they'd given her when she arrived and attached them to her skirts.

"Lady, ya clean up good. And ya look beautiful. It is an honor to be represented by you." Mouse bowed low and took her hand, kissing her fingertips.

She grinned at him. "Thank you. I'm going to try to make you all proud."

"We already are, lassie," Crab said.

"You look so beautiful. I can't believe you're mine," Ranulf said. He gently took her hand and led her across the deck to the gangplank and then held her hand as they walked along the dock. All the other people, though few, on the other ships stopped and watched as they strode along the dock toward the city.

At the end of the dock, a simple black carriage awaited them. On the door was a symbol of the sea and the cliffs in white. The footman opened the door and said, "Lord Densria sends his own coach for the lovely lady."

Ranulf nodded, helping her into the carriage. Jinhua marveled at it and wished she could walk around it. It looked much like the carriages at home, except the wheels were much bigger and fancier. But while the carts back home were practical, this carriage was beautiful. "I'm the luckiest woman in all the world to ride in such a beautiful carriage," she said when Ranulf joined her inside.

He grinned. "What a pair we make then, for sharing this ride with the most beautiful woman in the world makes me the luckiest man."

She grinned back at him. She wanted to swat him for his overindulgent flattery, but she felt her cheeks warm and her heart race. Would she ever tire of his fancy words? Would he ever stop saying them to her?

The carriage rolled on and Ranulf took her hand, rubbing his thumb along the top. He had cleaned up quite well too. He wore clean trousers, a vest, and a coat with tails. His shirt was clean, and she could smell his minty scent.

Jinhua shifted her other hand over his hand and squeezed. Then she slid the curtain so she could see the town as they rolled through it. She couldn't see much, however, as the carriage had picked up speed. She saw mostly blurs of colors and people in simple clothes waving as the carriage hurried through the streets.

When it finally slowed, Jinhua felt like her heart might run away with her. What would happen to her if this Lord Densria didn't like her? Would he send her back to Cerisa? Or just away? Would she become a prisoner?

"He'll love you, I promise," Ranulf said as he squeezed her hand.

At that, Jinhua realized she was not alone. She had Ranulf, her husband. He would stand by her.

The carriage door opened and Ranulf stepped out before her so he could help her down. When she stepped out, she faced the most exquisite building she'd never even imagined. It wasn't the biggest castle, but the sweetest and most beautiful. Its light gray stones were clean and scrubbed, and flowers and vines snaked across the facade. Five turrets pointed to the sky, capped in a gorgeous darker gray stone. The carriage crunched on the gravel behind her as it left, and Jinhua couldn't help but turn around to see the gardens. A lush green lawn—more grass than she'd ever seen—blanketed one side, and she imagined, the rear of the castle. Low flowering bushes and wild gardens filled the space between the drive and the lawn. Wild in its variety and colors, there was still order within each little patch and with the pathways lined with tiny rocks.

"Ranulf! My boy!" a man shouted as he ran down the steps. He was older, perhaps the same age as Ranulf's father might be. And if Jinhua had not known better, the man could have been his father. He had the same build, the same strong chin and jaw as Ranulf. But his eyes were different. Where her Ranny's eyes were a soft, kind gray, this man's eyes were a sparkling emerald green with laugh lines framing them.

He hugged Ranulf like he was his son, his straw hair streaked with white a contrast to Ranulf's dark hair, before turning to Jinhua. "My lady. I had a feeling Ranulf would come back from his travels with more than *stuff*." He grinned at Ranulf.

"May I introduce, my wife, Jinhua," Ranulf said, offering her hand to the old man.

"If I may, my lady," he said, gently taking her hand.

Jinhua noticed his hand was soft and warm but interestingly calloused in many places. "It would be my honor, my lord."

He grinned and brushed his lips against the back of her fingers. "Congratulations to you, Ranulf. And best of luck to you, my darling. You are the greatest beauty that has ever graced these hallowed halls, and I'm honored to host you first in Adanek, here, in my home of Densria." He bowed again and then turned to Ranulf. "May I have the great honor of offering your wife some refreshments indoors?"

Ranulf bowed. "Of course."

Jinhua tucked her hand in the crook of the lord's elbow. "I would be honored too." And with that, the amiable old man walked her up the smooth stone steps and through the giant double stone doors onto the plushy carpet lining the hallway.

"I find castles so cold. The carpet keeps my feet warm when I sneak down for some dessert in the middle of the night," he whispered.

Jinhua covered her mouth, not wanting to giggle.

"Oh, I'm so excited to have a lady to impress again!" He turned and added, "Though your company is plenty, Ranulf, I hope you don't mind my saying, fresh company is always exciting."

"Not at all," Ranulf said, grinning.

CHAPTER TWENTY-FOUR
Jinhua

JINHUA SMILED AS THE old man with the sparkling green eyes led her across a luxurious red-and-brown intricately woven carpet, warm and almost glowing with gray swirls, toward a grand staircase. As they neared it, they passed a massive open room on the right. He must have felt her pause because he stopped in front of it and said, "I just haven't figured out exactly what to put in this room. Or what to make of it."

"In some homes, I've seen indoor ponds that people fill with koi fish. It's believed that the koi fish protect the home's occupants from harm, that the fish will die in honor of their home's inhabitants," Jinhua said, at the same time thinking, *A pond here would be perfect*. The room had large, shuttered windows that could be opened in the summer and spaces that were dying for some plants and greenery. She'd turn this room into her own personal jungle if she could.

"Eureka! That's it!" he declared.

Jinhua jumped out of her skin. She wasn't sure if the old man was happy or angry, if he'd somehow seen what she had and thought it offensive.

"You, my dear, are brilliant. A hundred years later, and finally, this room will have beauty and purpose. Imagine a summer day with the big windows open and plants filling this room," he said. "A pond will make the perfect centerpiece."

Jinhua exhaled; she felt self-conscious, so she said nothing more.

"Tell me more about what you see in this room." His green eyes sparkled like emeralds. She wanted to glance at Ranulf, but Lord Densria was waiting for her answer, his expression open and sincere.

So, she described some of the variations in Cerisan receiving rooms in more detail.

"That sounds like a dream. Perhaps I could even put a little sitting area in the middle, so if you were to sit there, you'd feel as if you were in the jungle, all while being indoors. Ohhh, I can't wait to tell my gardeners. They might have a fit!" He giggled and then continued to lead her down the hall, past the staircase and to the left, where a set of wooden doors opened to an enormous library.

The old man watched Jinhua as she spun around in the huge room. "This is my study. I had them move my desk in here even though it's the library. I think the books help me look imposing." He puffed out his chest. He might be a short man, but his presence was large.

Jinhua was quickly liking this man more and more. "It's beautiful," she said.

"You're welcome to any of the books." Then he added, "Books should be read, not sitting on a shelf, so if you'd like to borrow one, just write the title over there in that open one." He pointed to the far right to an open book with scrawled writing upon it. "Anytime, my dear. You can come here anytime to find a book."

"Thank you. I am honored you would allow me such liberties," Jinhua said. She made a mental note to come back after dinner to get some books and start reading.

"Ahh,... now I'll show you to your rooms and let you and Ranny get settled before dinner. I know it must be wearing on your patience to entertain an old man."

"Not at all. Your home is beautiful, and it is my honor to enjoy the company of such an esteemed and kind person," Jinhua said.

"Ohhh, be careful, my lady. I might just keep you for myself." The lord giggled and led them to the right down a new hallway. "This is where the family rooms are supposed to be, but I have no family. My room is down there." He pointed down the hall to some huge white doors with gold gilding. "Ranny's room is all ready for him, but if you feel you would be more comfortable in another room, please do feel free to explore," he said.

"I'm sure it will be lovely," Jinhua said.

"I'll see you both at dinner then. This old man needs a nap!" he said before kissing Jinhua on the cheek and hugging Ranulf again. Then he nearly skipped down the hall to his room.

"My lady?" Ranulf took her arm and pushed open the white double doors with green gilded edges to their left. Her jaw dropped as she looked inside.

Warm wooden floors lined both rooms, the first a small sitting room and the second a bedroom. They were so spacious, all her family's bedrooms would have fit.

A massive four-poster wooden bed carved and painted white with horses was detailed all in a green that reminded her of jade. A rich blue edged green, and Jinhua thought it was the prettiest color combination in all the world. A bench seat with carved arms sat at the end of the bed, and along the wall was a matching carved table that looked out into the gardens.

Jinhua followed her nose to a bathtub of hot water in a bathing room next to the bedroom. The tub would easily fit her and Ranulf twice over, so she stripped her clothes off as quickly as she could and stepped into the tub. "I'm going to be here awhile," she said. She closed her eyes, letting her hair float wherever it wanted to.

She listened as Ranulf stripped out of his own clothes and stepped into the tub with her. Curiosity filled her when she heard him take the top off a container of some sort. Suddenly, he grabbed her toe and spun her feet toward him. He gently took her foot and started to rub, one toe at a time, kneading a gritty salve into her skin. He moved to the next foot, and Jinhua melted at his touch. Then he spun her around again as she floated in the hot water, gently gathering her hair next and opening another container. Gently, he massaged her head and worked the soap through her long hair. After rinsing it in the tub, he worked another thicker salve through her hair.

All the while, she relaxed and took it all in. She had so much of the sea to wash off, and all her worries from being with the crew, and her first days as a merchant washed off with it.

Chapter Twenty-Five
Ranulf

Jinhua was asleep in their bed, but Ranulf was restless. Their journey had been smooth, too smooth almost, and it worried him. Had Prince Feng really just given up after they'd outrun his ships? Were they planning something bigger? Why had there been no threatening letters?

He made his way to Mali's—Lord Densria's—study. He knew the lord would probably be awake, and if he wasn't, Ranulf knew the fire in that room was always burning and the room was always warm. At the very least, it would be a good spot to sit and think. He pushed the doors open gently and found Mali bent over some maps on his desk.

"Help yourself to some tea, or some stronger stuff if you want it," Mali said. He waved at the beverages on a little table between the desk and the hearth.

Ranulf noticed Mali had his day clothes on still. So he hadn't gone to bed yet, or even changed since dinner.

"How are you doing, my boy?" Mali asked as he left the desk and joined Ranulf by the table of beverages.

Ranulf smiled. Mali had taken him in at a time when his family hadn't much cared about him. Mali was like a second—well, third—father to him; they'd each filled a hole in the other's life. Tonight, Ranulf decided tea might settle his nerves better than the other beverages. The pot was still warm, so he poured himself a large cup of the soft chamomile tea. Mali chose a different drink, grabbing a bottle of amber liquid without hesitation and pouring a few inches of the strong liquid into a glass.

"Good. Fine," Ranulf said.

"So you're internally discombobulated?" Mali asked as they sat in the two chairs in front of the hearth. He looked around. "I shall move a third over here soon."

"That's very thoughtful of you," Ranulf said. He ran the pads of his fingers over the handle of the teacup a few times as he stared into the fire.

Mali didn't press him. He waited as Ranulf sorted his thoughts.

"I'm worried that she's going to change her mind, that the crew is only pretending to accept her, that she's going to resent me, that she'll miss her family terribly. I already feel guilty for it. Plus, I'm worried Prince Feng will find other ways to make our lives harder, that he'll find some political or manipulative way to cause us harm." Ranulf exhaled, feeling the tension leave his shoulders for the first time. He took a sip of the hot tea so his vision would clear.

Mali pursed his lips, thinking. "Do you resent me?"

Ranulf was so shocked at the question, he jerked his head up. "No! I could never. I'm grateful to you for taking me in."

"Jinhua is not the only orphan here. You have a family, but they do not have the resources to support you. Do you feel resentment toward them?"

"No. I understand there are many mouths to feed. They're simply overdrawn."

"Did you coerce Jinhua into marrying you?" Mali asked. There was no judgment in his voice, only curiosity.

"Of course not. I tried to dissuade her. I could tell family is important in Cerisan culture. And we knew that if we did this, we would be burning all ties to her family."

Mali drank the entire contents of his glass and then reached for the bottle. "So you're scared."

Ranulf hung his head. It felt shameful to say, but he realized he was.

"Change and new adventures are always terrifying. But that's how you know you're doing the right thing. If you'd played it safe, you wouldn't have a new wife. Think on that for a moment, my boy. What if you had come home without her? With a ship full of goods, yes, but not her? How would you feel?"

"Miserable. Even being parted from her within this home makes me ache for her. I want so badly to be next to her, touching her, even if it's just a fingertip on her shoulder. It's like my world lights up. I feel pride and joy, and when she looks at me, it becomes only the two of us and I feel like we can take on the world together."

Mali only smiled when Ranulf glanced over. Ranulf felt a little silly for saying such flowery things.

"I hope you've told her all this," Mali said. At Ranulf's nod, he continued. "And it sounds to me as if whatever the future—whether it includes Prince Feng or her family or yours—brings you, you'll be able to take it on together. Or is that not what you meant when you said you felt like you could take on the world together?"

Ranulf nodded. Mali had managed to make him feel better with his own words. It was his unique skill, and Ranulf hoped he would one day have half his wisdom.

"There will always be challenges, my boy. To have someone to share them with is a gift. Take time now to forge your bonds for the time ahead," Mali said. He patted Ranulf on the knee, then stood and finished his second drink. "I shall head to bed. But I look forward to seeing you two lovebirds in the morning." Mali grinned and waved as he placed his glass down on the table and left without putting the maps away.

Ranulf's tea had gone cool, so he threw back the rest and placed his cup with Mali's glass and left the room to join his wife in bed. He would take Mali's advice. This was their time to bond for the future. It was hardly a hardship to hold his beautiful wife in his arms. He crawled into bed and smiled as she rolled over and snuggled closer to him. It made his heart soar and settle at the same time.

CHAPTER TWENTY-SIX
Jinhua

I T HAD BEEN A blissful few days. They'd eaten, slept, and explored the town and Mali's home. He had been a most generous host and often feigned fatigue early in the evening to give them their privacy.

Jinhua stretched as she mulled over the delightful memories. She patted the bed space next to her and knit her brows when she realized Ranulf was gone. *Strange*, she thought, *I must have slept much later than normal.*

She got up, wrapped a silk robe around her, and went hunting for her husband. She looked around their spacious rooms. It was eerily quiet. Jinhua went back to their bedroom and tossed some clothes on. As she looked around, she noticed a few of Ranulf's clothes were missing. At least a few outfits were gone.

Where had her husband gone, and why hadn't he woken her? She felt her heartbeat increase. Her palms went clammy. Hopefully, she was panicking for no reason.

She left their rooms and went to the breakfast room, where they usually met Mali. She threw the door open more forcefully than planned and found Mali sitting by the window, a plate of food on his lap.

He looked sadly at her and handed her a letter. "I'm sorry, dear, I tried to convince him otherwise."

Jinhua took the letter and almost ripped it in two trying to open it. She sank to the floor, expecting the worst. Had everything been a ruse to get something from her? She hadn't anything to give but herself. Her sight blurred, and she had to focus and breathe so she could read the words.

> *My dearest, darling wife,*
> *I'm taking the coward's way out by leaving a letter with Mali instead of discussing this with you. The sea is a dangerous place. I love you so much that I cannot risk your life on the open ocean. Knowing you are safe makes my heart lighter.*
>
> *I know you wanted to come on this adventure with me, but it's simply too perilous for you.*
>
> *I was so glad when you got along with Mali. He's like a father to me, and I know he'll be good company and care for you while I'm away.*
>
> *I'll be back in a couple of months.*
>
> *-Your loving husband*

"Oh no he didn't," Jinhua growled, then read the letter again. "Did you know he was going to do this?" Jin looked up at Mali.

"Not until now. I tried to keep him here, but he explained and left me the letter, said he couldn't bear the thought of losing you, so he was going to make sure you stayed safe for his peace of mind."

"What about me? What about what I want? Besides, he won't survive without me! Did you know he got himself into three fights while he was in Cerisa? I saved his skin in two of those!" Jinhua said.

Mali didn't say he knew, but he nodded like it was easy to believe.

"How far away are they? Can I catch up to them?"

"I have a ship coming in tomorrow. I can order it to follow him. It could catch up."

"When did he leave?" she asked.

"Early this morning."

"Wait, did he even sleep?"

Mali only shrugged.

"AAARGH!" Jin yelled. She had taken her staff, found an old pole in the yard near the guards' training area, and begun beating it to dust. "I can't ... believe ... he ... just ... left ... without ... me!" Jin yelled. She continued beating on the pole, sending splinters flying in every direction with every crash. She didn't notice the crowd of guards that had gathered, nor did she notice when they pulled their shields out to protect themselves from the splinters flying at them. She didn't notice when she whittled the pole to a stump, and she didn't notice when it started to rain. Uncaring, she continued to beat the stump, even when it slid, even when her feet were in six inches of water.

Finally, a hand clamped on her shoulder. She spun around with her staff, ready to unleash her anger on an opponent, but Mali just knocked her staff over with one of his own. She realized she had no anger left. She was empty.

Mali's eyes were filled with gentleness and kindness. It undid her and Jin fell to her knees, sinking into the puddle of mud and unleashing a flood of tears.

Mali, strong even as an old man, picked her up like she weighed nothing and carried her, hands frozen as if she was still holding her staff, through the castle's side door. Both she and Mali were covered in mud and drenched to the bone. Jinhua buried her head in his shoulder and let him carry her. He gently put her down on a couch in the great library in front of the fireplace and wrapped blankets around her. She couldn't stop sobbing. She couldn't control her breathing as tears gushed from her eyes and her chest heaved faster and faster. Throughout it all, she tried to get up, feeling terrible for dirtying the lord's beautiful couch in his beautiful room in his beautiful castle but found she had been tucked in too tight.

Mali piled a final blanket around her and held her shoulder firm. His kind green eyes filled her watery sight as his hands rubbed her shoulders. "You're all right." He hugged her then, enveloping her in a tight embrace. He squeezed her as she inhaled and then let go as she exhaled, helping her slow her breathing by breathing with her. When she could finally see those green eyes through the fuzziness of tears, she began to steady.

She finally finished with a last hiccup and felt completely empty. Empty and tired. He burrowed a little hole through her pile of blankets, then passed her a cup of hot tea. He took his own cup of tea and sat cross-legged on a little footstool in front of her by the fire. He stared into the flames, and Jinhua noticed he'd left a few handkerchiefs at the edge of the mountain of blankets. She couldn't believe how sweet this man was.

"I used to travel often. I find it interesting to meet new people and discover new things, new cultures and languages. In the Far, Far East, I met a culture that lives in these tents high up in the mountains. They move from place to place and take their homes with them. They follow these deer-like creatures, you see. They use their milk and care for them and protect them."

His gaze flicked back to her, and Jinhua was ashamed when she found she had to look back into her teacup, taking a careful sip of the hot liquid.

"They were amazing. And do you know the most interesting part? They were a matriarchal people. Women led. Women decided. Women hunted. Men were tasked with the cleaning, the setting up, and the cooking."

He looked at her again, and Jinhua risked a peek, so he continued. "There's another culture that lives high up in the mountains, so high that it's so very cold, colder than you could possibly imagine. And yet they have these amazing hunters that have taught these great big birds to hunt—for the people."

Jinhua turned her head to better look at Mali, and she felt the cool air on her cheeks as a blanket slipped off her head.

"They raise these birds from babies, becoming their partners, and they go and hunt together. You probably guessed, but they're all women. The men are responsible for keeping their homes warm and clean and raising the children. They chop wood and such, but the women take care of the falcons, training them and caring for them. The falcon's care is their first priority. Those women even build warm, fleece-lined carriers. They feed the falcons the kills first, before feeding any of the people. If we come back as something else when we die, I wouldn't mind coming back as one of those birds."

Jinhua smiled and Mali smiled along with her. "You see, I'm telling you all this because I know you come from a culture where women are expected to be timid and meek and demure. Even though you, the daughter of a great warrior family and rumored to be the best warrior in the entire kingdom, are strong and capable, I understand that you were taught to be shy, quiet, and accepting."

Jinhua sunk an inch back into her blankets. She felt exposed.

"But you are here now. There are no expectations. You can be whoever you want to be. You can make your own rules. I know it seems Ranulf has his own expectations for you, but I also know he's open-minded."

Jinhua emerged once again from her blankets.

"There's another culture, I've never seen them, but I've heard they actually keep their men penned up like cattle." He chuckled. "The women don't trust them, so they keep their men in one building. They are to stay there, though sometimes the women trot them out to help build a new home or raise a building. These women even have a hierarchy among themselves, and it's said they can go to the barn and pick a male whenever they like for the night or the day." He chuckled again.

Jinhua grinned at the thought of such an upside-down world. Then she had another thought. A sly smile slowly grew as it took root.

Jinhua placed another pair of trousers in her bag. It was much more useful to wear trousers than dresses. She'd always hated wearing dresses anyway; they had so much fabric, movement always took more effort. She only packed one—at the bottom of her bag. Renshu had bought if for her because he couldn't resist the colors, so she kept it close to her more out of sentimentality than because she intended to wear it. That, and it was the only piece of her family she had anymore.

A knock on the door made her close the bag.

"I keep this room untouched. You can leave anything here, and I vow it will be safe. It will be exactly where you left it upon your return," Mali said as he entered.

Jinhua smiled. When you break down like she had in front of someone, they become a close friend. Her cheeks warmed as she thought about that night and how embarrassing it was. "I don't deserve any of your kindness, yet I am so grateful for it."

"You are like the daughter I never had, and Ranulf is the son I never had," he said.

"Thank you."

"I ... before you leave, there's something I want to tell you," Mali said.

Jinhua closed her bag and turned to give her full attention to the old man. She'd begun wondering if he wasn't as old as she originally thought. His strength and movements were that of a man much younger than he presented himself as.

He took her hands and made her sit down opposite him. She did so, looking into those wonderful green eyes. For a moment, she wondered if she'd met Mali first, would they be together? But she didn't feel the same electric zip up her arms or the fluttering of her heart as she did with Ranulf. No. She felt only genuine platonic love for Mali.

"I'll be going on a trip in a few weeks. If anything should happen to me, I will be leaving this estate, everything, even the lordship, to you and Ranulf."

Jinhua's eyes went wide, but she only asked, "What do you mean?"

"I mean that should I die, you will become a lady and Ranulf will become a lord. I've made all the arrangements and called in all the favors necessary," Mali explained.

"But—" Jinhua began.

But Mali had more to say. "I hope to have that pond installed in the front room before you return. And I hope I'm alive and well when you return, but if anything should happen, you will be the Lady of Densria and Ranulf the Lord of Densria. I have no sons or daughters, no cousins. The people here need someone to care for them, and this kingdom needs a lady and lord to ensure it prospers."

Jinhua sat immobile. She was stunned to think she'd one day be a lady. A little voice in her head reminded her she was supposed to have been a princess, but she shook her head because what this man was offering them was more generous than a stranger should offer. "Thank you," were all the words that came out.

"Now, that ship I mentioned arrived last night and is waiting for you. It's small and fast, so it should catch up to Ranulf without too many issues. It will take you to him and then return here."

"Thank you again," Jinhua said. She held the man's hands and smiled; she'd lost a family but somehow already felt like she was gaining another, more genuine one. "I don't know how we can ever repay your kindness."

"Speak nothing of it. I am the lucky one, to have such adventure in my life, such friendship."

Mali walked Jinhua to the door and even to the steep staircase that led to the docks. Up close, the staircase didn't look nearly as dangerous as it was well built and well maintained and even included a railing carved into the rock wall.

"Well, this is where I leave you, Jinhua. Please show Ranulf a little kindness. He is much softer than he looks, and he meant well leaving you behind," Mali said.

"I'll try," Jinhua said. She grit her teeth just thinking about it though. She hugged him, and they held each other for many minutes.

"I know most people like to say travel safely. But I like to say *carpe diem!*" And he flourished his arm out like it was a sword. "It means 'seize the day.' Adventure awaits you, my darling, and I know you won't let anyone get in your way."

"Thank you," she said. "I'm so grateful to have met you."

"And I you," he said in return.

"Where are you going on your trip?" Jinhua suddenly asked before they parted.

"Oh, somewhere out east. I'm not quite sure."

"*Carpe diem,*" Jinhua said, rolling the words around in her mouth.

"No, no, Jin. You must say it like this." He took a fighting stance, and with a flourish of his hand, said, "*Carpe diem!*" and waved his fingers in a little flourish.

"*Carpe diem!*" Jin said, and she flourished her fingers as he had.

He smiled and she turned to start down the stairs. She took two at a time; it would be good exercise. She turned to look up at every turn of the staircase, and there Mali was, still waving, so she would wave back with a little flourish of her fingers as she continued. When she got to the bottom, she looked for the ship Mali had mentioned. After spying it, she hurried over, greeted the captain, turned to wave to Mali one last time, then went belowdecks and threw her things into the room she'd occupy until she caught up to her husband. He was only two days ahead of her, but she was nervous about what he might say when she got there.

Her room was cramped. Jin realized she'd been spoiled with captain's quarters on her first journey, and her current quarters made her wonder what the crew bunks looked like.

She wanted some fresh air, so she joined the captain at the helm and nodded. He was a gray-haired man but had dark-brown eyes that glinted, ready for an adventure.

"Captain Sandi, at your service," he said with a bow.

"I hear you like to sail fast," Jin said, cutting to the chase.

"I do. And I hear you're chasing someone?"

"I am."

"Then we'll have a mighty fine adventure." The captain grinned, then gave the word to unfurl the sails.

Jin looked up to the cliffs and the castle and saw the tiny speck that was Mali and waved. He waved back, and she swore he even added his little flourish.

"What is your ship's usual purpose?" Jin asked the captain.

"We are the lord's flagship."

"He usually uses this ship on his travels?" she asked. He nodded, so she decided to be bold. "Where does he travel to?"

The captain grinned, and she knew he wouldn't tell her. "Here and there. Mostly new and exciting places."

"Interesting. Can you tell me how old he is?" She felt her cheeks warm; it was a rude question after all.

The captain only said, "Younger than he looks."

She grinned. "You're a good friend to him."

"As are you." He bowed again.

They started to pick up speed then, so Jin let the captain do what he needed to. They stood silently for a little while, though, just staring at the open ocean.

CHAPTER TWENTY-SEVEN
Ranulf

R ANULF WAS A CHICKEN. He was a coward. He hated himself, but she had looked so cozy and safe in their home, he had convinced himself it would be better for Jin to stay home. She would settle in, make the home theirs as Mali had invited her to. Maybe she had wanted to see the pond installation Mali was so excited for.

Ranulf had sent messages out to the crew in the middle of the night, and they'd left early in the morning, even earlier than when Jin liked to get up for training. He'd known it was wrong, but the letter he'd received had spooked him.

He put his hand to his vest where the letter sat.

The night before, Mali had given it to him as they'd sipped their night cap, saying it had arrived by messenger bird. Ranulf hadn't been expecting anything and had been curious and worried as he'd opened the small roll of parchment. There on the scroll, in bold letters, read, "Cerisans do not take kindly to being robbed. Because she is now sullied, consider both your lives forfeit. You will both pay for the insult to His Royal Highness, Prince Feng, future emperor of Cerisa."

Mali had said he'd already read the note. And because it had arrived by bird, it had meant there had to be a ship near enough for the bird to make the journey. "I suspect they're on a ship off the coast just out of sight. I've already sent word for the fishermen to keep an eye out," Mali had said.

A small part of Ranulf had hoped the prince had forgotten, had hoped they didn't want her as badly as they thought; the prince did, after all, have several wives already. But that letter had chilled his insides.

"My boy, we are not without our defenses," Mali had said. "And should they strike Adanek directly, it would be an act of war. That's not a risk I think they would take over a single person."

"We hope," Ranulf had said. If he had the prince's resources, he would. He would send an entire army to rescue his beloved Jin.

So, Ranulf had decided he would face the prince's forces himself—with his crew. He would do anything to buy her freedom, to save her. If they took him, then so be it, but he would put up a fight. If something happened to him, he knew Mali would take care of her.

Ranulf had sailed out with a heavy heart. His hope was that the prince's ship—or ships—would see his, mark it, and come to him. At least out on the open sea, he wouldn't pull an entire kingdom into a war over his actions.

"Ya should 'ave told 'er," Crab said from beside him now.

"She has a much better chance of surviving this if she doesn't know," Ranulf said.

"We have a much better chance at survival with her here," Crab retorted.

Ranulf had had to tell Crab what was going on but made him promise not to say a word to Jin. Together, they'd told the crew they were headed out on some errands. They'd all looked around for Jin when he'd arrived, but Crab had trained them well enough not to ask questions, so they hadn't said anything as they'd pulled away from the dock with one missing member.

"She's gonna to beat ya herself when she finds out, mark my words. She's a fiery one. She'll swim out 'ere on her own and climb up the side of the ship with daggers if she has to," Crab warned him.

Ranulf only nodded. He didn't want to continue talking about it. A small part of him wanted her to come to him. But he told himself that was foolish and dangerous. He was trying to give the Cerisan Navy a target—a target that wasn't her; he wanted to keep her safe above all else.

So, they sailed slowly in a wide arc to get the navy's attention—if they really did have a ship out here.

CHAPTER TWENTY-EIGHT
Jinhua

"Y A KNOW, IF YER ever lookin' to join another ship, it'd be an honor to have ya," Sandi said.

"That's awfully kind of you, thank you," Jin said. They had been sailing for three days now, and she was hoping to catch sight of Ranulf's ship today.

"Ship ahead!" came the shout from the crow's nest.

"Aye, raise the flag then!" the captain ordered.

Jin ran down to her cabin. She and Sandi had gone over the plan already, and since he was up for a little bit of the dramatic, he'd suggested they simply get close, and she could swing over with a rope attached to the mast. Ranulf's crew would recognize the ship as being Densrian. They would likely even think it carried a letter from her or Mali.

"The clothes are in the bag I left by yer door!" Sandi shouted after her as she ran down, found the small bag, and changed quickly. She completed the disguise with a cap and a messenger's tunic. Sandi's only request was that she write to him to tell him how their ruse went.

They started to pull up to the ship, and Jin could see Crab at the helm and Mouse on deck, waiting patiently. Sandi's ship sailed closer and closer since Crab had slowed down to let the other catch up.

Jin looked over at Ranulf's ship and realized how sorely she had missed it; it had become home. She found herself looking for everyone. They were all in their normal positions, and she hoped dearly they would all welcome her.

As they neared, Sandi nodded in salute to Crab.

"Send Mali my best," Jin said.

Sandi nodded, and as the two ships slid within feet of each other, Jin made a running leap, grabbing one of the ropes and swinging from one ship to the other.

"Must be an important letter if you came to deliver it personally instead of sending a bird," Ranulf said.

Jin looked up, taking off her cap to release her hair.

His eyes widened in surprise. "Jin. What are you doing here?"

She felt the anger rise in her whole body. She stood toe-to-toe with him and jabbed her finger into his chest. "How dare you leave me behind! How dare you leave just a note and not even discuss your plans with me! How dare you make that sweet old man break the news to me! How dare you leave yourself unprotected! How dare you leave your best warrior behind! I am not a porcelain doll to be kept on the shelf and only brought out on special occasions. I am a warrior. You are a merchant, and we are partners in this."

Ranulf's mouth hung open along with everyone else's. He reached for Jin's hand, and she slapped him across the face. He recoiled, face falling.

"You promised we would be partners. You promised we would be equals in all things. You promised we would explore the world together. How could you leave me behind?! Forget that you put yourself—and your crew—in danger by leaving your best fighter at home. Did everything we discussed mean nothing to you?" Jin's vision swam as tears flowed freely down her cheeks; she barely felt them as she blinked furiously to keep her vision clear.

"I ... I thought you'd want to settle in," Ranulf said, his voice tiny.

"And *why* did you not even discuss it with me?"

"I forgot to?" He visibly braced himself. He clearly knew that reason was as weak as it sounded and he was waiting for another slap.

But Jin didn't have it in her. Instead, she looked around. The crew was frozen, watching her spectacle. "All of you. I thought I was at least becoming part of your family. I'm hurt and angry that none of you came to say goodbye or tell me you were leaving." With that, Jin picked up her bags and went down to Ranulf's room and locked the door. She wanted to be alone.

Now that she was on board, she wondered why she had come at all. They obviously didn't want her here. Her family wouldn't want her at home anymore. A pang shot through her chest as she thought of Renshu and what he might be doing now. She hoped he hadn't been caught. Though even if he had been, he was Amah's favorite, so she hoped his good fortune would keep and he wouldn't be in too much trouble. Jinhua had left her family and had thought she'd finally made a new one. But if they didn't want her, what would she do? Where would she go? She thought of Sandi's offer to work on his ship; that might work. She'd probably rarely see Ranulf, so they could go their separate ways. The anger had drained from her body, and now she was just filled with hurt and sadness and loneliness.

A soft knock sounded on the door before someone tried to open it. Jinhua didn't bother to say anything or even move to go unlock it. She didn't want to hear their replies, their excuses. She curled into a ball, piled some blankets around herself, and let the tears fall, hugging her knees and just waiting for tomorrow. Maybe Sandi would still be nearby, and she could return to Densria. Maybe she wasn't as brave as Mali thought she was.

Several soft knocks came through that afternoon and into the evening. Jinhua didn't answer any of them. She didn't even care if Ranulf had to sleep in a borrowed hammock; she didn't want to talk to or see any of them. She was simply exhausted.

Eventually, Jinhua fell asleep in the pile of blankets, tears still streaming. When she woke, the sun was shining. She climbed out from the pile of blankets she'd nestled into and looked out the window. Sandi's ship was still there, though it had drifted behind. Maybe he'd thought to stay close and wait. She closed her eyes and thanked Captain Sandi. How had she been so lucky to come to know so many caring, thoughtful people?

Then came another knock on the door. "Lassie, it's Crab. I've got some nice rice soup from Carthy, and I promise I'm 'ere alone. Will ya let me in?" Crab's tone was gentle, like he was speaking to a frightened lamb.

Jinhua didn't want to say anything. She didn't know what *to* say.

"Lassie, it's not his fault. He was wrong to think ya needed protectin', but can ya fault him for wantin' to keep the one he loves most safe? And the crew assumed ya wanted to stay this time and join us next time. We weren't leavin' ya behind for good. We wouldda been back in a fortnight."

Jinhua still didn't say anything. She curled back into her ball, pulling more blankets around her.

"Jin, I'm sorry. I didn't know he hadn't told ya 'til later. It don' mean yer not part of the family, we all love ya. We were sad to leave ya, but we assumed ya wanted to stay."

Jin softened a little. Perhaps she was overreacting. No. They had left her. But she slowly tiptoed to the door, opening the lock and walking back to her blankets.

"May I come in, lassie? It's just me. I promise," Crab said.

"Yes," Jin croaked. She was surprised at how hoarse her voice sounded, and for a quick moment, panicked to think of what her face might look like.

The door creaked and Crab stood in the doorway, hunched over to fit, with a tray. On the tray was a bowl, a cup, and a teapot. He strode into the small room and softly closed the door behind him.

"Here. Carthy made it 'specially for ya." Crab was all tenderness and kindness. He lowered the bowl into her hands.

She carefully took a sip of the soup, keeping her eyes averted.

"I know we're terrible. We don' think of others as often as we should, and we didn't think about how ya felt or ask what ya wanted," Crab said. "We're an uncivilized bunch, and we've been stuck in our ways for a long time. I know all this because I grew up with three sisters and a mother who had no patience for male inconsideration."

Jin cocked her head.

"One fundamental difference in the way men and women are raised 'ere is that women are taught to always think of others, to be considerate. They're taught to be caretakers. It's easy for 'em to put everyone else first. Men, however, are often raised with responsibilities and duties to uphold and ways of life to follow. They're taught to do, not feel, to take care of 'emselves first."

Jin only took another sip of her soup.

"So now all the men on this ship—and Carthy— 'ave fallen into a pattern. We've known each other fer a couple years now, so we know the drill. We know where we need to be when and what to do when, and it's as simple as that. Then you came in and threw our way of life upside down—in a good way mind ya, and you'll be proud to know the boys have kept up with their training—and they didn't think. They just *did*. They know we're only ever at port for a few days and then they get ready to keep going: reload, restock, ship out."

Crab coughed. "We were sad ya weren't comin', but we assumed, newly married an' all with a new home, ya wanted to get yer home established first, to get settled before joinin' us on an adventure. Besides, we weren't goin' anywhere new or exciting. We were just goin' to do a normal run down south and back."

"To you."

"Sorry?" Crab stopped short.

"It was nothing new and exciting to you," Jin said. "It was new to me. I thought I had a family. And then you all just abandoned me."

"We thought you liked Lord Densria."

"I do. But you're my family."

"We're sorry. All of us," Crab said.

Jin raised a single eyebrow.

"Ranulf's been sittin' at the door all night and all mornin'. I finally sent 'im to the helm to get 'im outta the hallway."

Jin's heart melted a little.

"Will you see 'im now? Will you speak wiv 'im?" Crab asked.

Jin took another sip of the soup, finishing it off and putting it down. She nodded.

"I'm going to go take the helm and send 'im down. And ... well, just let him speak before you slap 'im again," Crab said with a wry expression.

Jin nodded and let Crab take the bowl and put it back on the tray. He placed the tea in her hands instead. Then he strode quietly to the door and left. What felt like seconds later, a soft knock sounded, the same soft knock she'd heard all night until she had fallen asleep. "Come in," she said.

The door creaked open, making Jin wonder if the door creaked on purpose.

Ranulf sulked into the room, shoulders drooping, eyes wide. He shuffled over to her, climbing up onto the bed but being mindful of her blanket pile and keeping his distance. He folded his large limbs around himself. "I'm sorry, Jin." His hand twitched as if he wanted to reach out to her, but he held back. "I didn't think. I just did. There's some business I need to handle, and I didn't want to wake you. I didn't think you'd want to go either. It's just a fortnight trip and ... and I ... I'm so sorry."

"You abandoned me," Jin said. She watched him visibly shrink.

"I'm sorry. I didn't mean to. I just thought you'd like some time to get to know your home."

"My home is with you, wherever you are. That's my home," she said.

"I ... can you ever forgive me? I promise we'll discuss all our plans. I won't assume anymore. I will wake you in the middle of the night even if you look like the most ethereal beauty as you sleep."

Jin couldn't help the grin that crossed her face as she reached for his hand. He was quick to grasp hers. He kissed the back of her hand, then turned her wrist over and kissed that too. He kissed her palm.

"I thought you didn't want me anymore," she said quietly.

Ranulf's eyes widened. "Never. It physically hurt to leave you. I was tempted to tell Crab to go on his own. But there's so much to purchase, and the lord of where we're going isn't particularly fond of Crab." He sighed and looked at her adorningly. "I missed you every moment we were apart. I kept wondering if you were content, if you enjoyed Mali's company. Then I worried that maybe he was actually a terrible person out of my presence."

"Mali is a wonderful man."

"Oh?" Ranulf said, raising an eyebrow.

Jin recognized his jealousy and decided to tease him just a little longer. "He is sweet and kind and generous. He's impressively thoughtful too."

Ranulf looked grumpy. "You're never staying there alone again," he said, pouting.

She took his other hand. "I'm not like other women. I'm not the delicate, fragile kind. When there's danger, I won't run from it. I'll protect you from it." She grinned.

He blushed and looked sheepish. "There's something else I've been keeping from you."

Jin froze.

"Prince Feng has sent threatening letters to Mali," Ranulf blurted out.

Part of Jinhua relaxed. She had expected something worse to come from her defection. But then she realized this was still bad. "How threatening?"

Ranulf winced as he spoke. "Bad enough that I'd hoped to lure him into battle with this trip?"

Jin's face fell as she realized how much danger Ranulf was willing to put himself in for her. "Have you seen his ships?" She wanted badly to be in the crow's nest to check for herself. Had she sailed right by them with Captain Sandi without realizing it?

"No. No, we haven't. Mali received the last letter by bird, which told us they were close enough to send a bird." Ranulf pulled the letters from his pocket.

Jin took the letters and read them. It eased the tightness in her heart to discover that only the adviser who had brought the marriage contract was chasing her. "These are all the letters?"

Ranulf nodded his head.

Then Jin looked up at her husband. "Will you promise me, no more secrets? Even from a strategic point of view, you cannot leave me behind. Making these kinds of decisions without me because you want to protect me"—Jin held the letters up—"That's as bad as not trusting me." Jin watched as Ranulf's face fell. She took his hands in hers. "We are partners."

Ranulf nodded, sitting up straighter. "I promise. No more of these decisions without you. I know you're the best warrior we have. You're probably the best in all of Adanek."

Jin grinned again, but then a thought blossomed. "Does it … emasculate you that your wife is a better fighter?"

"Crab is better than me too. Heck, I'd say half the ship is."

"That doesn't answer my question."

"No, it doesn't. I'm proud to have you as my wife. I feel lucky that you chose me. Of all the men—all the princes—in the world, you chose me, a bumbling fool."

"You are kind and gentle and sweet and thoughtful, most of the time. And apparently, you're also very good at charming people."

"I find people fascinating. We're all so different, but also so similar. We all generally want the same things, so you just have to discover what that is and make it easier for people to obtain it."

Jin chuckled. "Well, I can't wait to see you in action."

Ranulf pulled her gently onto his lap. He wrapped his arms and legs around her like a protective monkey and planted a kiss on her neck, behind her ear, on her temple and her face. "I'll try never to make you angry again. You were more terrifying than a dragon."

Jin winced. "It did have five days to build."

"I think I saw Turt wet himself." Ranulf laughed into her ear.

She snuggled closer to him. "Are they upset?" Jin asked.

"They're upset with themselves, like scolded children."

"Should I go talk to them?"

"You can beat them with your stick tomorrow. Today, I want you all to myself," Ranulf said. He tightened his grip around her, and she breathed in his scent. Mischievousness overtook her, so she nudged him until they fell over in bed. He untangled his legs from her, and she curled into her spot on his shoulder.

"I promise we will never be apart from this day forward," Ranulf said.

"Good."

CHAPTER TWENTY-NINE
Jinhua

JIN FELT NERVOUS AS she woke up the next morning and dressed. Facing the crew after getting so angry with them and then fleeing the scene in tears was daunting. She wondered if they would be kind or if she'd lost all the respect she'd earned. She also found herself wondering when the Cerisan Navy might show up and what they would do. She pulled at the hem of her shirt.

"Is that all you're going to wear?" Ranulf asked.

"Yes," Jin said. She wasn't sure what he meant.

"Maybe a coat or a vest?" Ranulf asked.

"Why?" Jin asked. Now she worried that she wasn't wearing enough clothing.

He threw his palms up. "I'm not saying you need to, but I'm going to have a tough time keeping my eyes on the seas ahead if you look like that all day."

"Well, that's your problem, isn't it?" She pulled her chin up and decided to tuck the ends of the shirt into the trousers she wore.

"Ready, my love?" he asked, grinning at her and taking her hand.

"Always," she said, smiling back. She felt strong with him next to her, even though she still felt her stomach flip-flop as they left the room and went up on deck.

The whole crew had gathered. They stood there until she neared, then they all took their hats off and bowed their heads.

Mouse approached her first, which really surprised her. "I'm sorry, Jin, that we left ya behind. Yer one of us, and we shouldn't 'ave left without ya."

The rest of the crew followed Mouse and proceeded to apologize. Jin's heart swelled in her chest until she thought it might burst. She grinned at them and even hugged the last man, making Turt's cheeks turn deep red.

"Now let's get back to training," Jin said, and they all spread out and began their routines. She wove amongst them, fixing the angle of an arm or moving a foot a little further over. They were all getting much better at the routine and would soon be able to move on to the next form, perhaps even doing some sparring.

She took her own favorite spot, on a railing at the bow, and went through the routine with them, this time demonstrating some variations so those who were ready could start working on a different variation.

Jin let her body take over and her eyes drift to the sea around them. She saw Mali's ship, with Captain Sandi, and waved at him. He nodded and blew her a kiss before turning around and sailing off.

Ranulf came up behind her. "Anything I should know?"

"No," Jin replied, smiling. She looked out at the ocean and the calm, dark-blue water that surrounded them and felt at peace. "Where are we headed, anyway?"

"We're going to visit a good friend: Lord Cambekton. He's buying some of the smaller goods we purchased. He's always interested in stone dragon sculptures and longswords," Ranulf said.

Jin brightened, excited to meet someone who liked weapons as much as she did.

"I know you're excited, but it's not like you think. He just likes pretty swords to hang on the walls."

"He doesn't use them?"

"Not that I've ever seen. He's a nice sort, though, just a little strange. He really loves pretty things. His estate is decorated very ... well, uniquely."

"He has no need of weaponry for combat?"

"He's protected to the south by the Henkramian border patrol, and there's not much but mountain to the east. His land is just a tiny little spot in a bay, hidden from most and of no interest to pirates or bandits, with waters too rough for most to get through."

"Does he have a wife? A family?"

"He does indeed have a wife. She's a little older than us but quiet and kind. I don't think theirs is a marriage of love, more a marriage of convenience."

"Oh," Jin said. She was surprised somehow that marriage contracts existed outside her homeland. "Are they happy?"

"They seem happy. You'll have to ask them. They're very friendly," Ranulf said.

Jin wasn't sure it would be appropriate for her to ask them.

The next day, their ship sailed into an unusual bay. It was like a painter had swooped and swirled a brush to create it. The land wasn't very usable, but it provided safe harbor for incoming ships. The castle was small, nothing to attract real attention. They docked and the crew went to work bringing out canvas and poles from storage.

"They like to set up camp on the beach 'ere," Crab explained.

"It's like paradise, fishin' and buildin' bonfires. The lord don't mind," Mouse said as he carried another set of poles out."

"What about the goods?" Jin said.

"We have one trunk," Ranulf said, jumping to help Crab carry said trunk onto the deck.

"That's it?" Jin asked.

"He likes small, pretty things remember."

Jin just nodded, then helped the crew haul more piles of canvas and helped Ranulf carry the trunk to the dock. She looked around but didn't see any guards or townsfolk.

"Will we be safe here?" Jin asked when she had a moment alone with Ranulf.

Ranulf nodded. "They're a quiet sort of people. They'd see anyone coming from miles away. But we won't see guards until we get to the castle."

When the crew broke off to start erecting their tents, Jin almost wished she could join them. It looked like fun.

Instead, she turned and helped Ranulf and Crab tote the trunk closer and closer to a looming stone wall. As they neared, she realized just how high the wall was. Even she would have difficulty scaling it without more strength and a long grappling hook.

Just as she was about to open her mouth, the creak of a hinge had her blinking as the stone wall opened.

Four guards emerged, unarmed, then jogged to meet them. "Master Ranulf." They bowed. "We've been sent to help you with your things."

Ranulf, Jin, and Crab put the trunk down and the four guards picked it up.

"I'll bring yer things and then join the crew," Crab said.

"Wait, you're not—" Jinhua said.

"Someone's gotta keep an eye on the crew, make sure they don't burn the place down. And I'm not much for the niceties." Crab winked.

"But—"

"You'll be fine, Jin. Come find me in the mornin' if you want to train. I'll be in the tent closest to the ship," Crab said.

Jin nodded. She threw her arms around Crab, and he hugged her back. Then he hugged Ranulf before turning and leaving.

The guards disappeared into the stone wall with their trunk, and Ranulf took Jin's hand, bringing it to his lips before they walked together through the big stone doors. Not five feet in, a block of stone bigger than the doors blocked their way. A ditch on either side of the wooden dock they walked on led to the enormous stone, and a narrow wooden walkway wound around each side of it.

"Is that ... to block the door?" Jin asked.

Ranulf smiled and nodded. He pointed to the left where an elaborate rope system was set up. "They can slide that big stone piece in behind the doors. It's why the doors open inward, blocking off all access to their home."

"It's brilliant."

"A bit of a pain when you're carrying supplies though, miss," a guard said.

Jin smiled. She supposed having to carry supplies around the stone every single time would be a bit cumbersome.

When they were finally behind the stone, she looked up and gasped. They were now in a forest with the tallest trees she'd ever seen. And from within that forest, a small castle jutted out. It looked like an egg nestled amongst the trees, its stone not the stark gray she expected of castles but a soft brown that blended in with the trees.

The wooden walkway melted into a moss-covered dirt path, and Jin craned her head around, looking for the ocean they'd just left. It seemed impossible that these two worlds existed so close together. She saw just a sliver of the ocean between the giant stone slab and the open stone doors.

As they approached the castle, Jin fell in love with the greenery around them. The path inclined more sharply then, and she saw beautifully carved wooden doors inlaid with iron. They were tall and open, revealing a buxom woman and an elegant, slender man waiting for them. They wore flowing, simple clothes in greens and golds.

"Lord Ranulf, welcome again. It's good to see you," the woman said, her eyes crinkling as she smiled.

Ranulf took her hands and kissed them both. "And you. May I present my wife, Jinhua?" He gently took Jinhua's hand and brought her forward.

"Someone has finally caught Ranulf's heart. Our warmest congratulations." The woman turned to Jinhua, and without missing a beat, came forward to offer an embrace.

Jinhua stepped into it, glad to feel the warmth and kindness of a stranger.

"I am Lady Cambekton, and this is my husband, Lord Cambekton. But please, we're not formal here. Call me Briemarie."

"It is an honor," Jinhua said as she curtsied to the lord.

He looked aloof, not quite present, as if he was thinking about something else. Then he shook his head and smiled, bowing to Jinhua. "Any woman who's captured Ranulf's heart must be a dear friend indeed." He took Jinhua's hand and kissed the back of it. Jinhua was surprised but honored by the gesture.

Briemarie took Jinhua's arm and led her into the castle. Once past the doors and the castle's double walls, a garden burst into view in the middle of the courtyard.

"This is beautiful," Jinhua said.

"Thank you. I just adore gardening, so Dale here turned our courtyard into a garden so I don't have to dig up some trees outside to do so." She smiled at her husband. She seemed to have genuine affection for him.

Jinhua looked and saw the men seemingly deep in conversation.

"Come, let me show you around our home. I hope you'll enjoy your time here."

"It's all so beautiful, I don't know how I couldn't."

That night, Jinhua contentedly retired to their rooms with Ranulf. Briemarie and Dale were wonderful hosts. Though Dale seemed a little absent-minded, it didn't seem to be purposeful; it was more that he didn't care for formalities and was always thinking of something else.

"What do you think?" Jinhua's husband asked as he slipped out of his clothes. Instead of wearing a nightshirt like most men, Ranulf preferred to sleep in only his undershorts or nothing at all. He said he didn't want to waste clothing when no one would see them anyway.

"I think they're lovely people, gentle, kind, and thoughtful," Jinhua said. "And this home is the definition of luxurious serenity."

Ranulf nodded. "Tomorrow morning I'm going to show Dale everything we brought. Do you want to be there?"

"Sure, if he doesn't mind."

"I'm not sure he'll even notice." Ranulf winked.

Jinhua smiled, then launched herself onto her husband.

CHAPTER THIRTY
Ranulf

RANULF SAT WITH HIS cup of tea by the window overlooking the training grounds. Even this far away, he knew which figure was his wife. She moved so beautifully, there was no mistaking her.

"Our ladies are beautiful, aren't they?" Dale appeared in the doorway, and Ranulf made to rise, but Dale waved at him to stay put. He came over and filled his own teacup before sitting down himself. "When I met my Briemarie, I didn't think there was any possibility in the world that she might choose to live here, in isolation, with me. I thought the entire court must not have eyes if they couldn't see she was the most beautiful woman in all the world. She's so strong and so graceful. I pale in comparison. I even considered bribing her to marry me."

Ranulf smiled. His gaze didn't leave his wife in the training rings below, but after nodding, he eventually forced his gaze away. "We had a bit of a tiff on the way here."

Dale offered a gentle smile. "Briemarie grew up in court and I grew up here, in the countryside. We had our differences at first too. I can't imagine the differences between two entirely different kingdoms and cultures."

"I'm terrified she's going to leave me, to resent me for taking her away from her family, that this life won't be enough for her," Ranulf said quietly. Admitting it to someone else felt like removing a stone from his shoulders.

"I thought the exact same. I was taking Briemarie away from her friends, from the life she knew, from her family. Their home is closer than Cerisa, of course, but still, it's a difficult journey to travel from court to here. I'm a recluse, and the road to the city isn't helpful either," Dale said.

"How did you come to terms with it?" Ranulf asked.

"I didn't."

Ranulf swallowed. The guilt was eating him up inside.

"There are never any guarantees, but time passed, and she stayed. We had our moments when I thought surely I would find her and all her things gone from her rooms. I made it a habit to wander into her rooms in the afternoons when I knew she was taking tea to make sure she hadn't packed up and left. One day, I went in, and they were empty." Dale laughed, though Ranulf had no idea how he could find mirth in that. "Turns out she was tired of being so far away from me, so she'd moved all her things into my room—our room now. Gave me a scare though. I ran to her tearoom to find she wasn't there and ran outside like a mad man yelling her name. She appeared before me in a field of flowers and grasped my hands, wondering what was wrong."

Dale shook his head and smiled. "She thought we were under attack or I was having a medical episode. When I embraced her and held her for dear life, it still took time for her to realize what was happening. We had a long conversation after that."

"And then?"

"And now we walk the fields together. She squeezes my hand as we walk to reassure me, and we speak more freely with one another. I'm the luckiest man in the world to love and feel loved in return."

Ranulf nodded. He was happy for Dale and Briemarie. He didn't want Jinhua to worry like that, and if he was being truly honest with himself, he *was* worried she would turn her back on him and choose to beg forgiveness of Prince Feng after a few months of living their simple life at sea.

Dale stood. "It's time I join my Briemarie for tea, but if I can give you one piece of advice, Ranulf, it's talk to her. Tell her how you're feeling and be honest about what you're thinking. Briemarie once told me that what she thought I was thinking was much more terrifying than what I was actually thinking."

Ranulf thanked Dale as he left. They hadn't seen another ship all the way here. He'd even asked Captain Sandi to stay near for a few days just in case. But now that they'd landed in Henkram, Crab thought they'd be safer. The ocean corridor between Henkram and Adanek was much narrower than between Cerisa and Adanek, so Crab had said it would be foolish for Cerisan ships to come near. Henkram and Adanek forces would be on them quickly if imperial ships touched their land or waters.

He only hoped he and Jinhua could stay here long enough that the Cerisan ships would run out of supplies and have to head back home.

CHAPTER THIRTY-ONE
Jinhua

EARLIER THAT SAME MORNING, Jinhua woke early and snuck out of her husband's arms. She wanted to get to training before their meeting with Dale. It made her smile to see Ranulf sleeping peacefully. She pressed a kiss to his forehead, slipped into her clothes and out of their rooms. She headed for the main doors and approached the posted guards. They stood at attention, though their staffs leaned against the wall.

"How may we help you, miss?" One guard broke away from the group and smiled brightly, standing a little taller as she neared.

"I was wondering if you could tell me where the training grounds are," Jin said.

"Absolutely. The guards all practice in the western courtyard. I just came from there, and I believe some of your crew are there already."

"Lovely. Thank you." Jinhua curtsied and slipped out the front doors and aimed for the western courtyard. She recognized her crew right away as they practiced their routine. She jogged to warm up and joined in behind them. Crab led the formations, and the castle guards were gathering to watch. She felt her crew getting self-conscious, so she signaled Crab, and they broke off into pairs to spar.

One guard approached Crab, and Jin listened in. "Would you like one of us to spar with you, teach you some of our skills?" the guard asked.

"That's very kind of ya, but I'll be workin' with Jin this morning."

"Oh, that's so kind of you to teach the lady a few things," the guard replied.

Crab grinned. "She's actually teachin' me a few things." He glanced at her.

The guards all grinned and nodded as if it was a joke they were all in on. Crab handed Jin a staff, and they started lightly tapping them to warm up.

The guards stood there watching, their expressions saying, "How adorable."

Jin angled her head and Crab nodded, so they started to practice in earnest. They hit harder, picking up the pace as they went through the motions. She leaped and he leaped, darting from side to side and sliding their hands up and down their staffs as they hit and blocked from different angles. Jin forgot about the guards, forgot they were in another land surrounded by great evergreen trees. She went into her meditative zone, where she noted Crab's every muscle movement and her body responded.

When they started to move even faster, Jin noticed her breathing was a little heavier than normal. She made a mental note to do more cardio and blocked Crab's next angled hit as she slid in closer to him and hit his abdomen with the butt of her staff.

"Ooof," Crab said. The hit was square in his diaphragm. He put his hands up, signaling he needed a minute.

Jin stopped, letting her breathing slow as she controlled her body's oxygen intake. She closed her eyes, smelling the sweet pine air. It was truly beautiful here.

Crab coughed and Jin opened her eyes. She looked at Crab, whose eyes flicked to their audience. Jin turned and saw the guards had gathered around them in a circle three people thick, their expressions shocked. Some of their mouths even hung open.

Her crew clapped, having prime viewing spots in the front. The guards blinked and then blinked again.

The guard who had spoken to Crab came forward. "That was the most beautiful thing I've ever seen." He offered her his hand and as she took it, he didn't turn her hand to kiss it but shook it up and down as men often did.

Jin smiled. "Thank you. My family trains warriors."

"Obviously. I don't think I kept up with half of what was going on. You moved so fast, both of you. It was … astounding to watch."

"That's very kind of you," Jin said.

"That routine your crew was doing before, how does that lead to this?"

"We learn various routines, beginner versions, until we've learned all the variations. Then we use our bodies' memory of those in sparring and combat. The more routines you learn, the more variations and options you have in a real-life situation."

"That's amazing," he said. "I'm the captain of the guard, by the way, Captain Ismuir. It's an honor to meet you. You must be the best warrior in all the known world."

Jin grinned. "The honor is all mine, Captain Ismuir. Thank you for letting us practice in your training grounds."

"Would you show us your routine?" he asked sheepishly.

"Absolutely," Jin said. She dispersed her crew to the perimeter so everyone would have someone to watch, and as one large group, they all started the routines again. After the first two times, Jin started to make her rounds, feeling very much like she did at home, correcting stances and postures and angles.

A messenger ran down then, in the gold and green of the Cambektons. The captain beckoned him over as he practiced the formation; Jin stood nearby, watching.

"Lady Jinhua, Lady Cambekton is looking for you," the messenger said.

"Thank you," she said as everyone stopped and bowed to her. Jin's cheeks warmed.

"Miss, will you ... will you come back tomorrow morning?" one guard asked.

"Yes. We train every morning no matter where we are, and you're all welcome to join us," Jin said.

"You are a kind and generous lady," Captain Ismuir said, bowing his head at her.

"Oh, I'm not a lady. Just Jin is fine."

"You are to us. We will be honored to learn from you tomorrow morning," Captain Ismuir replied. He bowed his head again, and Jin curtsied for lack of knowing what else she should do.

She waved to her crew and wished them a good day as she turned to follow the messenger back to the castle. With some directional help from the messenger, she made it back to her rooms to find her husband in bed, reading a book.

"How was your morning training?" he asked.

"You should have come to join us."

"It went well then?"

She nodded. "I met Captain Ismuir of Cambekton."

"And what's he like?"

"He was kind and generous. He's asked to join our training tomorrow morning."

"Revolutionizing the warriors of the world I see," Ranulf said.

Jin neared the bed, and Ranulf took the opportunity to wrap his arms around her. He pulled her closer and breathed her in. Jin cringed thinking of how she must stink.

"Even all sweaty, I could just sit here and breathe you in," he said.

"That's funny. Even I know I stink."

"I love it," Ranulf said. He peeled her shirt up off her body and let his fingertips trail along her skin, and she felt shivers race up her back.

But she jumped up and away from the bed. "I'm sticky. I'm going to bathe. Lady Cambekton is waiting," she said. Jin entered the bathing chamber and was so happy to see steam curling from the large tub. She grinned, thinking of the first night she and Ranulf had bathed together.

She poured some rose oil in and then tossed her clothes by the door so Ranulf would see them and know she was properly naked now. She slowly stepped into the water and massaged her tired muscles, eyes closed. When she opened her eyes again, she saw Ranulf, completely nude in the doorway. She grinned, slowly running her gaze up and down his body in appreciation. Ranulf strutted back and forth, smirking, before stepping in to join her.

CHAPTER THIRTY-TWO
Jinhua

Less than an hour later, Jinhua and Ranulf were dressed and holding hands as they went to meet the Lady and Lord of Cambekton. Ranulf led her to a room a few halls over, and Jinhua recognized it as a kind of receiving room. A great fireplace in the middle of the wall was accented with plush couches; long tables lined the opposite side of the room. Next to one table was the trunk they had carried in. Ranulf used the key around his neck to open it and gently took out the first sculpture. For the next hour, they carefully unpacked each piece and laid them out on the long table. Jinhua fawned over a few of the weapons—some too pretty—but one particular sword she kept coming back to. So Ranulf, looking around, put it back in the trunk and locked it.

Jinhua felt a little bad as she knew that sword to be worth quite a bit, but she was excited her husband had saved it for her.

"You should go through all our weapons first next time so you can have first pick," Ranulf said before going to sit on the couch as Jinhua made her way down the table of sculptures and weapons.

Then she eyed the decor adorning the walls. She noticed a theme amongst the items. Intricately decorated swords of varying lengths all had detailed carvings, reminding her of the temples in her own kingdom. The carvings, and weapons themselves, told the stories of old. "They're all so beautiful," Jinhua said.

"I knew I'd like you," a soft voice said.

Jinhua jumped. Lord Cambekton had entered the room silently, and Jinhua felt her cheeks heat at not having noticed. "Lord Cambekton," she said, dipping into a curtsy as she returned to the couches.

"Please, just Dale. And I'd be happy to tell you the stories about those. But perhaps after I get a chance to look at what you've brought me today?" he said.

Jinhua bowed her head and, with Ranulf, strode to the table. Dale walked along it, examining each piece. He didn't touch them on his first run, but on his second, he carefully picked up each one, looking carefully at the details. On the third round, Ranulf strode along the opposite side of the table, and they went from one piece to the next, Ranulf giving more details or telling the story of any particular carving. Jinhua, though fascinated, ended up sitting down and watching as they moved from piece to piece. She enjoyed the stories her husband told and was surprised at how much Cerisan lore he knew.

The doors opened again, and Briemarie entered with a tea service behind her. "Have you bored our guests to tears yet?" she asked of her husband.

He smiled at her. "Never." He gave her a peck on the cheek and moved away from the table, his eyes lingering on the piece before him. They all gathered on the couches, and Jinhua was happy to see food had accompanied the tea as she remembered she'd forgotten to eat that morning. She tried to be as delicate and ladylike as she could, though, when Briemarie came and sat with her.

"Captain Ismuir tells me you are the best warrior in all the world. He's asked me to beg you to stay a few more days to teach them all you can," Briemarie said.

"The best warrior?" Dale asked. He looked at Jinhua, then he shrugged. "You see that ivory dagger on the wall by the fireplace?"

"Ohhh, this is my favorite story," Briemarie said.

"Well, it tells the legend of a chief's wife who led her village into battle with a baby on her back after her husband was double-crossed." He grinned at Jinhua. "Women are stronger than men. I'll be the first to admit that. My own Briemarie had to uproot her whole life at court to come live with me. I could never do as she did."

Briemarie and Dale shared a smile. Jinhua recognized the affection between them.

"It was said that the woman in the story had grown up with her future husband, that he'd secretly taught her all the skills of a warrior because they'd spent so much time together. But that's usually an exception to the rule. How did you become so skilled, if I may ask?" Dale asked. His expression showed only curiosity.

"My family runs a school for training warriors. I've been training as a warrior since before I could walk," Jinhua said.

"Ah. I've heard of that. The whole family trains—daughters and sons—and then they all teach the students, correct?"

Jinhua nodded.

"And there are rival families, rival schools, correct?"

Jinhua nodded again. She wondered where this questioning would go.

Suddenly Dale pursed his lips in thought. Then he turned and continued to examine the items on the table, getting Ranulf's attention once more as he asked about this piece and that.

"You'll have to forgive my husband," Briemarie leaned over and whispered. "He loves learning and the arts. But conversation and politics are not his strong suit."

"No need for an apology. I'm happy to answer his questions. They seem to come from curiosity, not malice."

Briemarie smiled and nodded.

The next words left Jinhua's lips before she could stop them. "How did you meet?" She quickly covered her mouth, heat rising to her cheeks.

"Oh, it's all right. You and I are friends now. We're going to have to be because those two talk for hours sometimes, and it can get downright boring," Briemarie said with a wink. "I grew up at court. I'd only seen Dale a couple of times when he'd been forced to be presented with his parents. At court, we ladies usually fawn over the prince in hopes he picks us. Well, I knew from a young age that I wasn't delicate enough"—she pointed to her wide shoulders and thick arms—"to be considered a real beauty, so I aimed for noble lords instead."

Jinhua was about to open her mouth to object as she found the lady—maybe *because* she was thicker than most—to be beautiful in her confidence.

But Briemarie just shrugged and continued. "I was previously engaged to a lord, but he was a womanizer. When he was literally discovered one day with another lady, that family forced him to marry her—she was pregnant, you see."

Jinhua's eyebrows knit together, but she waited patiently for Briemarie to continue.

"I was considered too scandalous to marry after that."

"But it wasn't your fault."

"It rarely is. That's just what happened. So I was a bit of an outcast at court and then I started getting too old. All the other ladies were being married off, and I was starting to become two, then three, then four, then five years older than the other single maidens at court.

"One summer, Dale showed up to court out of duty, I think. He had waited to marry and found the giggling younger ladies annoying and too silly. I barely went to court functions anymore. But he must have asked around because I got a personal invitation to tour the gardens with him one day."

"That sounds romantic."

"It does, doesn't it? Well, when I met him in the gardens, my chaperone in tow, he introduced himself and then launched straight into how he needed a wife to help him run his estate because it had become bothersome for just him. He said he would provide a handsome allowance for whatever I wanted to do, and I could have the space to do as I wished as long as I didn't embarrass him or his family name and title. He was very direct. And I liked that." She sat up straighter, gazing at her husband and smoothing her skirts out.

"He told me I was very beautiful and what had happened to me wasn't my fault. The lord should have behaved with respect. He said I could even continue to live at court for half the year if I wished, but that he himself preferred a quieter life reading books and creating art at his estate away from court."

"Wait, your husband is an artist?" Jinhua asked.

"Yes. I'll show you his pieces this afternoon if you like."

"That would be wonderful. But please, finish your story."

Briemarie nodded. "Well, he said he would never hurt me or force me to do anything. And he didn't particularly care for children, so if I never wanted to bear children, that was fine by him. He also told me of his cousins, who would take the estate once we passed. They're decent people, he said, and he would make sure they took care of me if he passed first. Finally, he asked if I'd join him for lunch, and we had a lovely, peaceful time. I knew that if I chose this life, it would be a quiet one."

"Do you like it?"

"Yes, actually. I decided I wasn't going to get another offer, and he was known to be an even-tempered sort of man, so I agreed. I left court because it was getting to be too much, the continuous festivities, the silly ladies and their manipulative plots. I get to run the house here and read and enjoy nature."

"That does sound lovely," Jinhua said.

Briemarie smiled. "I think it was luck, but we fell in love. I've never met such a gentle and intelligent person. He dotes on me with utmost care and concern, and I think he's the most wonderful person in all the world."

They both turned to their husbands, and Ranulf winked at Jinhua.

"Please, would you tell me your story?" Briemarie requested. "How did you and Ranulf come to be married? If you don't mind my boldness, there were no announcements, so I assume it's an exciting story."

Jinhua felt her cheeks warm again. "He came to our village to trade, and I couldn't help but be curious about him after spotting him watching my siblings and I training our students. My brother and I"—Jinhua felt a pang in her chest as she thought of Renshu—"decided to teach Ranulf and Crab our culture and our ways so they didn't cause a scandal. Foreigners often do something that's taboo in our culture and get shunned and forced to leave."

Briemarie nodded, taking a sip of her tea.

"We fell in love. I couldn't help it, though I was, at the time, betrothed to another man."

Briemarie's eyes widened, and she leaned in, waiting for Jinhua to tell her story.

"Well, my family would not have accepted me marrying a foreigner and not honoring the marriage contract they had arranged." Jinhua didn't want to complicate matters by mentioning the contract had been with a royal prince. "But Ranulf offered me a life of adventure. If I had stayed and married, I would have had to give up fighting and become a true lady." She couldn't help but pull a face. "I don't mean to offend, but I enjoy moving my body and testing my skills."

"None taken," Briemarie said with a small smile.

"So I chose to leave my family. They've banished me by now, and I'm sure I can never go back, but I chose to follow love and adventure." Jinhua looked at Ranulf, who seemed to know when she looked at him and turned and grinned at her.

"That's a truly adventurous story. So romantic." Briemarie sighed.

"I think what you did was very brave," Jinhua said, "To move to the middle of nowhere with a man you didn't know very well."

Briemarie smiled. "He's a gracious, thoughtful man. And I've come to appreciate the quiet and the beautiful life I get to live." She smiled and leaned closer to Jinhua. "It helps, too, that I know the lord who broke my heart is miserable." She grinned.

Jinhua returned the smile. "Which lord?"

"Lord Pervalle. He spends most of his time at court now, vying for the attention of women younger than his wife. They have three children, and last I heard, a fourth was on the way."

"Oh my!" Jinhua said. That was a lot of children in a relatively short time, judging by Briemarie's still-young appearance. She thought back to all her own brothers and sister.

"Come, shall we see what our men are up to?" Briemarie offered her arm. Jinhua took it and they stood and moved to the table.

"Jinhua, do you know anything about this carving? What does it say?" Dale asked.

Jinhua squinted as she looked at the characters. "It says, 'Always look ahead in times of calm to receive the future with grace.'"

"Hmm ..." Dale said. He stared up and down the table. "I'll take them all," he said.

Briemarie, Jinhua noticed, didn't so much as flinch at that.

"I'm glad you like them," Ranulf said. A bright smile stretched across his face.

"Come, tell me the price and I'll make sure it's ready for you."

"Thank you, Dale. I'll be happy to discount the items given you bought the lot. Now I don't have to find other buyers." They shook hands and smiled.

"You are a true gentleman," Dale said. "Now, guests, how would you like to be entertained?"

"May we see your art?" Jinhua piped up.

"Of course. Come. It's nothing particularly special." He turned and left the room, Ranulf following and then Briemarie and Jinhua, arm in arm. They walked down a hall and turned left and then right, then did the same a few more times. It was difficult for Jinhua to keep track, and she made a mental note to draw a map later so she would know her way around better by the next time she returned.

They finally pushed a couple of doors open into a courtyard. A few trees and bushes dotted the open space, and various statues stood open to the elements. Along the awning-covered walls hung paintings of outstanding quality.

They were landscapes done so realistically, Jinhua thought they were looking out a window. She swore she could see individual trees in the dark-green forest he'd painted. "They're beautiful. You're very talented," Jinhua said. Taking them all in, she came across a piece that was of the sitting room, but a fire was burning in the hearth, and Briemarie was in the picture. You could see only her profile as she sat on the couch reading a book. There was no doubt in Jinhua's mind that no matter how they had begun, Dale loved Briemarie very much.

"Please, pick any one of these, my wedding gift to you both," he said.

Jinhua turned around, smiling. She couldn't wait to be able to look upon one of these beautiful paintings all the time. Walking along the walls, she searched for one that called to her. She wouldn't dare pick the one with Briemarie in it. Finally, she settled on one that looked like he had been sitting high up on the hill as he painted the sloping greenery below until it reached the beach and water's edge. She stood in front of it for a long time.

"This one then?" Dale asked.

Jinhua nodded. "That would be ever so kind. Thank you."

Ranulf came up behind Jinhua and put his hands on her shoulders. "This one's my favorite too."

Chapter Thirty-Three
Ranulf

B ECAUSE OF THEIR HOSTS' kindness, Ranulf and Jinhua, after speaking with Crab, had decided to stay another two days. Mali had already left, so no one was waiting for them at home, but they had sent a messenger to inform him of the change of plans so no one would be concerned.

Ranulf had come down to the training grounds to watch his beautiful wife put the men through their paces on this morning. He noticed they all stood tall and were quick to offer Jin their respects.

"Yes, just like that, Captain," Jin said. She took time each morning to train the guards, then took the afternoons to further teach the captain and a few guards who had picked up the formations quickly.

"Is it like this or this?" one guard asked as he angled his arm this way and that.

"Like that," Jinhua said. She moved his arm into the exact angle. "This form is modeled after a crane, so think of the way their wings move. It won't bend this way, but it will that way."

The guard's brows were furrowed as he concentrated on moving his arm in and out of position. He nodded and Jin moved on to the next person.

This was the last afternoon she had with them. She would get to run through the formations early the next morning one last time before leaving to sail back to Adanek.

"Lord Ranulf, a letter has arrived for you," a messenger said.

Ranulf nodded and took the letter. He calmed his nerves, hoping it wasn't from a Cerisan messenger bird. He hoped it was from Mali, but it was curious that someone would contact him while he was here. He thanked the messenger and turned around as he opened it so no one would see his expression. He felt Jin stop and watch him.

"Jin," Ranulf said, a broad grin spreading across his face. He beckoned her over and gave her the letter so she could read it herself.

She opened it and inside was a card decorated with fancy swirls and loops in gold ink. Her eyes went wide. It was a wedding invitation. "By personal invitation, you are invited to the nuptials of Her Royal Highness Princess Sayani and Lord Mupto."

Ranulf grinned. Somehow it didn't surprise him that their friend Mupto was about to become royalty. At the bottom was scrawled a message from Mupto himself: "Please come!"

Jin looked at Ranulf, eyebrows raised. They both looked back at the date. "Could we make it?" she asked.

"I think so," Ranulf said.

They grinned. Ranulf left to tell Crab, and Jin stayed to answer any last questions before she went to bathe before their next meal.

Jinhua

Captain Ismuir looked at Jinhua with a question in his eyes but seemed too polite to ask about her and Ranulf's excitement.

"A dear friend of ours is getting married," Jin said. "And it just so happens he's marrying into royalty." She started to laugh at the irony of it. She had ditched a prince, but a princess had chosen Mupto.

Ismuir smiled. "I believe it. You and Ranulf are friends to kings and guards alike."

"That's very kind of you," Jin said. She wasn't sure how she felt about his statement. "Any last questions?"

"Yeah!" one guard shouted.

Jin turned to give him her full attention.

"When are you coming back?" he asked.

Jin laughed. She had really come to enjoy their company in these few short days. "That's up to my husband," she said.

He looked disappointed. "Is there anything we can do to convince you to stay?"

"I'm afraid not. I'd really like to make it to my friend's wedding," Jin said.

Some of the guards sank to their knees in mock begging.

"If there's no other questions, then I'm going to bathe. I stink."

"Oh, please don't leave us ..." The guards reached for her, being overly dramatic.

Jin rolled her eyes at them as Ismuir gave them a stern look. She left them to their antics and returned to her room for her favorite part of the day: lounging in the hot bath. She let her body melt into the water and wished so badly that she could haul a bathtub onto their ship.

Jinhua cleared her mind of all thoughts, pushing them away for another time. She wanted only to enjoy the warm water and quiet time. When the water was cooler than her body, she finally pulled herself out and covered herself. She took her time getting dressed for supper and was surprised when Ranulf didn't return to change. She wondered if he had already changed and gone to meet Dale before supper as had become their habit.

She decided to put on a dress Briemarie had given her. On the third day, Briemarie had approached her with some dresses she'd had made when she'd had dreams of becoming a thinner woman in her younger years. But she had no use for them and thought they might look nice on Jinhua.

She decided to wear a lilac and moss-green dress that reminded her of the meadows she had found the previous day while she'd been walking with Ranulf. Checking the time, she saw that she would have to leave without Ranulf if she wanted to make it to supper in time.

When she opened the door, her eyes grew wide, and her vision started to blur as tears welled up in them. Before her, the entire Cambekton guard were dressed in their formal uniforms and had lined up along the hallway to accompany her to supper.

Captain Ismuir, looking dashing in his golds and greens and with his shiny golden helmet on, approached and offered his arm.

"You all honor me much more than I deserve," Jinhua squeaked out. She wiped her tears and took a deep breath before taking Captain Ismuir's arm. They all grinned from ear to ear at her reaction as they walked her to the dining room. Just before the doors, Captain Ismuir stopped.

"Lady Jinhua, you've taught us so much in so few days, and your generosity and knowledge will be something we will cherish forever. Please, accept this gift from us, the Cambekton guards, and know we will always have a place for you here." One guard knelt and presented an open wooden box with a dagger. He grinned as she looked at it. Inscribed on the gold-plated handle was the insignia of the Cambekton guards and three tiny emeralds.

"It's beautiful. Thank you," Jinhua said in a near whisper.

The guards smiled and opened the doors. Ranulf stood there, waiting. "When they asked if they could bring you to dinner tonight, I couldn't say no," he said as Captain Ismuir gently took her arm and returned her to Ranulf. "I'm sorry if you missed me."

She turned back to the guards. "Thank you. I'm so, so honored." She bowed her head, and they bowed in return. A part of her wondered how Briemarie and Dale felt about their guards showing so much loyalty to a foreigner though.

As Ranulf led her to the table, she saw Briemarie and Dale smiling. But rather than supper, a document lay on the table.

"I'm sorry to disappoint. I do promise there is food in the next room," Dale said.

"What's this?" Ranulf asked.

Jinhua was glad he was as surprised as she was.

"Please, have a seat," Briemarie said.

Glancing at each other, Ranulf and Jinhua sat down opposite Briemarie and Dale.

"You look so lovely in that dress, Jinhua," Briemarie said and winked at her. "I think, Jinhua, Captain Ismuir would have proposed to you if you weren't already married." Briemarie giggled.

Jinhua smiled, her cheeks warming at their attention; praise embarrassed her. "You've both been so generous and kind to us."

"This is a formal alliance," said Dale. "I know it's a little unconventional, but we would like to formalize our friendship. Cambekton will be beside you should you ever need our assistance and will be here for you anytime you need a place to stay," Dale explained.

Ranulf looked through the document. "You don't want anything in return?"

Dale nodded. "We do. We would like first claim on all the art you might find on your travels, particularly anything that tells a story. We'd even be willing to store some of your goods."

"This is incredibly generous. Thank you," Ranulf said.

Jinhua nodded, still a little in shock at the kindness.

Ranulf read through the document twice more carefully. Jinhua trusted Ranulf with the terminology, so she spoke with Briemarie and Dale about the art they were most interested in so she and Ranulf would know better what to look for.

Finally, Ranulf signed the document and Jinhua signed next to his name. Dale and Briemarie signed too; then they all rose. As Ranulf leaned over to shake Dale's hand, his stomach gurgled.

"And with that, we shall go to supper," Briemarie said.

They laughed and proceeded through the doors to the adjoining room.

"Did you like the dagger?" Briemarie asked.

"Yes, it's beautiful," Jinhua said.

"It was my idea, the emeralds."

"It's truly wondrous and such an honor."

"The honor is all ours." Briemarie reached across the table and took Jinhua's hand. "And Jinhua, know that you are always welcome here, no matter the situation. Our castle was built as a fortress, and we can withstand many different assaults. We shall be a shelter for you if you need it."

"Thank you. From the bottom of my heart, we are grateful," Jinhua replied. She hugged her friend. They sat down next to each other and chatted as they ate.

"To friends," Dale said.

"And allies," Ranulf said. They all clinked glasses. It was a joyous moment that Jinhua was proud to be a part of. It was their first alliance.

The next morning, they all gathered in the courtyard by the garden to say their farewells. Captain Ismuir and Crab had hauled Ranulf and Jinhua's things down, so the four friends embraced a last time before Ranulf and Jinhua strode down the path to the dock, Jinhua with her new dagger on her belt to show her pride.

A guard Jinhua recognized from morning training sped toward them, and Jinhua knew immediately something was wrong. He whispered something in Captain Ismuir's ear, and Jinhua watched as Captain Ismuir's face tightened in thought.

"Captain, please just spit it out. We all know something is amiss," Dale said.

"My apologies, my lord. It appears the Cerisan Navy is waiting just outside the bay. They're just out of range for Henkram's navy to take offense, but they are close enough to see anyone sailing away," Captain Ismuir said.

"I'm sorry to delay your travels, but I think it's time to devise a plan and I'm going to need some tea for that," Dale said.

Ranulf nodded and Jinhua tried not to let the thudding in her heart get the better of her. They would figure this out. They weren't alone.

In the same sitting room where Ranulf and Jinhua had presented their goods to Dale and Briemarie, they all huddled over a large map rolled out. It illustrated the waters between Adanek and Henkram.

Six little model ships represented the Cerisan ships waiting outside the bay, lined up along one side of the straight leading to the open ocean. There was no way for Ranulf and Jinhua to sail back to Densria safely.

"We might be able to sneak you across the strait into Adanek. But you'd have to cross the kingdom by land to get back to Densria," Dale said. "Your ship would be adrift."

Briemarie added, "Because even if the Henkramian navy pushed the imperial ships out of the bay, they'd catch you in the open ocean."

Jinhua nodded. She didn't know much about ships or ocean warfare, but it seemed silly to think their smaller ship would be able to outrun the half dozen warships without taking on serious, if not fatal, damage.

"So you need to get past them. Your ship is smaller and therefore faster, yes?" Dale asked.

Ranulf nodded.

"What if we invite them here?" Dale asked.

"What exactly do you mean?" Briemarie asked as she stood and turned to her husband.

Dale turned to Ranulf. "I mean, we sneak your ship around the back of the bay, then invite the leaders of the Cerisan delegation here. Then you sneak around them at night when they can't see out beyond the bay and get enough of a head start that they can't catch up. Their ships are slower."

"You want to entertain foreign guests? You?" Briemarie asked, blinking.

"For our friends and allies, I will if I must," Dale replied.

Jinhua looked to Ranulf and Crab, who were looking at the map now.

"We'd have to be careful, or we'd end up on the rocks. And we'd have to be out of the strait before it was light enough for them to see us. But it could work," Crab said. He examined the map again.

That night, Dale had a Henkram ship sail into the bay, and in the dark, they switched all the flags and markers to make Ranulf and Jinhua's ship look like the Henkramian ship. Then the now-unmarked Henkram ship moored in a sheltered cove.

"Here, put this on your ship on your way out too. You are a friend to Henkram and Adanek. Maybe it will make them think twice before they attack you, should they recognize you." Briemarie gave Jinhua a larger Henkram flag.

"Thank you. For everything," Jinhua said. The women embraced before sadly parting.

Ranulf

The next morning, Jin and Ranulf sailed out as if they were on a Henkramian ship that was making a mail or fruit delivery. They headed in the direction of the village, back around the bay, to hide their ship behind the cliffs. There, they would wait for one night and one day.

"Do you think this will work?" Mouse asked as they all sat in the galley. It was quiet. The crew didn't want to draw any attention.

"Lord Cambekton said he would drop a message from the cliffs above once the Cerisans were tucked into the bay and guests in his home," Ranulf said. The crew hadn't questioned anything, but he still nervously awaited objection.

None came. So they waited. And they waited some more. It was the next afternoon when Turt came running into the galley with a message. "Almost hit me square in the head." he said as he handed Ranulf the rock with a message tied to it.

Ranulf opened it and read it aloud. "This delegation enjoys their wine and will be feasting tonight. We have asked the village nearby to light the way for you."

"Now we wait again," Mouse said.

Crab picked up his knitting again, and the crew played cards halfheart-edly. Ranulf and Jin chose to take some time to themselves in their private quarters.

"If you gave me up, they'd probably let you go," Jin said.

"Never," Ranulf replied. He wrapped his arms around her. "You are mine." He kissed her forehead. "Mine." He kissed her cheek. "Mine." He kissed her shoulder. "Mine." He continued until Jin dissolved into giggles. That melted his insides. He would do anything to hear that sound.

"I'm sorry to make this harder. I wish they would just leave us alone. It's not like I was that valuable a bride for Prince Feng," Jin said.

Ranulf gave her another squeeze. "You are valuable."

"This adviser probably doesn't like being humiliated or something," Jin said.

"You're probably right. But I know this ship wouldn't stop searching for you."

"You don't think the crew want me gone for all the trouble I've caused them?" Jin asked.

"Nope. You're family now. We protect our family. Your problem is our problem." Ranulf smiled and added, "That's how a ship family works."

Jin nodded and buried her face in his shoulder. They sat and held each other, wondering what the next night would bring.

They waited until it was completely dark before they started to sail back out into the strait and around the bay. They only used what sails they absolutely needed, hoping their brightness wouldn't attract attention. It was dark enough that they could pass as a Henkramian ship if they were somehow spotted, but if lookouts with strong spyglasses looked closely enough ...

As they sailed around the bay, hugging the cliffs, Ranulf could see Jinhua holding her breath. He did the same. Their eyes were glued to the Cerisan ships, watching for any movement. He hoped they were all celebrating in the castle or asleep. His entire crew seemed to slowly relax as they passed the Cerisan ship and entered the strait.

It suddenly became pitch black as a cloud covered the moon, making Ranulf nervous as they started to sail into the darkness. It was easy to get an angle wrong in the dark. They could easily sail their ship right into the cliffside.

"Look," Crab said as he pointed up. The villagers had hung lanterns along the cliffs from above. They weren't visible from the bay, and they weren't bright, but they were enough to identify where the cliff was. They villagers had also lit the highest point where the strait widened.

Ranulf and his crew were lucky enough to have sufficient wind to sail, but not so much that it rushed them as they sailed through the strait toward the open ocean. Jin stood at the stern. She scanned the darkness behind them for movement. Ranulf's heart swelled with pride. He knew he'd forfeit his life for her. He'd learned she could be happy on this ship without him if she had to be. She'd be free, and that mattered more to him than he'd realized.

CHAPTER THIRTY-FOUR
Jinhua

ONCE THEY MADE IT through the strait, into open ocean, Ranulf handled the ship with more ease and by the time light peeked over the horizon, they were well on their way back to Densria. Because the imperial ships hadn't seen them in the strait, Jin felt more confident their trip home would be uneventful. She hoped Dale and Briemarie were all right, though, after hosting the Cerisans. She hoped to bring her friends something in gratitude the next time they met.

Once the crew saw Crab and Ranulf relax, they did too. That night, they celebrated their first alliance with Lord Cambekton as a crew, then enjoyed a smooth sail in perfect weather the rest of the journey. When Jin wasn't polishing her new dagger, which was almost every day, she was doing her part on deck, polishing, waterproofing, and swabbing. There was no sight of the Cerisan ships. They were safe for now.

When they arrived home, a letter reminding them that Mali was away lay on the entryway table, but it also said they were welcome, to stay in the castle as long as they liked. But by Crab's calculations, if they wanted to make it to Mupto's nuptials in time, they could only stay in Densria for a couple of days before heading back out again, with just one stop of a few days along the way to trade. Every crew member rushed until the last minute to resupply.

"Where's Crab?" Ranulf said on departure day. They needed to leave.

"He said he'd be back in time," Mouse said.

"I see him," Jin said. She spotted the mountain of a man as he waded through the people on the dock. Crab was carrying a tight bundle of fabric, and as he got closer and closer, Jin could see that the fabric was very fine indeed.

"What took you so long?!" Ranulf yelled over the rail.

"Yer goin' to a weddin'! You and I have fine clothes, but Jin's gonna need a new dress. So, I was gettin' some supplies!" Crab yelled back.

Jin froze. She hadn't even thought about what she would wear to Mupto's wedding.

When Crab boarded, she threw her arms around him in thanks. "What would we do without you?"

"Not a whole lot I imagine," Crab said with a smirk and a chuckle.

The ship left then, finally. The sails unfurled to catch the wind and bring them safely out of the harbor into the open ocean. Jin proudly manned the helm while Crab and Ranulf went below to confirm for the third time the correct direction. The first part of their trip would be easy. The crew had sailed that way a few times already and knew where they were going. It was the rest that was a bit hazy.

Jin took her task seriously. She watched the sea with one eye and the crew with the other as they performed their tasks. The ocean was quiet. Then she saw a blip to their starboard side. "What's that?" she murmured under her breath.

The blip disappeared. She scanned the starboard side again, flicking her gaze up to the crow's nest to see if Shelley had seen what she'd seen. Ranulf came up from belowdecks.

He must have seen the concern on Jin's face because he rushed over. "What is it?"

"I saw a blip," Jin said. As the words left her mouth, a large body surged upward like a column of water on their starboard side, and Jin's eyes widened as the body crashed back into the water, soaking that side of the deck.

Ranulf laughed. "That's a whale."

Jin was confused. Why wasn't Ranulf as concerned as she was?

"They're gentle creatures. That's the most violent we've ever seen, but only because it was pretty close to the ship this time. They jump out of the water for fun, I think, to surprise people. It's a marvel how they can jump so high out of the water."

"That was magnificent," Jin said. "Are there many of them?"

"Yes. I'm surprised we haven't seen them before now. And that *was* much closer than usual." Ranulf chuckled.

Jin stared starboard again, hoping to catch another glimpse of the whale jumping out of the ocean so she could enjoy it this time instead of worrying. But no luck. It was as if it knew she was looking and didn't want to perform to expectation.

It was another six days before they saw land, then another half a day before they got near enough to see more than just an interruption of the ocean. As they pulled closer, Jin could tell this would not be the quiet dock they had visited first. Already she saw two other ships, one coming in and the other on its way out, as Ranulf's ship approached the harbor. A small, irrational part of her scanned the ships to make sure they weren't Cerisan. She wondered what the Cerisan adviser's next move would have been once he'd discovered they were long gone from Henkram.

She returned to the moment and was thrilled to watch Crab guide the ship in as she helped tie ropes where needed. He skillfully moved the ship this way and that and shouted orders to the crew. There were ships everywhere amongst multiple docks. They made their way to an empty spot. Dog jumped off with Mouse to secure their ropes and pull their ship in snug with the wood. Jin hopped off then too and was securing the ropes on the dock when a hand cupped her butt cheek.

"I'm in the ship over there if you're looking for fun later." A black-bearded man with a few teeth missing pointed to his ship.

Jin leaped up in surprise.

Mouse, beside her, growled, staring the man down until he strode away. "Y'all right?"

"Yes, thanks." Jin said, blinking in surprise and shoving her feelings away for later.

Mouse nodded and went to secure another rope. Jin looked around, and since Mouse had the last one, returned to the ship a little faster than usual.

She went to the helm to determine her next task.

"Ya should've broken his hand," Crab said under his breath.

"I ..." Jin didn't really know what to say. She'd just been so caught off-guard. She nodded. "Next time."

"Yer the strongest and most skilled warrior I know. Don't forget it," Crab said. He placed a hand on her shoulder, and she nodded again and turned away as Crab ordered messengers to tell their customers of their arrival.

Some of the crew were setting up their positions and weapons on the deck as she went belowdecks to change. The crew would be on round-the-clock guard duty while they were docked to ensure their supplies remained untouched.

Jin, Ranulf, and Crab, however, were disembarking to trade with various nobles. They hoped to sell anything remaining at the market in two days to fund the supplies they needed to travel to Bulstan for Mupto's wedding.

Once regretfully in a dress, Jin took Ranulf's arm, and they strolled down the gangplank and up the dock. They entered the city and hired a carriage for the day to take them from house to house. That done, they watched the crew load five heavy trunks on the top of the carriage, then hopped in themselves and rolled through the stone streets. Each bump of the carriage wheels over the cracks between the stones made Jin nauseous.

All the buildings were painted white here. Low walls surrounded some houses, and most were built into the hilly land, making it difficult for Jin to tell which were singular buildings or which were multiple. She'd never seen houses so bright and white.

They pulled up to their first house; it, too, had a low stone wall that opened to a tall archway. When the carriage stopped, they got out and stepped through the archway into a small garden. Plants of all kinds bloomed all around her. "These gardens are gorgeous," she said. Many of the leaves and flowers had strange shapes to them.

"Thank you," someone said.

Jinhua looked up in time to see an elderly woman come out of a wooden door to greet them.

"Lady Margaret." Ranulf bowed, and Crab and Jinhua followed suit. "You remember my partner, Crab, and this is my wife, Jinhua."

Jinhua stayed low in her curtsy as he introduced them.

"It's a pleasure to meet you. And congratulations on your nuptials," Lady Margaret said. She turned and walked back into the house; the three followed.

"So, what have you brought me today, Ranulf?" She sat on a chair and Jinhua noticed they hadn't been invited to sit and she hadn't called for refreshments. This must be a lady who liked class separation.

Jinhua turned and saw Crab bringing a trunk inside. She helped open it and lay some of their wares out for the lady to inspect.

"Bolts of silk, in orange and purple like the flowers you showed me last time I was here. Also some of the crockery you requested in earthenware brown." Ranulf removed the fabrics and placed them on the table between them. Jinhua gently removed the brown bowls and cups tucked ever so gently in the trunk and placed them softly on the table.

"Lovely. Ranulf, you brought me exactly what I asked for. You are the first to deliver that so precisely," Lady Margaret said. She smiled and nodded her approval. "Eva, bring refreshments for our guests," she said, barely raising her voice.

Jinhua was pleasantly surprised to be wrong. Perhaps this lady just preferred to get business out of the way first. Moments later, a maid arrived with drinks in clear glass cups. Jinhua bowed her head in thanks to the girl and got a smile back.

Lady Margaret reached into her pocket and took out a small bag of coins. "Here. This is the rest of what I owe you from our bargain. Now, let's talk about what I'd like you to bring me next time."

Jinhua took out her parchment and started to scrawl the list down since neither Crab nor Ranulf were doing so. At the top, she wrote "Lady Margaret," so she could keep it straight.

"Do you think, Ranulf, you could bring me seeds?"

"Depends upon the plant, my lady."

"Well, I've heard there are these flowers that bloom red as blood with a yellow center. Have you ever seen them?"

"I have seen flowers like that, yes."

"Would you be able to bring me the seeds? So I may add them to my garden?"

"I will try, though I have not transported many seeds."

"The key will be to keep them dry. Moisture will germinate or mold them. Keep them dry and in a parchment pouch so they can breathe, and they should be fine for years." Lady Margaret smiled excitedly.

"I will do my best," Ranulf said. He glanced at Jinhua, who had written "red flowers, yellow middle, seeds, keep dry in parchment."

Ranulf, Crab, and Jin had to drink their tea quickly before they were shoved out the door. They climbed back into their carriage with their trunks and headed to the next noble's house. This time, Jinhua looked out the window to watch the white walls pass by. Some houses teemed with vines and gardens and flowers, and as the carriage rolled on, some began to boast larger and larger splashes of color. Always on the windowless side were plates with small pieces of colorful glass or stone arranged in vibrant patterns. With each home they passed, the plates got bigger. The first was no larger than a dinner plate, but they got larger and larger as they traveled. Jinhua loved the colors, and as they rolled on, she tried to make out the shapes within the patterns of glass pieces.

"Just wait 'til you see the next residence," Crab said, leaning over to glance out the window.

Jinhua only raised her eyebrows as she kept watching the different plates fly by. "Why did the previous houses not have plates but these do?" she asked.

"The different colors represent the different noble families. The high nobles of this place can trace their families back to five original couples, siblings who journeyed here on the last wishes of their father. He had dreamt of an island that would provide for his family," Crab explained.

"And what did the island provide?"

"Salt," Ranulf said.

Jinhua's mouth almost popped open in surprise, but she kept her lips firmly together. "Who's the next family?" She peeled her gaze away from the houses and guessed that as the plates got bigger, so too did the prestige.

"The ruling family," Ranulf said. Then he scoffed, "Well, the ones that deal with us common folk. The true ruling family don't see many people outside their circle."

"I see," Jinhua said, wondering what this family would be like. "Why didn't Lady Margaret have a plate outside her home? She's noble, yes?"

"She is. But she ain't considered pure enough fer a plate." Crab rolled his eyes.

Jinhua was surprised that she felt badly for Lady Margaret.

The carriage started to slow, and Jinhua turned her attention back to the window. The low walls doubled in height, though everything was still white. They came around a corner and Jinhua's jaw dropped. Set far away from the low walls and the main road, across from a rock-and-sand garden, was an enormous white house with gold trim.

"Is that—"

"It certainly is, lass," Crab said. He grinned and glanced at Ranulf. They both grinned at Jin's reaction.

How ... Jin thought. She knew her mouth was hanging open still at seeing actual gold gilding the outside of someone's house, open to the elements and thieves.

Chapter Thirty-Five
Jinhua

THE CARRIAGE PULLED UP alongside the huge building. When it rolled to a stop, Ranulf climbed out first, and Crab followed, turning to help Jinhua.

Ranulf had gone to heartily embrace a short, stout man, a greasy, darker version of himself. His hair was black, and his skin was tanned from the sun. "Lord Tenson, it is so good to see you again!" Ranulf expressed with enthusiasm.

Lord Tenson embraced Ranulf, but Jinhua thought it looked as if someone had made him do it.

Ranulf was grinning from ear to ear, but Jinhua recognized it as a fake smile, a mask to put his customer at ease.

"And what have you brought me?" Lord Tenson said as he turned to look at Jinhua. She noticed his eyes rake down her front and felt as if he might ask her to turn around to inspect the back of her before her husband cut in.

"This is my wife, Jinhua," he said.

"Oh my. You dirty dog, you. Congratulations are in order! You rascal, getting married so quickly. I don't believe we received an invitation!"

"It was a small, private ceremony," Crab said, stepping up to join them.

"Well then, does she speak our language? Or is it purely ... body language?" Lord Tenson asked.

"While I cannot say that I have mastered your language, I do have a good handle on it," Jinhua said as Ranulf beamed.

"My, my! She speaks!" Lord Tenson said. "Come, Jinhua, lend your arm to an old man and help me into the house. We'll start with refreshments while Crab and your husband bring the goods in."

Jinhua didn't see a polite way to refuse, so she plastered on her own smile, the very smile her sister had made her practice for the prince, then let him lead her through the large white archway into the courtyard. At the far end was an outdoor sitting area. Drinks awaited them and Lord Tenson smiled far too widely as he handed her a glass of creamy pale-yellow liquid.

"We musn't forget the last ingredient." Lord Tenson reached over, took some salt, and sprinkled it on top of the creamy yellow liquid.

Jinhua raised her glass to her lips and took a careful sip. While she didn't really think he would poison her, she knew it probably was filled with strong spirits specifically designed to impair guests and give the lord the upper hand.

Crab and Ranulf carried in a trunk each and set them near a couple of tables beside the seating area. Jinhua, bringing her drink with her, went to help them unload the goods. She was a little surprised to find a couple of curved daggers among the goods, plus a box Jinhua knew was filled with jade and other precious stones.

"Ranulf, Crab, here! We must start with refreshment!" Lord Tenson said.

Jinhua noticed he only said it once he was sure they were done pulling the goods out. She also noticed neither gulped the liquid but instead sipped it as she had.

"Tell me, tell me, gentlemen, of your adventures! There must be a story in all your travels worthy of the telling!"

"Well, yes, there is," Ranulf said. He puffed his chest up, opening his arms wide as he dove into the story of how he had met an old hunched man who must have been the oldest man he had ever met. "While I was drinking and playing cards with some townspeople in a tavern, an old man came up behind me, tapping me ever so slightly on the shoulder with his staff.

"Then he whispered, 'Put all your cards on the table.'

"For some reason, I felt compelled to. I won the round, winning the highest purse that night. Afterward, I realized the old man was gone and went to chase him down. The old man led me to his hovel of a home, where he showed me some stones he was selling. 'They were meant to be with you,' he said, but he wanted a fair price. I pitied the old man, so I barely bartered and paid almost the full price. But then suddenly, the old man grasped me by the front of my shirt and said, 'Now you hear me, never use these. Do you understand? They should only be pretty baubles, but they hold more power than you could ever know.'"

Lord Tenson was riveted. He hadn't even taken another sip of his beverage since Ranulf had begun his story. Jinhua wondered how much of the story was true, but it was still impressive that Ranulf could tell such a tale just to sell a few rocks.

Once he was done, Lord Tenson stayed very still for a few moments before asking, "Have you showed anyone else these stones?"

"No. Not at all. We visited one other client, but she does not have the resources for such things, and I dare not show them to anyone without the ability to buy them. I fear they might go mad trying to obtain them," Ranulf said.

Jinhua thought that was laying it on a little too thick, but Lord Tenson took a sip of his beverage, then a gulp.

"What'll you have for them?" he asked.

"Well, I'm not sure. They are so very valuable. I mean, if what I said proved anything, it's that these are one of a kind." Ranulf stood tall and proud.

Jinhua glanced at Crab and saw his expression was schooled into indifference.

"I will offer you ten bags of salt per gem," Lord Tenson said.

"Which salt?" Ranulf asked.

"The everyday kind," Lord Tenson said.

Ranulf pushed his lips out, as if thinking hard on it.

"Fine, I will send you two of our finest and eight of our ordinary salt per gem. That's plenty for you."

"Did I mention that when we were returning, we ran into bandits searching specifically for rocks just like these? I took great pains to change our route to shake them and keep these gems safe."

"Fine, five bags of our finest, and five of our everyday."

"There are six gems here," Ranulf said. "Forty bags of your finest salt and twenty of the normal stuff."

Lord Tenson looked concerned. He shifted his weight back and forth a few times, his gaze lingering on the gems. Jinhua, who stood closest, decided to add to the urgency and started to pack them up.

"No, no. You can stop that. I'll take it." He stuck his hand out for Ranulf, who did indeed shake it.

Jinhua wasn't sure what they would do with so much salt but stood back from the table, waiting for Lord Tenson to take his goods. Without much fanfare, he grabbed them all, counted them, and put them in his inner vest pocket.

"Now, are these the other things you've brought me?"

"Yes. We have curved daggers, at your request," Ranulf began, and so went the rest of the trading session.

When the carriage started to roll away from the massive gold-adorned house, Jinhua turned to her husband. "That story with the old man, that was a lie, right?"

"Yes. Lord Tenson likes a good story with mystery."

"Do you do that all the time?"

"Some of the nobility require ... well, an exciting story to tell their friends," Ranulf said.

"Was there any truth to it?"

"I did buy them from an old man."

Jinhua laughed. Ranulf continuously surprised her. "Where are we off to now?" she asked, feeling a little giggly.

"How much of the lemon drink did ya have?" Crab asked.

"Not much, maybe half a glass?" Jinhua said.

Crab grinned. "We're getting ya back to the ship."

"Why?"

"That drink is potent. I drank half once, and I was on the floor pukin' my guts out for half a day. I never drink any more than a quarter now."

Jinhua thought back to Crab's glass; it had been a little less than half full when they had left.

"I dump half into a plant when he's not lookin'," Crab said.

"Oh," she said, her vision beginning to swim.

"We have to go back to load the salt anyway," Ranulf said. He put his arm around his wife, and she snuggled into him, hoping if she closed her eyes, the world would stop moving so much.

The next thing she knew, she felt Ranulf carrying her and heard the creak of wood underneath her. Then she felt the soft bed they shared, their scents absorbed into the thin mattress. "Are we ... done for the day?" she asked sleepily.

"Yes, *you* are. Crab and Dog are unloading the salt. Then Crab and I will tie up a few more appointments. But then I'll be right back," he said. He kissed her forehead. "Rest now." He grinned from ear to ear.

"Why are you smiling?" Jin asked.

"Because you're brilliant," he said before turning and leaving.

Jin slept—for hours. When she woke, she had a fierce headache.

"Here, this will help." Ranulf pushed a cup of warm liquid into her hands, and she took a sip. It was glorious. It slid down her throat, and she felt the heat radiate from there to the rest of her body.

"Crab says you have to drink this after." Ranulf pointed to a small cup of black liquid.

She knew enough to know it wouldn't taste good. "Where did he get that?"

"Crab keeps a stock of various herbs and remedies. We are on the ocean for a very long time, after all."

"Crab's a healer?"

"He searches for specific ingredients for an apothecary back home. In return, the apothecary teaches him. Plus, he has an amazing memory."

"Oh. That's good for the crew."

"Yes. Eventually though, we'd like to employ a true healer for our longer journeys. Now drink up," he said.

She took another long draft of the hot liquid before leaving a third in the cup so she could have it after the vile black liquid. Jin took a couple of deep breaths before tossing the black liquid back as quickly as she could and then slamming her mouth shut so she couldn't spit it all back out. It was like drinking ashes. It was disgusting. She closed her eyes and focused all her energy on keeping it down.

Ranulf pressed the other cup of warm liquid and a tiny pile of sugar into her hands.

She carefully stuck her tongue out and licked the sugar from her hand, letting it dissolve and slip down her throat. Then Jin took a few more deep breaths and swallowed, taking another swig of the hot liquid. After a few minutes, she opened her eyes. "That was vile."

Ranulf grinned. "I know. I've had it a few times. But you should feel better soon."

Jin nodded slowly. Unfortunately, she'd actually had worse from her town's apothecary. She took another sip of the hot liquid, letting it slide down her throat. "If you don't need me today, I think I'm going to stay on the ship."

"That's fine. Crab and I are only at the market today."

"I think I'm going back to sleep."

"Carthy left you some bread, when you think you can stomach it," Ranulf said, pointing to the little table next to the bed. "If you need anything, Carthy's going to stay with you."

"Who's on watch duty today?"

"Shelley and Turt."

"I can take an afternoon shift," Jin said.

Ranulf nodded, making her dizzy.

She closed her eyes and could feel his grin as he tried not to laugh.

"That lemon drink *was* pretty strong," Jin said.

"Yes." He moved in slowly and kissed the top of her head, then left a trail of kisses down her arm to her hand. "I'll send word later today."

Jin nodded and then regretted it as her head spun again.

Ranulf shut the door behind him, and Jin fell back to sleep until Carthy came with more food a few hours later. Jin hated feeling like an invalid. So, after eating Carthy's soup, she pushed herself to at least walk around the ship while everyone was at the market.

She barely made it back to bed after that. Perhaps she wasn't quite as ready as she thought. She pulled a blanket over herself and lay down for a minute, welcoming the blackness that enveloped her but promising herself she'd still take that afternoon shift.

Chapter Thirty-Six
Ranulf

After putting Jin to bed and meeting with their last noble clients, Ranulf and Crab had prepared for the market the next morning. The bulk of the work was hard, physical labor as they loaded trucks, crates, and barrels onto wheeled platforms for transport to the city.

The sun's first rays were lightening the sky with cotton-candy colors as they set up their table. Crab pulled a length of cloth out of a crate and draped it over the table.

"What are you doing?" Ranulf asked.

"Many of our wares are dark in color. Jin said puttin' a piece of light cloth on the table under 'em would help 'em stand out. Plus, it would make our table look nicer and we can hide things underneath easier," Crab said.

Ranulf nodded. Part of him ached to be back on the ship with his wife. He wanted so badly to hold her in his arms even though she was still out cold from the strong lemon drink.

"Yer gonna chase away all our customers with that lovesick expression on your face," Crab said. All they had to do now was wait. So, he pulled out a couple of sticks and a ball of yarn.

"What are you doing now?"

"I'm knittin'. I can never find socks big enough for my feet, so I'm gonna make 'em. It's also better than dancin' from leg to leg," Crab said as he looked down at Ranulf's restless feet.

Once the market opened, they would be busy; waiting was always the difficult part. Combined with how badly he wanted to be snuggling his wife, Ranulf was ready to run around the market just to burn off energy.

"Ya better sit, or yer gonna scare off the early-mornin' shoppers," Crab said, standing. He put a hand on Ranulf's shoulder and eased him onto a barrel.

"You think she'll be all right?" Ranulf asked. His thoughts raced through the possibilities. Logically, he knew she had simply imbibed too much, but anything from allergies to sickness to poisoning were also possible.

Crab took a deep breath in and out, loudly enough that Ranulf followed his lead.

After several moments, Crab spoke. "Jin 'll be fine. She's strong, and she'll be more embarrassed than anythin' else, just like us all. In fact, it'll probably make the crew bond with 'er more than anythin' else."

Ranulf nodded and drummed his fingers on his knees, trying to wait patiently.

Crab sent Dog and Mouse to scout out the market before he turned back to Ranulf. "Have ya heard anythin' else from Cerisa?" he asked quietly.

Ranulf shook his head. "Nothing. Mali's still away, but nothing's happening in Densria. They sent a letter saying nothing else arrived."

"Do ya think they'll come after us again?"

"I don't know what to think. I'm caught between my hopes and nightmares."

"I think it makes me more nervous that they haven't sent another threatenin' letter or anyfin," Crab said.

Ranulf nodded. Silence could well mean they were planning something bigger, something more than just a threat. *When would the anchor fall?* he wondered.

They were quiet a moment as Ranulf wondered what they would do if they were confronted by the Royal Cerisan Navy. Could they outrun them? Their ship was smaller, therefore faster. Would they see the enemy coming soon enough to turn around and run? Or maybe they could sail close enough to Adanek that they could dock if need be to avoid interception. But that would only delay the inevitable. Maybe they could bargain their way out of this predicament?

Crab looked thoughtful too before he finally nodded. "Let's hope they've gone home."

Light began to streak through the clouds, and the first set of early shoppers appeared at the edges of the market.

"Time to work," Crab said as he nodded his chin at the first few people to enter the market.

Ranulf nodded and put on his most charming smile as he nodded to Shelley and Turt returning to the table. They all glanced at it, grabbed an item, and strode off.

Ranulf approached an older woman who walked well given her many wrinkles. "May I offer you my arm?" he asked as he presented his arm to her.

"Why thank you. It is always a pleasure to walk with a gentleman," she said, taking his arm.

Ranulf bowed his head and strode down the aisle with her. "What are you looking for today?" he asked.

"Just my normal groceries. The baker over there has the best bread." She narrowed her eyes at him. "I haven't seen you around here before. What do you sell?"

"Oh, I have a table over there, but I wanted to meet the locals, get to know what people here need for my future trips," he said.

"That's a smart move," she said, stopping at the baker.

"The usual?" the baker asked, and she nodded. He grabbed a small loaf and a few triangle pastries, put them in a cloth, and wrapped it for her. Then he looked at Ranulf. "Want anything?" he asked.

"I'll take five loaves and thirteen of those triangle things," Ranulf replied.

The baker's eyes widened in surprise as the woman clutched his arm.

The old woman chuckled. "Oh, you won't regret it. He has the best bread in the whole city."

The baker handed Ranulf a bundle, and they continued to walk down the aisles. Ranulf listened as she explained how to pick the correct carrots and zucchini.

As they rounded a corner, the old woman gripped Ranulf's arm. "You know, I've just remembered I broke my bowl the other day. Do you sell bowls?"

"We do. I'd love to show them to you," Ranulf said. He smiled and escorted her to his table; there, he showed her a range of bowls, pulling more and more out as he narrowed down her preferences and prices.

"Auriel! I thought I might see you here." Another older woman strode up to their table. Ranulf stayed quiet as the two chatted and caught up.

"Beatrice, weren't you saying you needed some better cups? Didn't that nephew of yours crack some last time he was over?" Auriel asked. She winked at Ranulf, and he dipped his head to hide his smile.

"Why yes, he did. He says he barely tapped it on the table, but the whole bottom came off and tea went everywhere. It was such a mess, I tell you," Beatrice replied.

"May I interest you in these? We use 'em on our ship and 'ave fer two years now. Even in a sailor's hand, they haven't broken," Crab said as he slid in with some clay cups they had bought from a blacksmith-turned-potter in Adanek.

"I'll take four of those bowls if you have them," Auriel said as she turned back to Ranulf.

He nodded and wrapped them up as she exchanged coins for the beautiful bowls.

"Well, thank you for walking through the market with me. I'm going to head home to use my new bowls and cook up something tasty before it gets too hot to cook," Auriel said. Beatrice was also done, so together they hustled out of the market, leaving Ranulf at his table.

Before he could even turn to Crab, another woman came over. "What did the old biddies buy? They know quality when they see it, so I want to see what you sold them."

Ranulf smiled and obliged. The rest of his day flew by after that, and only at the end of the day as he made his rounds of the market to get their own supplies did he remember his bundle of baked goods stashed under the table. Their walk back to the ship was lighter in crates but heavier in coin.

Walking with Crab deterred many thieves, so he was glad they'd all returned to the ship together. Once aboard, he went to check on Jin, who was still asleep. He opened his little package and pulled a pastry and a crust of bread out for her before taking the other loaves to Carthy. Then he offered her a triangle.

"Mm, good. Why don't ya share those with the other laddies, while I finish cleaning up?" Carthy asked.

He'd rather have gone back to Jin but knew he'd been holed up with his wife a lot lately, and even Crab had mentioned he needed to spend some time with the crew.

So, Ranulf returned to the deck with his pastries. The crew had gathered crates and barrels together and pulled up the gangplank. Crab had night watch, so the rest had gathered around to enjoy the food, stories, and ale fresh from the market. This was everyone's favorite meal because it was the freshest. Carthy didn't even have to work tonight; instead, everyone had bought something at the market and shared it.

As Mouse pulled a barrel over for him, Ranulf handed out the pastries, and they sat and talked and drank ale well into the night. When the stories began to wind down, Mouse nodded at the crew, and they put away their crates and barrels. Then he handed a plate with a meat pie on it to Shelley, who added a piece of cheese, then Dog added a sausage. The plate went around until Turt put a cookie on it and took it to Ranulf.

"For Lady Jin. I'm sure she'll be hungry when she wakes. Hopefully she feels well enough to eat," Turt said.

Ranulf blinked, surprised at the thoughtfulness. He wasn't an emotional sort, but he had to swallow to keep the tears at bay. He nodded at Turt, thanked the crew, and took the plate to his chambers.

Ranulf put the plate down, adding his little pastry and crust of bread to it. He'd forgotten how much he enjoyed his crew. It had been a long time since he'd sat with them and talked of what they'd seen and heard in town. They were their own little family. He quickly wiped a tear from his cheek as he stared at the plate of food.

Jin stirred and he quickly undressed and pulled her close.

CHAPTER THIRTY-SEVEN
Jinhua

THE NEXT MORNING, THEY were off to Bulstan.

Since Crab and Ranulf had never been this far southeast, they were nervous. Jin noticed how often they checked their maps and calculations and direction and how often they stayed up late to check the constellations against their position. She even started to learn the constellations since they repeated them so often. It surprised her that they were the same ones as in her kingdom; they only had different names. Looking up one night, she saw the small and large dragons and felt a pang pierce her heart as she thought of how they had always represented her and Renshu.

When she was younger, she'd injured herself and Renshu had taken care of her. She was so rough in her practice that she cut her hands and they swelled. Renshu took her by the shoulder and steered her to the training building's rooftop. There sat a bucket of water and a tin of salve, with packs of linen tucked under a roof tile. The pain was too much for an eight-year-old, and she was sobbing uncontrollably. She couldn't even do any of her chores with her hands like this, so she felt guilty too.

"Don't worry. Qiao is going to do your chores for you today," he said, hauling the bucket of water over. "Do you think you can dunk your hands in here?"

Jinhua was so afraid of the pain that would come.

"It'll hurt at first, but this water is very cold. It'll numb the pain and stop the swelling," Renshu said. He didn't force her to put her hands in or grab her hands and shove them in like her other brothers would have.

She nodded and dunked her hands in. She squeezed her eyes shut against the pain and counted to ten over and over. Renshu had taught her that she could do anything for ten seconds. So she counted to ten. Then counted to ten again, taking it ten seconds at a time.

"You're such a brave girl, Jin. All right, you can take your hands out now," Renshu said. He gently took her hands, covered them in salve, and bandaged them. She was riveted, watching carefully so she knew exactly what he did so she could do it next time.

"You see up there?" Renshu looked up and turned his face to the sky.

Jinhua nodded.

"See those stars that make a weird square with a tail?" Renshu asked; she nodded. "And then to the right, that bigger one? The four stars that make a square and a tail?" She'd only nodded again, forgetting the pain in her hands and squinting to make out the squares in the sky.

"Those are the small and large dragons," Renshu said. "Just like you and me."

"I'm the small dragon?" Jin asked.

"No, silly, you're the big dragon. Dragon sizes are determined by the size of their heart, not their age. You are the big dragon, and I am the little dragon. I'll be fast and agile so I can protect you."

"Jin," Ranulf said, bringing her back to the present.

She smiled at the memory of her brother. She blinked and looked around, re-orienting herself to the ship and the present time. When she looked at her husband, she saw curiosity in his eyes.

"What were you thinking about?" he asked, sitting on the barrel next to hers.

"The sky. What you call the big ladle and the small ladle, we call the big and small dragons. Renshu used to make up stories about the two dragons going on adventures. He said we were the dragons. I was the big one and he was the small one."

"You miss him a lot?" he said.

"Yes," Jin said, realizing her vision was blurring. She wiped at her eyes.

"I'm sorry you had to leave them."

"I am too. But Rennie was right. Every day is an adventure and this is where I'm happiest. I just wish he could have come with me, or at least I wish I knew if he was all right."

"I understand." He took her hand, and she squeezed it. "I bet Renshu will come see you next time we go there," Ranulf said.

"You don't know my family. I've been banished by now, dishonored. I'm dead to them. We probably can't even go to that town ever again."

"So we go to the town south of it. It has a decent market, I'm told. We contact Peng. I know your brother will come find us, if only to make sure you're all right."

Jin grinned, turning to kiss Ranulf on the cheek.

"What was that for?"

"Because I can. And for your optimism and thoughtfulness."

CHAPTER THIRTY-EIGHT
Ranulf

L AND LOOMED BEFORE THEM in the early-morning hours. They, were, however, unsure if they were in the right place. Mupto's letter had said to sail to the southernmost point of the island to a channel. They were to sail their ship into it, and if they weren't recognized, to state Ranulf's name and they would be admitted.

"Strange instructions to leave, no?" Crab said.

"Yes indeed. I wonder why?" Jin asked.

They all shrugged as they sailed south around the shore to find the channel.

It was afternoon by the time they found the channel; it was wide, and Crab expertly sailed right in. It made them nervous though. It was a vulnerable position. They would be closed in and at the complete mercy of their hosts. Ranulf gulped as they approached; an enormous wall awaited them, a large net spread across it.

A few men on the wall signaled for them to approach the net. Crab, Ranulf, and Jin looked at each other warily.

Then Crab shrugged. "Well, we gotta be in the right place. I mean, that channel is exactly what Mupto described."

"I suppose," Ranulf said. "I've heard of these, but I've never heard mention of walls and nets. I guess we have to take a chance."

As they approached the net, the men on the wall shouted and scurried about. Their ship slowly and steadily approached the net, hit it, and stretched it as it slowed their momentum.

"Ropes! Ropes! Ropes!" the men shouted at them.

Ranulf finally gave the order to toss their ropes to those on the wall. Catching them, the men ran along the wall with them, and their ship slowly moved along with them. When they reached the towers at the end, the wall itself started to move.

The wall split in the middle and retracted the net their ship was in; the water levels evened out. Teams of men and women pulled their ship through the open gap toward another wall. They moved slowly, and Crab didn't have much to do but to keep the ship straight.

Once they were beyond the wall, it started to close again. Once closed, the wall before them started to open. Ranulf joined Jin taking in the island itself. As they traveled upward, they edged closer and closer to ground level. All around them was grass and huge trees with tall trunks and an explosion of wide leaves at their tops.

As they made their way into the next area, the second wall closed behind them, leaving them two options. On the left was a harbor. Several ships were docked, so Ranulf thought surely they'd pull in there. But another wall, to their right, was starting to open. Crab kept the helm steady as they sailed slowly through a third gate. This time, instead of a wall was a sparkling palace of bronze. Each tower had a round top that tapered to a point like a dollop of bronzed whipped cream.

One small figure stood on the shore as their ship was pulled closer. Ranulf grinned when Jin's jaw dropped. The palace glowed orange with the sunset reflecting off it.

Their ship was pulled up against a dock that led to the palace gardens. Only wide swaths of sand with tiled, raised beds and a gentle, gradual slope lay between them and the bronze palace.

The gangplank was lowered, and Crab, Jinhua, and Ranulf descended to see Mupto standing, arms wide open and smiling broadly. He was dressed in much finer silks now, colorful and oozing wealth.

"I'm so happy you came!" He enveloped the three in a huge hug.

"Ya have a lot to tell us," Crab said.

"First, I must congratulate you, Ranulf, Jinhua. I only hope to be as happy as the two of you in my marriage." Mupto took both their hands in his and squeezed.

Jinhua threw her arms around Mupto again; she was so glad to see him. He might not be from her home, but he felt familiar, the way home did.

"So ..." Crab said, looking behind his shoulder at their ship.

Ranulf guessed Crab wasn't sure what the crew was supposed to do.

"The ship will be safe here within our walls. I reserved space in our barracks on the west side for your crew if you like, so they can sleep and eat and relax to their hearts content," Mupto said.

Crab nodded and turned back to the ship. Then a neigh to their right caught their attention. A magnificent black horse stood atop a hill, an equally magnificent rider—a woman with long, black wavy hair flowing behind her—astride it.

"That is my fiancé," Mupto said, smiling widely and waving at her. She waved back just as enthusiastically. Then she turned abruptly around and galloped away. "You'll meet her a little later. I told her I wanted to welcome you on my own." Mupto turned back to them, looking happier than Ranulf had ever seen him.

Jinhua nodded. Ranulf wondered if she felt a matching sense of adventure in Mupto's fiancé even with the distance.

They walked along the coarse sand, their dirty boots marring the perfectly combed wavy lines. Ranulf felt bad about walking on such carefully manicured ground. At the gardens, they waited for Crab and the crew to catch up. Ranulf knew Crab would have left at least two men on board for now. There was maintenance to be done, plus it was second nature for Ranulf and Crab to worry their ship would be stolen. If that happened, they'd be stranded. They'd never leave it completely unattended. However, he was glad the crew would get some rest. They would switch out often.

Mupto led them along the pebbled pathway then, every shade of tan and brown represented in the rocks. On each side were squat but huge squares of tiled garden beds exploding with colorful flowers surrounded by the same brown rock they walked upon.

At the end of the path, guards appeared and led the crew to the right where Ranulf guessed the barracks were. While he and Crab were fond of Mupto, Ranulf found himself questioning whether he really knew Mupto well enough to trust him so wholeheartedly with his ship and crew.

"You can visit them later if you like. They aren't prisoners here but guests. If they find the ship more comfortable, they can go back," Mupto said.

Apparently, Ranulf's face was easy to read.

CHAPTER THIRTY-NINE
Jinhua

THIS PLACE WAS SO beautiful that Jinhua investigated the trees, expecting them to hold jewels that sparkled as brightly as the palace. They ascended some stairs to another garden, but it was a garden of water; sprays of water danced and shot up everywhere. Mupto suddenly stopped, sticking his arm out so they would stop too. They watched as an arc leapt from their right to their left, passing right in front of them. Then he proceeded onward.

"How was your trip here?" Mupto asked as he continued.

"It was uneventful. We stopped in a town north of here to do some trading. You wouldn't want any salt, would you?" Ranulf asked.

Mupto laughed. "I will inquire as to our salt stores and let you know." He slowed a beat, walking next to Jinhua for a moment. "And how are you adjusting?" he asked.

"We had a rocky start, but we're much better now," Jinhua said. She smiled and he narrowed his eyes. She wondered if he would accept her answer. He had always felt strangely like a brother, a kindred to her beloved Renshu. Mupto didn't question her further but nodded as if he wanted to save that conversation for another time.

They continued up another set of stairs, this time back to flowers Jinhua had never seen before. Some didn't have petals but looked like birds; others looked more like vines with tiny purple flowers on them. "These are beautiful," Jinhua said.

"The queen likes to keep rare flowers," Mupto said.

Jinhua kept that in mind, wondering if she would find the red flowers with yellow centers here and could trade something to obtain them for their client.

They strolled onward, and Jinhua turned her attention to the looming palace ahead. Despite the bronze, it reminded her a little of the island homes they had just seen. An entire wall was a mosaic of colors just as the previous homes were adorned with mosaic plates. Jinhua stared at the pieces, seeing animals and swirls. "Does the wall tell a story?" she asked Mupto.

"It does. It tells of an ancient legend where creatures from our imaginations roamed the lands. The ones on this side of the palace are our allies. The ones on the other side—the official entrance used for visiting officials—are our enemies."

"It's incredibly beautiful. It must have taken years to create."

"I'm told it took a full century to finish it all," Mupto said. He stopped to look at a red bird that pulled your eye to the middle of a wall between two large open archways.

"Where are you taking us, Mupto?" Ranulf finally asked.

Mupto grinned. "I'm sorry. I should have explained. My fiancé would like to meet you. We're meeting her in the inner courtyard for refreshments." As if he couldn't contain himself, he quickened his pace.

Jinhua's face fell. "I'm not dressed to meet royalty."

Ranulf and Crab looked at their own appearances, pulling at the hems of their vests.

Mupto grinned. "What am I then? Chopped fish liver?"

Ranulf looked appalled. "You can't be serious, Mupto. We'd like to make a good impression. I thought you were just showing us around."

"I am showing you around—on the way to meet my fiancé. She will not care what you wear."

"Why?" Jinhua asked, immediately suspicious.

"I've told her all our stories," Mupto said, his chin in the air.

"You told her about the time I got beaten to a pulp?" Ranulf asked, his cheeks going pink.

"Yes, and she's excited to meet you especially," he said. With that, they proceeded through an archway. Guards appeared, so Ranulf, Jinhua, and Crab couldn't do anything but follow him. They may have walked through a set of doors, but they entered an open, breezy hall. They strode past two more archways on either side that led to unknown places. Jinhua tried to straighten what she could of her clothes before they arrived after she caught her reflection in a small mirror hung on the wall. She attempted to braid her hair back, but the salty ocean air made her hair impossible to manage, and she was forced to abandon the attempt.

"You look beautiful," Ranulf whispered, taking her hand. She felt its warmth radiating, and it soothed her anxiety.

The halls they walked weren't filled with tapestries like they were in Densria, nor were they empty—punctuated with only a vase here and there—like the walls in Cerisa. These walls were embedded with small gems that sparkled and caught the light.

They strode through yet another archway and finally found themselves in the inner courtyard. A pool filled the middle of the space, fed by a waterfall gushing down one side. There, the woman they'd seen earlier from afar, with the beautiful wavy black hair, was holding the horse's reins as it stood in the waterfall. She was dressed in fine clothes as a princess might be, but she looked so un-princess-like as she tried to bathe the horse. She was half soaked and covered in suds. Jinhua watched as the bubbles ran down into the pool of water they stood beside.

Mupto coughed, grinning. She turned and smiled widely at him. Then she waved, flinging more soapy water before clearly realizing she might get her guests wet. Biting her lip, she wiped her hands on her already wet skirts. She looked up again and beamed when her eyes met Mupto's. Jinhua recognized their love and wondered if she looked at Ranulf with the same dreamy face.

She invited them to come closer as she led the horse out of the waterfall. "Please, don't tell my father about this. He doesn't appreciate how much easier it is to bathe him here."

Ranulf, ever the charmer, pretended to lock his mouth and throw away the key.

She laughed. "You must be Ranulf." She guided the horse forward, tossed the reins over his head, and gently tapped his back end. He trotted along the edge of the courtyard to where a stable boy looked very out of place. "Go with Hasan. He'll dry you off. I'll see you later," she told the black horse, and Jinhua knew she'd like this woman.

Ranulf bowed, reaching for the princess's offered hand and kissing the back of it. "It is an honor to meet you, Your Highness. Especially given you stole our friend's heart."

"It is my honor to meet all of you." She turned her attention next to Crab, who went a little pink in the cheeks as she went to greet him.

He bowed low.

"Crab, Mupto was never brave enough to ask how you got that name, but I would very much like to know. So you must promise to tell me." Her eyes were warm.

"Of course, Yer Highness," he replied, smiling.

"Oh, and none of that formality. Please, call me Sayani."

"Of course, Sayani."

She floated over to Jinhua, who was utterly stunned by this princess-from-a-book come to life. She expected to see flowers dancing near their feet at any moment.

"And you must be the Lady Jinhua." Princess Sayani took both of Jinhua's hands, not even glancing at what she wore, instead, looking only into her eyes. "When Mupto told me about how you and Ranulf met, and how you left to follow your heart, my heart broke at how sweet your story is and how difficult it must have been. I'm also secretly thrilled you're such a fearsome warrior and hope to see you knock my dear fiancé to the ground a few times. I know we will be great friends."

"That's very kind of you. Thank you."

"Now come, I have refreshments waiting so I can fawn over all of you." She turned with a flurry, not letting go of Jinhua as she led her to a table filled with colorful, tantalizing pastries.

They all sat, Jinhua feeling at ease much faster than she thought she would have amongst royalty. In moments, they were all relaxed and chatting about some of the stories Mupto had told Sayani about their adventures together, Ranulf and Crab correcting a few times when Mupto had been humble.

"Well, Ranulf, if anything, I owe you a great debt. For you stepped in to help my Mupto when he could have been killed even though you were outmatched. That is bravery beyond words and I'm grateful. Without you, I would never have met my Mupto. I owe you much of my happiness." She smiled.

"Daughter!" A voice boomed.

Jinhua whipped her head around to see a large, round man with a full beard striding toward them. He wore robes embroidered with gold and silver thread. The king strode up to them, obviously angry. They all scrambled up, and Jinhua wondered if they were about to be thrown out, or worse, into jail.

"Daughter, why is it I just saw horse hair and soap bubbles floating in my koi pond?" he asked. Then he looked up, clearly surprised at the strangers, who all sank to one knee as they bowed. "Oh, my apologies, I didn't realize you were entertaining guests—wait, are these Mupto's friends?" His gaze scanned each of them, landing on Jinhua last. "You must be the warrior." His voice softened, his expression awed as he took Jinhua's hands in his and guided her to stand.

Jinhua nodded. "It's an honor to meet a man of such high esteem, Your Majesty." She bowed her head, but the king held her hands so she couldn't dip into another bow.

"The honor is mine. Mupto has told me of your stories, and it is a brave thing you've done, leaving your family, especially one so famous as yours. Will you be training with us tomorrow? I would love to watch your matches."

"The honor would be mine," Jinhua said.

"Father! They're here for our celebrations, not for your entertainment!" Sayani said.

"You're right, daughter. So have you even shown them their rooms? Traveling is a weary task, yet you keep them here for your own entertainment." The king looked sideways at his daughter, whose cheeks turned a little pink.

"My father is, of course, right. I hope you'll join us for supper tomorrow night? I know Mupto would like you all to himself tomorrow morning, but if you're bored in the afternoon, come find me in the stables," Sayani said.

Mupto stood then, bowed to his future father-in-law, and kissed the back of his fiancé's hand. He led his friends away toward an archway behind the waterfall.

"We've managed to get you two rooms near each other but trust me when I say it's about to get a lot busier. The wedding is in two weeks. That's why I asked you to come earlier. Most everyone arrives next week, and it will be madness here," Mupto said.

He led them down a hallway, again surrounded with sparkly, colorful walls. He continued walking until he came to a hallway where people were busy bringing linens in and out of rooms all up and down the hall.

"Here," he said and turned to face a set of double doors made of solid wood. He pushed them open to reveal a large living space.

"Crab, your room is attached through that door there. It's also the next door in the hall. You have a living space, a bedroom, and a bathing chamber. And Jinhua and Ranulf, your bedroom is through those doors there, the bathing chamber beyond that."

Jinhua looked at the beautifully carved stone furniture. It was all worthy of a king, not lowly sailors. "This is all too much," Jinhua said.

"Actually, it's not. Because ... well, Crab, Ranulf, I was hoping you would stand with me at my wedding."

Crab whooped and Ranulf's jaw dropped.

"I'd be honored," Ranulf said.

"As would I," Crab said.

"Jinhua, I'd have asked you too, but I'm only allowed to pick men," Mupto said.

"That's all right. I think I'll have my hands full getting these two presentable," she replied, smiling to reassure him.

"Good. I'll send supper up to you here tonight, but I'll come find you for training tomorrow morning. We'll have breakfast and a whole host of appointments to get you ready for the wedding," Mupto said.

Jinhua could see he was worried his friends would back out. "Sounds wonderful." She smiled again and hugged Mupto. "We're so glad to be here to help," she said when she let him go; he was clearly relieved. "What are your plans tonight? Would you like to join us?" Jinhua asked.

"I would love to, but I'm dining with my future family tonight," Mupto said.

Jinhua nodded. "What time will you be here to collect us for training?"

"Before the sun rises. You'll hear five chimes."

She nodded and walked him to the door. Ranulf and Crab still looked a little stunned as they nodded.

When Mupto left, they drifted to the seating area. Jinhua's eyebrows rose. "What a whirlwind." Before they could dirty the furniture, she ushered them to the bathing rooms, then rushed ahead so she could have fresh, clean water before Ranulf sullied it with his dirty traveling self.

CHAPTER FORTY
Jinhua

JINHUA READ THE NOTE again. She thought it a bit strange to meet someone for tea in the stables, but she was glad for the informal setting. She looked forward to getting to know Sayani. "I don't know if I have anything appropriate to wear." Jinhua looked through the trunk of clothes she'd brought, at the same time wondering whether the fabric Crab had procured would be fine enough to wear at the wedding. This whole place sparkled like jewels. Would she be accepted?

"You're going to have tea with horses. Wear something you can ride in. We can safely assume she loves horses," Ranulf said, peeking up from his book.

"I actually meant for the wedding," Jinhua said. "I know Crab generously thought to get me some fine fabric, but I don't know if it's fine enough for a royal wedding or if we know anyone who can fashion a fine enough dress."

"We could ask Mupto for the name of a dressmaker and commission something for you if you'd like," Ranulf said.

"Do we have the coin for that?" Jinhua chewed her lip.

"I'm good at bargaining. We can go into town, and I can speak to the dressmaker. You'll have the most—second most—beautiful dress," Ranulf said.

"We'll go tomorrow then, after tea. Thank you, Ranny."

"I look forward to it." He reached out and grabbed her, wrapping his arms around his wife and hauling her into bed for a snuggle.

Once they were all cleaned and refreshed, the couple joined Crab in their shared living area and enjoyed a quiet dinner. They weren't sure what the meat was, but they didn't really care. It had been days since they'd eaten fresh food, and they could only hope the rest of their crew was eating as well.

"Jinhua, I have something fer ya after dinner," Crab said.

She was puzzled but excited. She declared herself finished, so Crab got up and retrieved a small bundle of folded cloth.

"Try this on. I'll need to make a few more adjustments, but I 'ave time in the next week or two," he said.

Jinhua pinched the fabric between her fingers and let the rest of it fall. A beautiful pink dress waterfalled to the floor. "It's beautiful, Crab. I didn't know you could sew."

"It's a hobby I picked up. I prefer crochet and knitting, but when you're at sea fer as long as I am, it's easier to mend your own clothes with needle and thread."

"It's more wonderful than I could imagine," Jinhua said. She pressed the dress to her front, then spun on her heel and ran to the other room to change. When she put it on, she was amazed at how well it fit and flowed. Now they wouldn't need to commission a new dress. She returned to their common rooms twirling, skirts flying around her.

"You look beautiful," Ranulf said, his eyes shining.

Crab chewed his lower lip and tilted his head. He looked around and picked up a hefty book, then placed it on the floor.

"'ere, step up on this," Crab said. Jinhua gladly did so, and the mountain of a man got down on his hands and knees, looking carefully at the seams and hem. He opened a little pouch on his belt that was filled with pins. "Spin slowly please," Crab said. He placed pins along the bottom hem, and Jinhua bent down to look. "Stand up straight please." Crab looked up, an eyebrow raised.

Jinhua straightened.

"Ya can still breathe," Crab mumbled, his mouth now full of pins.

Jinhua relaxed her shoulders. Ranulf laughed, making Jinhua realize what a strange situation this was. She chuckled in response.

Crab stood up and looked at the dress. "How do ya like it?"

"I love it!"

"These lines 'ere, do ya like where they are?" Crab gestured at the gold-threaded detailing that draped around her neck and down both sides.

"Yes, I adore it," Jinhua said.

"I was goin' to add some flowers 'ere, but then I thought that might be too much," Crab said.

"Can we add a collar here? Like on my other dresses?" Jinhua asked.

"Yeah, that should be easy," Crab said.

The dress went up to her collarbone and she was glad for the conservative feel, but she missed having a bit of a collar. She also thought a collar would add a touch of her own culture to the dress.

"What would ya think if I removed the sleeves?" he asked.

Jinhua pursed her lips. It would be more skin than she'd shown in a long time, but she saw what he was saying. There was a lot of fabric. And she wasn't a large person, so she was rather swimming in it. She got to decide who she was and what she wore now. She didn't have to pass her mother's scrutiny anymore. Jinhua nodded. "I think I'd be alright with that."

"Good," Crab said, standing up. "Ya can change now."

Jinhua gave him a kiss on the cheek. "You are amazing." Then she dashed off to the bedroom to change. She didn't close the door all the way, so she overheard their conversation.

"She's right. You're much more talented than I am in more ways than I can count," Ranulf said.

"Ya know I've always dabbled in this and that," Crab said humbly.

"I know it must feel strange to add Jinhua to our partnership, but I appreciate how easy you've made it for her," Ranulf said.

"She keeps ya tamed, so I welcome her addition," Crab said.

Ranulf grinned. "This is still a partnership though. So I hope you know how much I value you."

"I do," Crab said. "I'm a simple man, Ranulf, ya know that. I'm perfectly happy with this life."

"All right, well, if you ever need to talk about anything."

"I know where to find ya."

Ranulf was nodding as Jinhua strode back in. She caught his gaze and smiled.

Chapter Forty-One
Jinhua

THE NEXT MORNING, JINHUA and Crab met in the common room so early it was still dark. Jinhua was wondering whether she was dressed appropriately, but she wore what she always trained in, so it would have to do. A soft knock on the door sounded, and she creaked the door open, hoping not to wake Ranulf.

"Good, come," Mupto said as he poked his head in. Mupto himself was dressed in similar clothes, putting Jinhua at ease. "I've been waiting to show you off, Jinhua. I haven't told anyone other than Sayani and her father of your incredible skills." He grinned and she grinned back. It felt good to be among friends again.

They made their way through the maze that was the palace to the side lawn. There, dirt rings were surrounded by a line of staffs and guards dressed like Mupto.

Jinhua's crew stood on the sidelines in the grassy area but walked over when they saw her. She used their usual routine as a warm-up. She tested her muscles and spent a little more time on areas stiffer than others. But she felt good otherwise. The adrenaline started to pump through her as she looked around at the guards beginning to watch.

During a discussion with Mupto, Jinhua had learned that their training methods were similar but different in discipline and effort.

"Instead of doing specific routines named after different animals, here, we move from position to position, sometimes holding a position for hours to focus our minds and muscles on the finer details of each form," Mupto had explained.

So now Jinhua told herself, "All right, I'm ready." She added another level of complexity to the crane form, excited by how her body felt.

"Lady Jinhua," a voice behind her said.

She spun around and found a large, burly man with a dark beard and dark hair dressed a little finer than the other guards.

"Mupto has said you'd like to test your skills against ours," he said, his tone polite.

Jinhua guessed he was the captain as she remembered seeing him supervising the guards' training when she had snuck a peek in that direction. "I would, if it's not inconvenient." She bowed her head.

"Not at all. My name is Captain Navin."

"It's a pleasure to meet you."

"Please, come and join us when you're ready. Mupto mentioned that your weapon of choice is the staff?" he asked.

She nodded. When she turned back, she saw her crew inching closer, clearly excited for the show. When she raised an eyebrow, they all pretended to look away.

Crab came over and asked, "Ya want me to move 'em along?"

"No. it's fine. If I get my butt handed to me, they might as well watch as a cautionary tale," she said.

"I think you'll surprise 'em," Crab said.

"Mupto wasn't the highest-ranking officer and probably not the strongest fighter."

"I don't think they're matching ya with their best," Crab said, nodding at the guards, where the captain was approaching the group of beginners. "Well, to be fair, ya are a woman, and a small one at that," he added, but he pursed his lips, not quite preventing his laughter.

Jinhua knew he was trying to rile her up for the spar, but she shook it off, already feeling the adrenaline speeding through her body. She didn't want to make a stupid mistake.

Taking a few deep breaths to calm herself, she made her way to the guards. She gulped a little as she neared; she only came up to their biceps. She'd never felt so short before but continued to the selection of staffs to the side of the ring. Her own crew fanned out along the edge of one ring, and the guards eyed her.

The captain nudged one guard who looked no older than sixteen. But she didn't judge him. At sixteen, she had beaten her older brother for the first time. Maybe Crab was wrong, and this was their best warrior.

He bowed to her, holding his staff at the ready. Once she selected her staff and entered the ring, he did the same. He started to circle, and she decided to strike first. She slammed her staff downward at him, and he threw his up just in time to intercept. He stood a little straighter, obviously surprised at the strength behind her hit. He moved in to strike, but Jinhua felt like she was watching him in slow motion. She disarmed him and moved to whack his middle before bringing the butt of her staff to his throat.

He threw up his hands and bowed.

"I told you so, Navin," Mupto said. He stood between Crab and the captain and grinned at Jin.

"Nasir," was all the captain said.

Nasir looked a little younger than Navin, but Jin knew age had little to do with skill. Nodding his head, staff in hand, Nasir entered the ring. He didn't make the mistake of circling her but went straight to a hit. Jinhua met his strike with her staff and then used the opportunity to sweep her leg behind his and force him to fall as she danced away and brought the butt of her staff back up to his throat. He threw up his hands and bowed out.

"Mohammed," the captain said. Another man, closer to her age if she had to guess, stepped up, and again she watched his muscles and frame. She had to adjust some of her moves as their moves were stylistically dissimilar, with different angles she could appreciate. It took her five extra moves, but again, the battle ended with the butt of her staff against his throat.

She looked over at the captain, whose brows were knit together.

They were waiting for him to name the next person when he finally nodded and grabbed the staff behind him, removing his jacket in one swift movement as he entered the ring himself. "Mupto, you've been dishonest about this lady's abilities," he said.

"I never said she wasn't talented," Mupto said. He hid a grin behind his hand.

"You, lady warrior, must be a lady of one of the more prestigious fighting houses?" the captain asked.

Jinhua nodded.

"Are you from the fighting house Mupto trained at?"

"No, we're better," Jin said with a smile. She was excited for a challenge and knew the captain wasn't being malicious; he was only as excited as she was to test his skills.

The air filled with the *clack, clack, clack* of their staffs, each feeling the other out, testing speed and agility, looking for injuries or weaknesses in the other. Finally, they launched into a real spar and Jinhua smiled widely.

Captain Navin moved as quickly as she could and had as much skill, possibly more. She felt her body settling into the calm her mother always encouraged her to slide into. She wasn't thinking anymore, but reacting and enjoying, observing with every stroke she matched and parried.

However, Captain Navin was larger and heavier, therefore slower to stop and not as agile as she. Though he was better than most men of his size and weight, she moved faster and pivoted more quickly just given the size difference. She met him strike for strike until she saw an opening; she didn't take it. Was he setting her up? Would he realize she'd missed the opportunity?

He did and she only grinned wider. He *had* set it up. She was patient, and though she'd fought a couple of sparring matches before this, she still loved this moment and would wait for her chance.

But then a realization came to her. For the captain of the guard to lose against a stranger—a woman at that—would be humiliating, so she set him up and then followed through, taking the hit she'd planned to. When he struck her middle and slid up, knocking her off her feet, she threw her hands up and backed away. He approached her and offered her a hand. He said quietly in her ear, "You set me up to win."

"I am not the captain of the guard," she muttered before backing away with a huge grin.

He smiled widely as his guards surrounded him and patted him on the back. He nodded to her. "I'll see you tomorrow morning, lady warrior." He turned and returned to instructing his men.

Crab and her own crew surrounded her as they walked back to the palace. "You let 'im win," Crab accused her.

"I don't know what you're talking about," Jinhua said.

"I saw it."

"He's the captain of their guard. I don't have as much riding on a fight with a foreigner," she said quietly.

"And 'ere I thought you just liked to fight," Crab said. He grinned and put a hand on her shoulder.

Her own crew congratulated her on a good spar and returned to their barracks, but she could have sworn Mouse had a glint in his eye as if he, too, knew what she'd done.

CHAPTER FORTY-TWO
Ranulf

WITH A KNOCK ON their door, Mupto peered in at Ranulf's common room while Jinhua was bathing. Ranulf had just been about to join her, or help her, or both ...

"Would you mind walking in the gardens with me?" Mupto asked. He looked nervous, so Ranulf quickly agreed. He'd never seen Mupto this agitated.

Ranulf poked his head into the bathing room to let Jinhua know he'd be with Mupto in the gardens and had to tear himself away from her nakedness.

Mupto was quiet as they walked through the palace, out the doors, and into the gardens. They were walking along the tree line when he finally spoke. "Why did she choose me?"

Ranulf blinked; he wasn't sure what Mupto meant.

They stopped and faced each other, and Mupto let all the words spill out. "I love her with everything I am and everything I have, but so do many of the guards. You should see the way they look at her. I was one of them. It's almost like an admiration club. We fought about who got to walk nearest her when she walked in the garden or who would rush to help her when needed. When she started to call upon me, I thought perhaps she liked that I was one of the quieter guards, that she needed someone to listen. I couldn't even let myself admit that perhaps she had some affection for me, and then ... and then she chose me. And I don't know why. I need to know so I can keep doing whatever it is that she loves so much about me. But what if she chose wrong, Ranny, what if I disappoint her, and what if she cancels the wedding at the last minute and I'm shamed, kicked out of the royal guard, and banished from Bulstan?" Mupto was breathing so shallowly that Ranulf wasn't sure he was taking in enough air.

Ranulf took hold of Mupto's shoulders and shook him gently. "Breathe in ... slowly ... and out ... slowly." Ranulf breathed with his friend until Mupto could finally stand tall again. He looked as bewildered as a stunned animal, but at least his chest was moving more normally now. "You are an incredible man. Sayani sees in you what everyone else sees: a generous, welcoming, friendly man she wants to cherish as much as you cherish her. Everyone gets nervous. And no one knows why people fall in love. It's the greatest magic we have in this world. What you feel when you see her, what you feel when you talk with her, when you hold her hand, she feels too. I've seen the way you look at each other. It's as clear as we see each other right here and now. You are in love with each other, and it's both your jobs to foster that love, to adventure together," Ranulf said.

Mupto closed his eyes, breathing deeply, then finally opened his eyes again. Gone was the frantic wildness; the calm, cool, confidence had returned. "You're right. I suppose Sayani and I *have* talked about it. I still don't know what I did to earn such love, but I have my whole life to show I deserve it," Mupto said. He still sounded a bit shaky, but at least he wasn't hyperventilating.

"I might suggest you post the other guards in your unit far away from the palace though," Ranulf said.

Mupto laughed. "I will certainly do so." He took a last deep breath and seemed to come back to himself. "We are lucky men."

Ranulf smiled and nodded. "We certainly are."

They continued walking along the forest path. Ranulf kept a close eye on Mupto and was glad to see his friend was more relaxed, less stiff. His pace slowed, too, and Ranulf was glad to take the time to look up and around. "Is that a treehouse?" he asked.

Mupto grinned. "It's said Sayani tried to build it herself, but it was so terrible and dangerous that the guards had to fix it and build it properly overnight so she didn't hurt herself the next day because she was convinced she would move out of the palace and live in a tree."

"Why would she want to live in a tree?"

"I think it was closer to the horses? From what I hear, she was six years old," Mupto replied. He was smiling like an idiot, so Ranulf knew Mupto would be all right.

Mupto started to climb the tree, so Ranulf followed. It had been a long time since he'd done so, but it was something his body remembered well how to do.

"I received an interesting letter the other day," Mupto said. They stared into the canopy of trees as they sat on the edge of the platform.

"Oh?" Ranulf asked. His palms suddenly broke into a sweat.

"Indeed. The prince of Cerisa, Prince Feng, offered me a good deal of money if I arrested and handed you, Jinhua, and your whole crew over to them." Mupto's gaze slid over to Ranulf.

Ranulf laughed nervously.

"I told him, of course, that I last saw you going north," Mupto said.

Ranulf's shoulders relaxed. "Thank you."

"Does Jinhua know?" Mupto asked.

Ranulf nodded.

"We're partners in life. She knows."

"What does she think?"

"I'm worried she'll turn herself in, worried she's going to say I'm not worth this much trouble, that she'll regret having made this choice and want to go back to her family. I'm also worried that the Cerisan Navy will surprise us and blow my little ship to smithereens while we're out in the middle of the ocean and we'll all drown."

Mupto was quiet. "In the same way that you think Jinhua will run from you, I think that Sayani will turn me away. It's terrifying. But perhaps we shouldn't be starting our new lives together scared," Mupto said. "She's already chosen you, Ranulf. She left her kingdom, her family, her home. For you. That decision has already been made. Any fool who has seen you two knows you love each other."

Ranulf nodded. He wondered when he'd feel secure in their love.

"As for the Cerisan Navy blowing you up in the middle of the ocean, I don't know if there's much I can do about that. But you're all welcome to stay here as long as you like," Mupto said.

"We might have to take you up on that if they show up outside your locks." Ranulf laughed, then asked seriously, "How long do you think it'll take before they realize we didn't go north?"

"I'm not sure, but they'll find they have to sail quite far north to find supplies for their ship."

"What did you do?"

"I might have bought all the supplies along the coast ..."

"No ..." Ranulf said, his eyes widening.

"I need you here for moral support as I get married. I'm not about to let some silly navy ruin my and Sayani's special day." Mupto winked at Ranulf.

"Thank you, friend." Ranulf said, and he folded Mupto into a hug. He didn't deserve the kindness his friend showed him.

Chapter Forty-Three
Jinhua

T HAT AFTERNOON, JINHUA PULLED at her sleeves as she walked through the palace to the stables. She tugged at the hem of her shirt and then retucked it into her trousers, hoping against hope that she'd made the right choice wearing riding clothes.

She passed a few guards as she neared, and they all nodded and smiled at her. It seemed her little spar with their captain had become quite the story. She was glad for their friendliness but worried about their attention.

Pushing through the west palace doors, she found herself facing a lovely green slope and a low building. She descended to the building and opened the doors to see the princess brushing one of the horses in the middle of the aisle. "Hello," Jinhua said.

"Oh, hi!" Sayani said. She looked at Jinhua and grinned. "You passed the first test." The princess was also wearing riding clothes, though the material was very fine.

"Can I help you with any of that?"

"No, no. Artemis doesn't love strangers, so I'll just get you to stay there for a sec. I'm almost done." She used a beautiful creamy hairbrush to brush through his tail. The horse turned its head sideways to look at Jinhua, but she stayed exactly where she was. She wasn't afraid of horses, but she didn't have the most experience with them so she gladly gave them their space and hoped they would give her the same.

"So, Mupto told me you and Ranulf fell in love the moment you met," Sayani said.

Jinhua grinned. "We definitely felt strongly for each other, but ..." Her words trailed off as she tried to decide how much to tell the princess. Suddenly, she decided to just dive in. "... but he was a foreigner, and I was betrothed to someone else."

"How scandalous," Sayani said, sounding excited to hear the story.

"I started to teach him our culture, our ways, so he and Crab wouldn't look like fools in my kingdom."

"Just you?"

"No, my brother too. Crab and Ranulf met Mupto on their own, and I was introduced later."

"So exciting, foreign lands and clandestine meetings," Sayani said, grinning.

"Well, they weren't secretive. Everyone knew we were teaching them."

"What did your fiancé think?"

"Well, he didn't know. It was an arranged marriage. I'd never actually met him."

"He never wrote to you? Or came to visit?"

"No. He has many wives."

"And you would have been just another one of many?"

"Yes. Something like that."

"You were engaged to the royal prince?"

Jinhua blushed. "Yes, how did you guess?"

"I got the same proposal. I mean, I've had similar proposals from princes. It's overrated if you ask me."

"How did you and Mupto get together?"

"Here in Bulstan, things are a little different."

"Oh?" Jinhua asked, hoping to learn more.

Sayani put the brush down and glanced over her shoulder at the stable boy waiting for her to finish. He calmly approached, took hold of Artemis, and led him out of the stables.

"Come, let's sit down for the juicy parts," she said. She led Jinhua to another room, and Jinhua blinked as she walked out of a stable and into a luxurious sitting room. All the couches were various colors of pink and orange and had gold-gilded feet. Creamy pillows lay on the couches, and a tea service sat waiting for them.

Sayani sat down and poured the golden-brown liquid into two ornate teacups. "There's already a little sugar in there, but feel free to add more if you like." She handed Jinhua a cup and took one for herself. "Anyway, Bulstani princesses have the right to choose. We can choose whomever we want as our betrothed, and we can also, after ten years of marriage, choose whether our husbands remain prince consorts or ascend to king. However, the true bloodline will always rank higher."

Jinhua thought it was refreshing for a society to let women choose. "And the princes?"

"That is a much different situation. They are matched with local girls at the age of five, with a princess-to-be and a spare chosen and raised alongside the prince until they are adults and ready to be married."

"That is very different."

"Yes, yet it still doesn't prevent creeps from seeking me out," Sayani continued as Jinhua took a sip of the sweet minty tea. "I've had twenty-two requests to marry from princes from other lands."

"How do you respond to them?"

"I let Mummy do that now. I used to write back asking if they would come meet me or if they would answer my list of questions, but they rarely ever wrote back." She took a sip of the tea and readjusted her position, kicking off her boots and crossing her legs. "But you asked how I met Mupto." She grinned. "As small as this island is, I hadn't officially met Mupto before he left for your country. I'd seen him in passing since he was attached to my security contingent, of course, but perhaps it was because he was young and quiet that I didn't notice him at first. His superiors, though, said he worked hard and was a good fighter, so they sent him and one other to your country to learn. The other man fell ill on the journey there and died before they reached land." She thought a moment, sadness for her people in her eyes.

"Then Mupto was called back. Upon his return, I was out riding along the shore—I like to race the ships you see—and he stood in full uniform on deck. I remember thinking how handsome, proud, and confident that guard looked. I raced that ship back to the gardens, where Captain Navin stood at the dock waiting. I stood with my horse right next to him out of curiosity. Captain Navin has always had a soft spot for me, so he nodded and let me stay. Mupto marched off the ship and straight to Captain Navin, but he addressed me first.

"'It is an honor to be greeted by the most beautiful sight in the world upon my return home,' Mupto said, and he bowed. Most guards never usually bother with my presence, so I was a little thrown off. Then he turned and greeted Captain Navin. They started to walk off as Mupto began his report of his time away, and I found myself following them. They walked the long way around the courtyard and circled it a few times. My horse spooked at something, and instead of grabbing my horse's bridle—which is what most guards would have done—he leapt in between my horse and me." Sayani smiled and gazed dreamily afar at the memory. "As we passed the stable, I left them, but I loved the stories Mupto told about his time away. So after I returned my horse, I went to my chambers to bathe for dinner and then called for Mupto to meet me in my public sitting room.

"When he arrived, I ask him many questions about his travels, and we ended up talking for hours. We watched the sun rising over the horizon before he finally excused himself and left. He told me later that he had a full day's work the next day and was happily exhausted for it." She giggled before taking another sip of tea.

Jinhua, too, giggled and sipped her tea. Sayani and Mupto's story was delightful.

"I was fascinated by Mupto. He was so vibrant and kind and funny," Sayani said. "My father noted the difference in me right away. He'd been waiting years for me to find a husband. That much at least never changes." She rolled her eyes.

"I wrote Mupto a letter that day. It was three pages long. He was working but still managed to send me a reply—an equal three pages—by suppertime. I asked if he would come and visit me when he was off duty. He agreed but suggested that we meet in a more public place like the gardens." She looked around her.

"I chose my prettiest dress and even put some berry juice on my lips and cheeks before I met him in the gardens that night. But it was cold, and the moment he saw me, he took off his cloak and slung it around my shoulders. I loved the scent of him. I could have sat there and breathed it all night long. But we continued talking. It was like we'd been together forever, and we talked again late into the night.

"That night, I asked if he would mind being assigned back to my security rotation so I could see him more often. He didn't object, so I went to Captain Navin the next day to make the request."

"Let me guess. Navin said no," Jinhua said.

"Exactly! He said he couldn't have a guard distracted from his duty. In reply, I asked if it wouldn't be good to have someone I know so well protecting me. Wouldn't someone like that put extra effort in should I be in danger?

"'Or,' the captain said, 'He'd be more distracted and that causes an incident.'

"I left in a huff, but it wasn't my decision, so I wrote to Mupto again, telling him all the captain had relayed to me. He replied in half a day fully respecting the captain's orders. He said if I would like, he would meet me for tea that evening in the rear courtyard." Sayani smiled. "I was surprised he always wanted to meet me in public places. Of course, though it was cold that night, I purposefully forgot a cloak so I could borrow his." She giggled conspiratorially.

Jinhua chuckled but didn't dare interrupt the story.

"Five evenings in a row, I forgot my cloak and Mupto lent me his. He tells me now that he caught a cold from not having a cloak all those nights, but it was worth it. He loved seeing me in his cloak." She smiled down at her tea.

Jinhua sighed. She was a sucker for these kinds of stories.

"Anyway, as princess, it was a bit of a strange courtship. You see, princesses have all the power and make the decisions in Bulstan. I couldn't figure out if Mupto really loved me or if he was just indulging me out of duty. He couldn't act on his desires, so I was at a bit of a loss as to what to do next."

"I know Mupto is a rule follower, but I have a hard time imagining he wouldn't have told you how he felt," Jinhua said as she sat back.

"You're exactly right. We spoke and spent every evening together in public for two weeks." She smiled and sat back herself.

"He sounds like he was the perfect gentleman," Jinhua said.

"Frustratingly so," Sayani said as she rolled her eyes.

"So how did he make the leap from guard to prince-consort-to-be?" Jinhua asked.

Sayani grinned. "I proposed."

"You didn't!" Jinhua breathed.

"One night, he seemed agitated. I thought for sure he'd just been doing his duty and just didn't want to tell me and break my heart. But he sat me down and started to pace back and forth. Then he suddenly stopped and sat down very abruptly next to me. He said, 'Your Highness'—I'll never forget how serious his face looked, his eyebrows all knit together. My heart was racing faster and faster, and I braced myself for the worst'—I know I'm not supposed to ask you, so I suppose it's unofficial, but I cannot stand by any longer like a timid mouse. I love you. I would like to marry you, even if I'm not allowed to ask you, officially.'

"The look on my face must have been shock because he stopped dead, and the color drained from his face. He must have thought I didn't feel what he did.

"'Your Highness, would you like me to leave?' he asked quietly.

"I rushed to explain. I said, 'No, no, it's not that. I thought ... I thought all this time you had been indulging a princess. I hadn't ... hadn't dared to hope you truly felt that way for me.'

"He rushed over and knelt before me, taking my hands in his and putting his head on my lap. 'You are more than I deserve in so many lifetimes,' he said. And then I ran away, back to my rooms."

"What?" Jinhua asked. She could see Sayani liked drama, but she was such a good storyteller, Jin was happy to oblige with an appropriate response.

Sayani paused to pour her more tea. "I knew I loved him. I've met many men, had many men try to seduce me for my crown, and I knew from the first time we spent time together that Mupto was my love. So the next day, we rode out to the cliff and sat in the cave there. He seemed a little dejected, but stoic. I'd dragged all these pillows to the cave ahead of time so it'd be comfortable and private"—she wiggled her eyebrows—"but he wouldn't take advantage. I tried everything, even pulling my sleeve off my shoulders! Anyway, he turned around for a moment, and that's when I whipped out a ring. Have you seen it? The gold one with the ruby?"

Jinhua nodded. *No one would miss that ring,* she thought.

"Well, I told him that I knew I loved him, and I knew he loved me, and he should marry me." She stuck her chin up in the air and smiled.

"What did your father think?" Jinhua asked, curious about how her family reacted.

"I thought I'd get more resistance from him. But I think he knew it was coming. I only have the power to make him my prince consort, for now anyway, so I think that helped my father feel more secure and involved," Sayani said.

She spoke of it so lightly, as if love was a picnic for her family. Jinhua felt a knot of jealousy at the strife in her own family because of the man she'd chosen to love and marry.

Sayani put a hand on her arm. "I know you've had a difficult time choosing the man you love. And I'm sorry for it. Please know you and Ranulf always have a place here. Mupto would love to offer you a place in our court, and I would too, if you'd be willing to stay. But Mupto says you're travel crazy and Ranulf is a merchant through and through."

Jinhua smiled. Sayani was not what one imagined a princess should be. She was beautiful, kind, thoughtful, and adventurous.

A loud neighing interrupted their thoughts, and Sayani rushed out of their little room. Jinhua was right behind her and watched as she calmed the horse and led it outside, where the staff had been trying to lead it.

Once she put him back in his paddock, she returned to Jinhua's side and stuffed her feet back in her boots. She looped her arm in Jinhua's and then together, they started up the little hill toward the palace.

CHAPTER FORTY-FOUR
Jinhua

A S THE NEW FRIENDS strolled back to the palace arm in arm, Jinhua felt happy, lighter. Though they'd only just met, she knew they would be friends for a long time. "Are you nervous?" she asked.

"Not to marry Mupto, I'm excited for that. But the ceremony, the people, it's a lot."

Jinhua's eyebrows shot up before she could control herself.

"What?"

"I just thought, well, you grew up doing this, so it wouldn't be so nerve-racking."

Sayani laughed and it sounded like a wind chime. "I'm still me. And as me, I would prefer to ride my horse and run through the forest than stand in front of hundreds of people. I'd even take meeting people one-to-one instead of a crowd."

"I'm definitely better one-to-one than in a crowd too," Jinhua said.

"You're glad not to be royal, aren't you?"

Jinhua jerked back, then stared at her hands, unable to look Sayani in the eye. "How did you know?"

"I get the feeling you're relieved not to be in my position," Sayani said gently.

"I'm sorry."

"Don't be. *I* often wish I wasn't."

"When I ... I was betrothed to a prince of my kingdom, I would have been his eighth wife. I ran away with Ranulf instead. I feel more relief than I'd like to admit at not having to be a princess," Jinhua said.

"All the more romantic." Sayani sighed. "It must have taken a lot of courage to leave everything and everyone behind for love."

Jinhua could only manage a nod as a lump filled her throat.

"I know it's not the same, but if you'd like, know that you are family here. Mupto has told me so much about you and Ranulf and Crab. Please know I'd like this to be your home now too." She took one of Jinhua's hands in her own.

"That's so kind of you. Thank you."

"I'll even ensure you have your own bedroom. Come, let's go pick one. It will always be yours, waiting for you."

"Truly?"

"I swear it on Bulstan. You can do whatever you like with it, leave whatever you like, and it will be a safe place for you and your family."

Jinhua smiled as she followed Sayani into the palace and down a corridor. They explored each one, and as they did, Jinhua realized she wouldn't ever have half the poise or kindness that Sayani did. Then she remembered something. "Sayani, do you have a red flower with yellow centers here?"

"Yes, I think so. Would you like some seeds?" Sayani asked.

"Please, for one of our clients," Jinhua replied. She smiled to think of Lady Margaret as one of *their* clients, not Ranulf's, but theirs, together.

"Consider it done," Sayani said. "Oh, how about this room? There's a view of the forest from here."

They continued to stroll from room to room until Jinhua finally picked a room, and Sayani promised her it would be theirs by the next morning. Jinhua had picked it not only for the view, but it was also in a quiet wing and out of the way; they wouldn't take prime space away from the palace that way.

"Now, shall we find out what the boys are up to?" Sayani took Jinhua's arm, and they went off in search of the boys.

They searched the whole palace but didn't come upon them until they rounded a corner and the garden came into view. Mupto, Ranulf, and Crab all sat in the garden drinking tea, Crab engrossed in an intricate knitting pattern.

"May we crash your tea party?" Sayani asked.

"Absolutely. There's enough for all," Mupto said, turning pink.

Sayani smiled mischievously. "Oh, what a rather … relaxing hobby for such manly men like yourselves."

"A fine mint tea is appreciated by all," Ranulf said, pouring some for the ladies.

"So, Ranulf, you now have a permanent residence in our palace," Sayani said.

"Oh?" Ranulf asked mildly.

"Call it a second home. We shall all be married, and we shall all have children together, and they will be the very best of friends, just like we are," Sayani said.

"Sounds like a wonderful life," Mupto said.

"And Crab will knit them all hats and socks," Jinhua said.

Crab looked up from his work—just then noticing the ladies and looking chagrined—and rose to bow to the princess.

"What are you making, Crab?" Jinhua asked as he took his seat again.

"More socks. My feet are much too big. It takes time just to make a few pairs, so I figure I should make 'em myself," he said, raising the plain gray tube of yarn in his hands.

Chapter Forty-Five
Ranulf

TWO WEEKS FLEW BY. Ranulf was happy for the reprieve. Jinhua became such good friends with Sayani that she became a last-minute addition to the maidens accompanying Sayani up the aisle. Ranulf smiled as he took his hot cup of coffee to the back garden. He didn't really like this hot dark-brown liquid, but he enjoyed the ritual and it seemed to liven him up quickly. Jinhua had been swept up in preparations before he'd even woken, and now he watched the staff scurrying around putting the final touches on the celebration.

Standing on the highest point of the garden, he was careful not to get in the way as he gazed upon the spot where Mupto would marry his bride. An explosion of colorful flowers all in pink, white, and yellow covered an enormous arch and pulled attention toward the palace, which shone like a gem. Ranulf watched two guards follow a couple of young men as they carried something gleaming and red to the arch. Climbing on ladders, they secured it to the archway's interior. He stared another moment before realizing that the string of luminous red was a strand of some of the largest rubies he'd ever seen in his life.

"It's a bit much, isn't it?" Mupto asked, sidling over with his own cup of coffee.

"It will be a ceremony fit for a princess and her prince," Ranulf said.

"Have you seen the rest of the gardens?" Mupto asked. He looked content and calm.

"Are they different?" Ranulf asked.

Mupto laughed and invited Ranulf to walk with him. They slowly descended some stairs and followed a path to the rear gardens, where the reception was to be held. Ranulf's eyes widened as he took in bushes bursting with blooms, jewels nestled amongst the leaves: rubies with roses, diamonds with lilies, emeralds with ferns. Stone benches waiting for guests sat row upon row amongst the flower boxes.

Ranulf had tried to stay out of the way the last few days, training with Crab and moving their ship to a little bay as the canal would be part of the ceremony. He and Crab had also taken the opportunity to prepare the ship to leave. They were getting antsy, making Ranulf wonder if it would be rude to leave in the next three days.

For now, he asked, "How are you feeling?"

"What do you mean?" Mupto asked.

"I mean, are you nervous? Excited?" Ranulf raised an eyebrow.

"How did you feel the morning you married Jinhua?" Mupto asked.

"Excited." Ranulf smiled. "I couldn't wait. Time moved so slowly. I just wanted the moment to arrive so I could kiss her properly."

Mupto stopped to watch as someone knelt in front of a bush of daisies, stringing jewels amongst the leaves and flowers. "The moment I met Sayani, I knew my life would be different. I would happily be anything she wanted me to be. If that meant being only a guard or a friend, I would happily do it for the rest of my life. I would do anything to be around her ever-shining light," Mupto said. "To be completely honest, friend, I don't know what she sees in me, but I hope to be married before she finds out I'm just a regular person."

"That, Mupto, I can assure you, you are not," Ranulf said.

Mupto elbowed his arm softly so they wouldn't spill their coffees and smiled. "Oh, I was wondering, Ranulf, if you would stand witness for me?"

"Sorry? I thought I already was."

"You were my best man. Rather, I'd like you to stand with my family as I marry into the royal family. I've asked Crab to take your place as best man, and he's agreed."

"What does that mean, exactly? What's the difference?"

"It means you get the best seat in the house," Mupto said, grinning.

"I'm honored, Mupto, but I thought you'd want your true family—"

"You are the family that matters most to me. Please, Ranulf, you and Crab and Jinhua are my closest friends. I know we've not known each other long, but I feel like we've known each other forever."

Ranulf smiled. After having been part of two of his siblings' weddings, he knew the best thing to do was agree. It was Mupto's wedding day, after all. "I'm at your service." He bowed his head.

"Good, let's get back so you can learn your parts," Mupto said. At Ranulf's expression, he added, "I'm joking. You don't have all *that* much to do." Then Mupto burst into laughter as the color drained from Ranulf's face.

Five hours later, Ranulf found himself standing next to Crab on a staircase leading to the archway. A golden carpet, made of true gold fibers, lay atop the stairs and draped along the back wall of the palace, so the archway looked like it was filled with gold.

Strange, thrumming music with clear brassy notes made the atmosphere ethereal. As a horn sounded, the audience turned to the canal. Three lights glided through the fog toward them. As they neared the dock—now covered in flowers—the lights became small, flat boats. Six maidens glided off the first boat when they reached the edge of the platform, and the six figures fanned out as a new figure, on horseback, disembarked the second boat. Just then, the fog melted away and revealed the princess, a vision in shining gold. A ray of sunlight shone down on her, making Ranulf squint as the light reflected off every inch of her.

Ranulf recognized the horse as the same one she'd been bathing in the inner courtyard, and he was surprised to see it walk calmly off the boat, down the dock, and to the edge of the crowd. Six more maidens filed out of the last boat, following the horse in two rows of three, and the first six followed suit behind them.

The maidens were completely covered, head to toe, in pale-cream cloth, though he thought he might have seen some pink through the folds of the skirts, but he couldn't be sure. Ranulf squinted, trying to see beyond their veils to find his wife. Each maiden, starting from the first, spun around then, their skirts changing color as they did so. His eyes were pulled immediately to the second maiden in line; it was Jinhua. He'd recognize her movements anywhere. Their bouquets of flowers now sparkled, and it took Ranulf a moment to realize they were now bouquets of jewels, switched during the spin. He took in the bigger picture as it was meant to be seen. Each maiden wore a different colored skirt, and it reminded him of flowers with jeweled pistils floating down the aisle. They finally came close enough for Ranulf to see through the gauzy veils. He kept his gaze on the second maiden and smiled when he saw Jinhua smiling at him. They stared at each other as long as they could as she took her place on the opposite side of the second step.

She turned to the bottom of the steps, and Ranulf did the same as he watched Princess Sayani ascend. She was a vision of opulence, beauty, and grace as she dismounted and walked up to meet Mupto. Ranulf turned to watch Mupto and saw his eyes shining with tears as he smiled the widest smile Ranulf had ever seen on him.

The ceremony was foreign to him, but Ranulf continued to drag his gaze away from Jinhua as they watched Mupto and Sayani perform various motions and listened to the ancient texts as the two melded their lives together.

"Congratulations again," Ranulf said, embracing Mupto. Jinhua and Ranulf stood on the dock, preparing to board their ship and start their journey home. They hadn't had time to trade, but he was happy to be a part of his dear friend's ceremony.

"When will you be back?" Sayani asked.

"Whenever you'll have us," Jinhua said. They held each other's arms.

"Then you must stay, for I want you both to live here," Sayani said with a smile.

Jinhua smiled back. "You'd get sick of us and banish us in no time."

"Please, though, will you promise to come back at least in half a year? And you must stay here for a month!" Sayani said. "Promise!"

"That would be lovely," Jinhua said.

"You are always welcome here. We expect you to come visit us every half a year. Do you promise as well, Ranulf and Crab?"

"Yes. We do. It would be lovely to visit with ya both and take a break from our merchant lifestyle," Crab said before Ranulf had a chance to interject.

Mupto hugged Crab at that, and Sayani hugged Jinhua again. Then it was time to board. Once aboard, they waved and waved. Even as Mupto and Sayani jumped onto their horses and disappeared into the forest together, Ranulf and Jinhua watched the cliffs. Moments later, they smiled and waved to the newlyweds riding atop the cliffs.

Ranulf turned to Crab. "Are we moving slower than you'd expect?"

Crab's brow knit. "Yes, it does seem slower, now that ya mention it."

"It's the cargo," Mouse said from behind them.

"What cargo?" Ranulf asked as they all turned to Mouse.

"The trunks Mupto sent this morning," Mouse said. He looked worried.

Ranulf ran to the cargo hold and leapt in, Jin and Crab right behind him. He opened the closest trunk, and sparkling gems of all colors stared back at him.

"Great goddesses above," Crab said.

Jin ran to the next trunk, and Ranulf was right behind her. Crab stood motionless as he stared at the three strange trunks around him. He had already flipped them all open, and they, too, were full to the brim with gems.

When they came back to their senses, they climbed back on deck only to find a note tucked between two rubies on top of a barrel that read:

> *We couldn't let you leave without something to trade!*
> *-Mupto and Sayani.*

They spun around.

Mupto waved and Sayani covered a giggle as they smiled and waved. "See you in a few months!" Mupto shouted.

"We don't have a choice now, do we?" Jin said.

"No. But I'll happily come back in half a year," Ranulf said as he waved enthusiastically back.

Chapter Forty-Six

Ranulf

THE TRIP HOME FELT much faster than the trip out, and it was mostly uneventful. Ranulf made sure to spend time with the crew, and Jin joined the card games once in a while too. They were also careful not to touch too often when they were with the crew, which they made up for in their quarters.

"I think we've finally hit our rhythm," Crab said one morning. He and Jin had just finished their training, and Ranulf dragged his feet as Crab took the helm again. Sometimes, Ranulf got lucky and escaped morning training because someone had to man the helm and Jin would get caught up teaching someone a specific form. Before he knew it, it was time to eat, and they had completely missed his training.

Today was not one of those days. Jin appeared at the helm, and Ranulf couldn't help himself as he circled his arms around her. She had a layer of salt on her just as everyone did after so many days at sea, but he'd never tire of holding her.

"Ready?" Jin asked.

"Ready for what?" Ranulf asked. He hoped playing dumb would get him out of it.

"You've missed too many training sessions already, so let's get to it." She took his hand and led him to the space on deck they'd cleared for practice.

"I really hoped you'd forgotten or gotten caught up."

"Your safety is important."

"But that's why I have you." Ranulf smiled his most charming smile and hoped it would soften her.

"And that's why you should be a better warrior than you currently are," Jin said.

Ranulf tried once more as he held her close and whispered into her ear.

Jin danced away. "Later. You must be able to defend yourself or I have failed."

"What if I just say I won't ever leave your side?" Ranulf asked.

"And what if we're outnumbered?"

"Crab is worth at least two people. And you can easily take down six. I don't think we'll ever be outnumbered." Ranulf said.

"Ranny, please. For me. Learn some, so you can at least take care of yourself. It's important to me," Jin pled, widening her eyes as she neared, and he melted into a puddle at her expression.

How could he say no to that beautiful face? "All right," Ranulf said.

"Good." Jin bounced away giddily and grabbed a staff for him. "All right, show me your stance."

Ranulf took his stance and then felt the ship list this way and that, challenging his stance. He threw a look at Crab at the helm, who pointedly did not look at him but grinned. He was being ganged up on.

"Good, good. Now, let's go through the first form together."

Ranulf moved his staff and his body as she'd drilled into him.

"Good, again, but this time, I'm going to counter what you're doing. I won't push, but our staffs will touch," Jin said as she started to move opposite him. This was new.

She moved with him, from one point of contact to another; he kept to the exact same moves he always did, but she moved with him. Their staffs kissed at times, and sometimes her foot stepped between his as she moved around him.

"This is interesting," Ranulf said.

"Focus on your pattern," Jin said. "This time, we're going to hit with a little bit of force, just a little push. You'll feel it, so resist enough so you don't move." Jin started to move a bit faster, forcing Ranulf to move faster too.

As they moved together, he felt his wife more and more and felt his own body responding to her dancing around him: a brush of a hand here, a rub of a leg there. He swallowed his emotions and stumbled.

Jin stopped and looked up. "Remember, you need to focus."

"I don't think we're replicating the feelings I'd have when faced with an enemy—"

Jin grinned. Ranulf realized she was doing it on purpose.

"I thought it would motivate you," she said as she put him back into position and started from where they'd left off.

His body began responding in a way he would not be able to hide for long.

"Ran, Jin. We 'ave a problem," Crab said, interrupting them.

They stopped and looked at him, then to where his gaze was focused.

"Several ships, Captain!" Turt called down from the crows' nest.

"How many exactly?" Ranulf asked. He ran up to the helm to stand with Crab, and Jin did the same.

They squinted but could only make out the horizon and little lumps on it. Their ship had just turned toward home and were a day out.

"Umm ... a lot? I stopped countin' after twenty, Cap!" Turt called.

"Did he say twenty?" Jin asked. Ranulf saw her face fall as she grasped for any other explanation. "Maybe Mali arranged a welcome, or perhaps the Kingdom of Adanek?"

Ranulf swallowed. He knew in his heart this was the trouble he'd hoped they could avoid.

"Umm, Cap?" Turt asked from above. He had the only spyglass.

"Spit it out, Turt!" Mouse yelled from the deck.

"They're definitely flyin' Cerisan flags."

Ranulf felt his heart sink into the pit of his stomach. He looked to Jin and Crab. They looked as scared as he felt.

"Crab, no one is to disturb us for the next ten minutes. Slow the ship. Don't get closer." Ranulf reached out a hand to Jinhua, and they went to their quarters.

Without looking at Jinhua, Ranulf started to grab a cloak, some rope, and rations he'd stored in a trunk. He dug into a chest and grabbed a heavy bag of coins. He moved around their quarters looking for a larger bag until Jin grabbed his arms and spun him to face her. "Ranulf, you better tell me right now what's going on," she demanded.

Ranulf blinked. His heart was pounding, and his hands were sweaty as he wiped them on his trousers, but that didn't work, so he grabbed handfuls of fabric.

"We have a small rowboat. If you and Turt get in and slip to the back of the ship, they won't see you. You two can get yourselves to shore. Mali will take care of you. If not, there's enough in this bag for you to start fresh. Go see Marco, the baker in the village. He's young, but he's a good person. He'll know what to do."

"Ranny," Jin said more softly this time. She pulled him to their bed so they could sit down. She sat across from him, crossing her legs, and placed a hand on his cheek. "Did you forget? We're in this together."

Ranulf took a deep breath. His racing heart was hard to calm. "I need you to be safe," he said quietly. He didn't even feel the tear slide down his cheek until Jin wiped it away with her thumb.

"I understand what you're feeling. I was terrified when you faced down rogues that first time, and it felt worse the second time. My heart is so tight right now, I think it might burst," Jinhua said.

They hugged each other so tightly, it was as if they might crumble to pieces if they let go.

"Are you sure you don't want to leave me?" Ranulf squeaked. "I feel like it's a good time to remind you that I can't offer you a life of royalty. This"—Ranulf pulled away for a moment to hold Jinhua by the shoulders as he looked around at the bare-bones captain's quarters, at their few maps, navigational tools, and a chest"—is it. And I always worry something will happen to Mali, that we'll return to a lord only distantly related to him and we'll have to pay for all of Mali's generosity. We don't have a home. I have nothing to offer you but this." He waved at the room. His face twisted in a pained smile as he lifted the getaway bag once more.

Jin looked into his eyes, "He's never told you, has he?"

"Told me what?"

"Mali told me he intends to leave Densria to us," Jin said, "but I don't need it."

Ranulf hung his head. He had hoped and dreamed of that, but until Densria really became theirs, he didn't want to depend upon it. It could be taken away from him at any moment—just as she could be.

Jin wrapped both her hands around Ranulf's face and rose so her face was only a few inches from his. "When will you get it through your head? I chose you," Jin said. "I don't care about fancy clothes, or jewels, or any of it."

"Now, maybe, but what about in six months when we haven't bathed in days and you're wearing the same clothes you are now?"

"I hope we figure out a way to wash the clothes, but that's fine with me."

A knock on their door interrupted them.

"Hate to break up whatever's goin' on, but they're gettin' closer!" Dog shouted.

"We will get through this together," Jin said. "Trust me. Trust that I've chosen you, and promise me that we'll face whatever the future holds together."

Ranulf nodded. They kissed and then touched their foreheads together, closing their eyes to breathe each other in for one more moment. "Let's go figure this out."

She took his hand, and he squeezed it, feeling ten times bolder than moments before.

CHAPTER FORTY-SEVEN
Ranulf

"D O YA THINK WE could slip by them and into Densrian waters before they blow us to smithereens?" Mouse asked.

Crab shook his head. "It's a tight squeeze and gettin' tighter by the second."

"Do you think they'll talk? Or is this an execution situation?" Ranulf asked.

Crab tipped his head from side to side, considering it, but didn't answer.

"He promised to kill us both. They will attack," Jin said.

"Do you think he wants to kill us together or have one watch?" Ranulf asked.

"Why are we talkin' about so much killin'? I thought we wanted a plan to get outta this alive!" Crab said.

"I think he'd use one of us to get to the other," Jin replied. "I don't like your plan."

"What plan? I've not 'eard a plan yet," Crab said.

Ranulf looked at his two favorite people in the world. "I go in alone, to talk. They won't consider me a threat. We offer them"—Ranulf swallowed. He hated to part with them, but for Jin's freedom, for the crew's safety, he would—"the three chests of gems Mupto gave us."

Jin looked pained. "I may not like it, but that might work. Prince Feng likes shiny things."

Crab shook his head. Then he put a hand on Jin's shoulder. "Yer worth more than three chests of jewels, lass."

"Not to them," Jin said.

Jinhua

Jin placed and strapped leather armor on her husband before letting him dress, "I'd feel better had you been training with me everyday," she said.

"I'll pay better attention to my training in the future," Ranulf promised.

"You will definitely be trained better after today." She rose and crossed her arms.

Ranulf took a deep breath in and then out. "I'll be fine."

"I'll murder and string them all up by their intestines if they so much as touch you."

Ranulf grinned, cupped Jin's head in his hands, and pressed a kiss to her lips. "I love it when you're protective."

"I'll be watching. If they so much as twitch, I'll be there."

"That's what they want, remember," Ranulf said with a wink.

How he could be so calm before walking into a death trap was beyond her. He barely knew how to defend himself.

They emerged onto the deck. Mouse was waving a white flag as they sailed closer to the prince's ships. The closer they could get to Densria, the more hope they had that at least some of the crew could get home should everything go south.

They loaded Ranulf's arms with two chests and put the other one beside him. As they neared the lead ship, they saw weapons drawn, but no one rushed at them.

The same royal adviser that had come to their village to evaluate her for the royal marriage contract was on board, making her wonder if her sister, Qiao, was too. Would she be assigned this duty to witness the disloyalty of her own sister?

Jin shook her head; she had to stay focused. She was armed to the teeth beneath her clothes, and she tensed as Ranulf walked across the gangplank, the two chests in his arms.

Jin stood at their end of the gangplank. Their crew sat in the sails, armed with bows, keeping watch for hidden archers on the opposing ships.

"Thank you for accepting our offer to parley," Ranulf said.

The emperor's representative smiled, and Jin kept her face neutral. The man had taken opulence to the next level; his smile was filled with gold. "I'm known for my intelligence. What have you to offer?" he asked.

"Three chests of gems directly from Bulstan in return for our freedom: the Lady Jinhua's, my crew's, and mine," Ranulf said. He opened the chests and tilted them so the light would catch the gems. The diplomat looked like he was about to drool as he took in the gems.

The adviser's gaze finally slid to her crew. The other chest of gems was open beside Crab, and it caught the light too.

Jin wanted to add more to Ranulf's words. But she trusted him. If Ranulf was quiet right now, it was for a reason. He knew how to read people and make deals better than anyone she'd ever met.

"The freedom of you, your whore, and your crew, in exchange for three lifetimes worth of gems," the representative said.

Jin ground her teeth, and she saw Ranulf's fingers around the chests turn white as he gripped them tighter. She felt her crew tense. Jin knew Ranulf could control himself though.

And he did. He only nodded. "You have yourself a deal."

Two guards came to collect the chests, and as Ranulf walked across the plank connecting the two ships, the diplomat followed. Only once Ranulf was safely on board did Crab hand the last chest to the diplomat. He took it and left, and Dog pulled the plank.

Jin couldn't help but scan the other ships. She didn't see her sister on any of them; she hoped that meant they'd left Qiao out of it.

The Cerisan warships had started to sail away when Jin heard, "Fire at will!"

"No!" Jin said.

Then the first cannon went off, hitting their ship in the bow.

"I promised you freedom, but not your ship. Nor did I promise safe passage past my navy!" the emperor's royal representative shouted.

"Unfurl the sails!" Crab yelled.

Their ship bordered land to starboard, but they would have to pass three warships to get to safety.

The crew in the rigging unfurled the sails as they fell with their ropes. Jin prayed the wind would pick up at the right moment—and it did. She felt the breeze as their sails caught. More cannons blasted, and Jin could only hope they'd make it by.

Ranulf took the helm, and Crab leapt down to the lower deck, rope in hand.

"Hold on!" Ranulf shouted. His shout was drowned out by two more cannon blasts. Wood splinters flew and the ship lurched forward, leaving bits of wood behind them.

The crew rushed around to secure ropes, but Jin didn't know what to do. She held tight to a railing beside the helm. At least she was out of the way. Though she wanted to help, she could see the crew's familiarity and experience working together shine through. No one ran into each other; no one crossed ropes. They all moved together seamlessly, and the ship lurched further forward.

They made it past the first ship. Movement caught Jin's eye to her right. She squinted to see if she really was seeing what she thought. Mali, in a billowing cloak, stood on the cliffs with a much smaller figure, also cloaked.

"Mali's here," Jin said.

Ranulf was near enough to hear, and he nodded but kept his attention on the helm as they continued onward. The ship was sailing slower than she knew it could, and she wondered if they would make it.

As they passed the first ship, soldiers on the second ship leapt over the short distance between their ship and hers and headed straight for Ranulf.

Jin funneled her rage and drew her swords as she intercepted them. She took three on at a time, moving with precision and sliding into the calm of trusting her body, trusting her weapons as extensions of herself, as she ran through one, sliced the neck of another, then turned to kick a third in the groin before finishing him off with her blade. The sailors didn't stand a chance. She was a warrior, and these soldiers threatened her love. No one would get through her.

Some of her crew must have climbed back up into the rigging with their bows and arrows because she saw some sailors trying to cross fall before making the leap onto hers. Finally, they passed the second ship; there was only one more in front of them. Then she heard explosions behind them.

Jin turned to see the cliffs were lined with people from Densria. A row of catapults launched bundles of something that exploded as they hit the Cerisan ships.

Thankfully, her ship was far enough away from the third ship that Jin could stop fighting. She panted as she took in her surroundings. Twelve soldiers lay slain around her, and Ranulf—still concentrating on steering them to safety—was untouched.

Then Jin noticed the cannons weren't firing at them anymore. It was odd because they were close enough that the third ship should have hit them. She turned to look to port and saw the crew frozen, watching the other ship.

Jin looked at the Cerisan warship's cannons. Vines had grown from the wooden deck up and into the cannons. They plugged the cannons, and as fast as the Cerisan soldiers tried to clear the cannons of vines and plant matter, the vines doubled and tripled.

Jin instinctively turned to starboard, where Mali held the smaller figure's shoulders. His hood had blown off, and she saw brown hair flying in the wind and a serious expression on the boy's face. She didn't know how, but she knew Mali and that boy were responsible for the vines.

They cleared the last Cerisan warship, and they could finally see the Densrian harbor ahead. The warships could still chase them, so Jin held her breath. She turned to see whether the Cerisan ships would follow them into Adanekian waters. Though attacking them while docked would be a declaration of war, the Cerisan Navy might not care at this point.

The diplomat had long since sailed further away and commanded his navy from afar. When she turned back, she saw two small groups of people on the bay's tips. Ranulf sailed in too quickly and would probably run aground, but if it meant their safety, she didn't think it would matter.

"What are they doing?" Jin asked as her gaze was drawn again to the two outermost points of the harbor.

"I think Mali set some traps of his own while we were away," Ranulf said. His shoulders relaxed as he kept an eye behind them. The Cerisan war ships did not follow but waited further out.

As soon as they passed the two points, the two groups of people started shouting. Jin ran to the prow to watch as a massive net was raised, the groups pushing a wheel that raised the net behind her ship as it sailed in. Any ship sailing in now would be snagged and caught like fish.

Jin turned to look at Ranulf. He exhaled as if he hadn't breathed for some time. Then he grinned as he looked at her, and she grinned back. He let go of the helm, and they threw themselves into each others' arms.

"We did it," Ranulf said. He glanced back at the dozen bodies on the ground. "Did you do that?"

"No one threatens my love," Jin said.

Ranulf grinned and held her face as he kissed her on the lips in front of the whole crew, who whooped and cheered. Their ship lurched as it hit the beach, but it stopped.

Crab came over and hugged them both. "We're alive. I can't believe we made it."

"I can hardly believe it either," Jin said.

"I knew we could do it," Ranulf said. He grinned as the other two looked at him incredulously. Then they walked toward the crew.

"Did ya see what happened to those cannons?" Turt asked.

"Did ya see Jin take out those soldiers?" Shelley asked.

"Can ya believe they'd fire on us after letting us go?" Dog asked.

They all helped toss the ropes to the nearby dock workers, who slowly hauled them backward so they could tie up properly in the harbor. Between her crew and the dock workers, they pulled their ship into position so they could unload the goods as quickly as possible in case the ship sank.

"We owe Mali a lot," Crab said.

"We owe that boy, too, whatever he did," Jin pointed out.

"We owe the people of Densria," Ranulf said, glancing at the cliffs and the enormous net. Then he looked to the catapults lining the cliffs further away.

"Then let us go thank them," Jin said.

"Together." Ranulf grinned. He held his hand out, and she took it.

Jinhua knew then that whatever their futures would bring, they would adventure and face danger together.

Join my newsletter to access free stories from the Threads of Magic World by clicking this link or scanning this QR code:

Note from the Author

THIS BOOK STARTED WITH my wondering how it was that two people from very different cultures come together. Thali is a mixed-race human and I wondered how her parents would meet in my fantasy world.

I do apologize that there aren't many critters, nor much magic in this book. Mostly because the critters and magic really start with their daughter's story.

CONTINUE READING IN...

Start from the beginning with their daughter's adventures in Of Threads and Oceans...

Or dive into Camilla Tracy's new story in The Dancer and The Magician...coming summer 2026!

Buy here: https://geni.us/theDancerandMagician

Or scan this QR code

QR code for a link to buy
The Dancer and The Magi-
cian

ACKNOWLEDGEMENTS

T HANK YOU, DEAR READER, for choosing to pick up this book and spend your valuable time with it.

I'm grateful to my communities – friends, family, and chosen family that are so incredibly supportive and loving with my work. My writing groups, fellow grapes and hearties both for your support, encouragement, and commiseration. I always look forward to our meetings.

Thank you to my early readers, Char and Paul, I always appreciate the perspective you bring to my stories.

Always so thankful for my editor, Bobbi Beatty of Silver Scroll Services. Your ideas, edits, and careful eye are essential to making this story its absolute best.

Thank you to Lorna Stuber, my dear author friend/proofreader! Your attention to the nitty gritty are unmatched.

I'm grateful to the very talented artists at MiblArt. Your talents and teamwork bring the story visually to life.

These books are possible because of the amazing support I have from my family. Thank you to my dear husband for his support and being a sounding board for all kinds of ideas. And to my mother for her support and enthusiasm.

Since the last book, we said goodbye to my heart dog Truffle. While a part of me will forever be changed, I'm so grateful for the time we had together. As I raise my next best puppy buddy, I'm extra grateful for the lessons we learned together.

To my furry puppers, Udon and Enoki, thanks for reminding me to get up every few hours and napping while I tip-tap away. To Kali, thank you for making sure I get outside for some fresh air and dirt under my nails once in awhile.

About the Author

Camilla is a lover of many mediums of storytelling. She loves to write strong heroines with animal sidekicks, who can triumph and find the love of their life. She always has projects on the go and loves to consume stories of all kinds—books, shows, movies, plays, amongst many others.

When she is not writing, Camilla is often found exploring animal behavior, crafting, drinking a hot beverage, and clicker training her animals.

Come visit her at CamillaTracy.com or on instagram @camilla_tracy. Sign up for her newsletter by visiting: https://geni.us/CamillaTracynewsletter or by scanning the QR code below: